Gripped by Fear

Special Limited Edition

FIRST EDITION

To my friend and fellow writer, God bless you

John

A CHICAGO WARRIORS THRILLER

Also by John M. Wills

Chicago Warriors
Midnight Battles in the Windy City

TotalRecall Publication, Inc.

Houston   London   Toronto

Gripped by Fear

A Chicago Warriors Thriller

John M. Wills

1103 Middlecreek Friendswood, Texas 77546 281-992-3131 281-482-5390 Fax
6 Precedent Drive Rooksley, Milton Keynes MK13 8PR, UK
1385 Woodroffe Av Ottawa, ON K2G 1V8

Copyright © 2009 by John M. Wills

All rights reserved. Printed in United States of America, England and Canada. Except as permitted under the United States Copyright Act of 1976, No part of this publication may be reproduced, stored in a retrieval system, or transmitted in any form or by any means electronic or mechanical or by photocopying, recording, or otherwise without the prior permission of the publisher.
Worldwide exclusive content publication / distribution by TotalRecall Publications.

Hard Cover
ISBN: 978-1-59095-772-1
UPC   6-43977-35772-4
eBook: Adobe Acrobat
ISBN   6-43977-67741-9
UPC   6-43977-68268-0

Paper Back
ISBN: 6-43977-47733-0
UPC   6-43977-87825-0
Audio Book
ISBN   6-43977-57750-4
UPC   6-43977-68268-0

The sponsoring editor is Bruce Moran and production supervisor is Corby R. Tate.
Book editor Barbara Weingartner
Jacket Design by Bruce Moran
Photo Illustration by Jaquelynn Tramble

This is a work of fiction. The characters, events, views, and subject matter of this book are either the author's imagination or are used fictitiously. Any similarity or resemblance to any real people, real situations or actual events is purely coincidental and not intended to portray any person, place, or event in a false, disparaging or negative light.

Judgments as to the suitability of the information herein is the purchaser's responsibility. Further, the author and publisher do not have any control over and does not assume any responsibility for third-party websites or their contents.

Printed in the United States of America with
simultaneously printings in Canada, and England.

1 2 3 4 5 6 7 8 9 10

FIRST EDITION

To my wife, Chris, whose faith continues to amaze me. She is the centerpiece of our wonderful family, her strength and beauty, truly a gift from above. I am so blessed to have her as my partner; thanks for everything, babe.

The Author

John spent thirty three years in law enforcement, working the streets in Patrol, Special Operations, posing as an undercover agent, and as a street survival instructor. He is the recipient of two of the highest awards given for valor by the Chicago Police Department, and has worked violent crime, organized crime, and drugs while an FBI Agent. He has published dozens of articles on training and police survival. This is his second novel in the Chicago Warrior thriller series.

John is retired from the Bureau. His last assignment was as an Instructor at the FBI Academy, in Quantico, VA. He lives with Christine his wife of thirty-nine years. They have been blessed with three fantastic children and four marvelous grandchildren.

Contact John via www.johnmwills.com

Acknowledgments

Thanks to the Riverside Writers of Fredericksburg, Virginia, for their guidance and support.

My heartfelt gratitude to Bruce Moran for taking a chance on a total stranger.

Be strong and courageous! Do not be afraid of them! The Lord your God will go ahead of you. He will neither fail you nor forsake you.
Deuteronomy

John M. Wills

~ 1 ~

First Victim

It was done. He stood and fastened his pants, then became one with the darkness as he slipped out the door and into the alley. This time of night welcomed only demons and devils. It was good, but not nearly enough. He would need more...soon.

It had already been a long day for Maria, watching three of her neighbor's children as well as tending to her own five had worn her out. Now she was headed downtown to Chicago's Loop where she would spend the night vacuuming floors and emptying waste baskets in some of the tallest and most important buildings in the world. This had been her lot for the past two years; this is the plight of "illegals," as they were called. Unable to find traditional jobs, they worked at what they could to earn money to pay their rent and food bills. Her husband was a day laborer, getting up at dawn each day to stand en masse with others at the local convenience store in hopes of being picked by a landscaper or painter looking for temporary workers.

Walking from her apartment on Chicago's South Side to the bus stop on Pulaski Avenue at this time of night had always unnerved her, but she had gradually gotten used to it. So when she saw a man walking in her direction she didn't think much of it. She assumed that, like her, he was probably also a laborer and may have been returning home from a long day. As he drew near that all changed. An alarm went off inside; her senses went to full alert as her muscles tensed in preparation.

"Hello...,"

No answer from the stranger as he passed. She willed herself to relax; relief washed over her. Suddenly, a vicious blow to the back of her head knocked her to the ground. Before she knew what was happening, the stranger picked her up and carried her toward one of the houses. Still reeling from the attack, but becoming aware of yet more danger, she struggled to regain her senses.It was dark. She saw a house...no lights...no one to hear her. Passing between two dwellings moving toward the back...a garage.

"No!" She tried to yell but her cry for help came out as a whisper, barely audible to anyone but herself. Total darkness. *Inside the garage, have to get out!*

More pain as she was dropped awkwardly to the ground, her already throbbing head bouncing off the concrete floor.

Disoriented, battered, and terrified of what might happen next, a fist smashed into her face. Dazed from the pain she sensed more movement...*my clothes*, her pants and underwear—gone. She tried to struggle but her body wouldn't respond. She felt him as she slipped further away; welcoming the coming abyss that now was the only thing that could rescue her from this demon sent from hell. Helpless, unable to do anything to save herself, she did what her mother had taught her whenever evil was present: she prayed. *Our Father who art in Heaven.... My babies, Father, please take care of my babies.*

***

"Did you bring it?" Billy asked, looking around. He was hoping that his friend Jose had brought a cigarette that they could share.

"Yeah, I got one from my brother's pack; he'll never miss it."

The two young boys walked down the sidewalk to the vacant house. They were on their way to school, but every once in a while they liked to sneak a cigarette here in the abandoned garage. They had seen the high school kids smoking and thought that it made them look cool. They'd found this place several weeks back, part of a house left vacant months ago, and had made it a custom to stop here a few times a week to indulge in their new found ritual.

"I got matches, Jose."

"Big deal...I got a lighter, man. It's a lot better than matches."

They were proud of themselves as they strutted through the side door of the garage, anticipating the thrill of acting like the big kids. But their normally quiet and secret safe haven held a surprise for them on this morning.

"Holy shit! What's that?" Jose stopped dead in his tracks as he saw a woman's body lying on the ground.

Billy, taking baby steps, approached the body. "She's got no pants on, man; I think she's dead."

Both boys moved in closer for a better look.

"Man, somebody beat the crap out of her. Look at all that

blood!" Jose was getting curious...and bold. He knelt down and stared at the woman's private area. With his pupils wide open to illuminate and process the unbelievable sight in front of him, Jose said, "Billy, you ever see a woman down there before?"

"Not in person man, but I seen pictures. Hey, what are you doin'?"

Jose slowly reached down and touched the woman, then yanked his hand back quickly as if he had just touched a hot skillet. "I just wanna feel it...."

The woman stirred, one arm reaching toward the boys. "Help me...."

Startled, Jose fell over and landed on his backside; Billy jumped, "Holy shit, she's alive!"

"Help...hurt me...his eye...."

Jose stood up. "What she sayin', man?"

"I don't know but we gotta get outta here." Billy turned to leave, "I'm callin' 9-1-1."

Both boys ran from the garage and headed to the convenience store where they used the phone. "Hey, police, you gotta come quick; there's a naked lady in the garage. She's hurt bad."

~ 2 ~

Violent Crimes Unit

Five o'clock. Pete Shannon rolled over and kissed his wife, Beth, on the cheek then quietly got out of bed and headed down the hall to the guest bedroom. On the way he poked his head into his son's bedroom. Pete, Jr. was sleeping peacefully. *How blessed am I?* They had waited fifteen years for this precious gift from God; he was sent from above at a time in their life when they needed a miracle to keep their marriage together. Pete, Jr. was that miracle.

He continued to the guest bedroom where he dressed in his shorts, tee shirt, and running shoes, and then slipped out the door without disturbing anyone. He loved running at this time in the morning; the normally noisy, congested city was still asleep, only a few cars and delivery trucks on the streets. It was the perfect time for prayer and reflection, as well as for planning his day. He took off on his jog into an early morning fog that quickly swallowed him up like a leviathan scooping up a school of fish in the sea.

Just a couple of months ago, he and his partner, Marilyn Benson, had started their new assignment as detectives at Chicago Police Headquarters. The Violent Crimes Unit was quite a departure from their previous assignment as plain clothes officers on the Tactical Team (TAC) in the 8th District. Their extraordinary police work and heroism had earned them meritorious promotions. But both he and Marilyn, or "Bens," her nickname among friends, were still trying to adjust to working normal shifts. Two years of straight midnights had changed their biological clocks.

He finished his run around the campus of St. Xavier University, "Xavs," and walked down 103rd Street toward his house to cool down. *Thank you Lord!* Walking in the back door and into the kitchen he saw his wife and son, "Mornin' babe! Mornin' little guy! How's daddy's boy today?"

Pete, Jr., smiled as he looked in his father's direction, and then quickly got back to the business of finishing his first formula bottle of the day.

"How was your run, honey?"

"Great! You know this five a.m. stuff isn't bad. The streets are empty, it's quiet and cool…I could get used to this."

"How long will you and Marilyn be on the day shift?"

"I guess that I'm not really sure. King said that he would keep us on it for a few months, at least until we learned the paperwork and stuff associated with being a detective."

King was Lt. Jerry King, the Commanding Officer of the Violent Crimes Unit. He had been in charge for the last seven years, before that he had been in Patrol and Homicide. He was a tough, seasoned cop who could see through people; he didn't suffer fools well and hated liars and excuses. If you did your job you were golden with him, if you fudged it or were delinquent with paperwork, you were on his list. It was not a good thing to land on King's list.

"I hope that you stay on days for a long, long time, babe. I'm getting used to having you next to me in bed every night. Those two years that you spent working midnights was a lonely time for me."

"I know, I'm beginning to like it as well but I know that it won't last forever. All the guys take turns working shifts so we'll eventually have to get into that rotation."

Pete started moving toward the hallway. "Wow, he's polishing off that bottle like he hasn't eaten in days."

Beth smiled and said, "He does that every morning—gives him energy to get through his busy day."

"Yeah, he's got a busy day alright," laughed Pete. "He'll be asleep again in another hour."

"C'mon, honey, he's a baby!" Beth snuggled him and kissed his cheek.

"Okay you two, I've got to hit the shower."

Thirty minutes later he was in his truck headed toward Police HQ on the South Side at 35th Street and Michigan Avenue. He pulled around the back of the building to the parking lot just in time to see Marilyn getting out of her car. "Hey, Bens!"

"Hi, Pete! What's up?"

"Not much, little Pete and Beth were up and at it when I left, and I got my run in again this morning; I'm really getting used to this day shift."

"Good for you, I guess that I'll get my workout in tonight.

Kim and I are hitting the gym around seven."

Kim was Marilyn's best friend and workout partner. She was a Chicago Firefighter and was also a fitness buff. She and Marilyn had entered several bodybuilding contests, and Marilyn had recently won the Miss Illinois contest. But Kim had also taken a beating at the hands of Marilyn's old boyfriend, Gary, who had drugged and raped Marilyn. After learning that he was wanted by the police for the crime, he became incensed with getting even and searched for Marilyn early one morning. Thinking she was at Kim's apartment, he burst in, beat Kim, and then lured Marilyn there only to be arrested for his crimes. He was out of the picture now, serving 25 years to life for attempted murder and kidnapping.

Pete and Marilyn walked toward the rear of the building to the employees' entrance and stopped short. He turned to Marilyn and asked, "What do you think so far?"

"About what?"

"About the job...being detectives."

"I like it, Pete; we're working some good cases and using our interviewing skills. I think it's a good fit. Why, aren't you happy?"

"I don't know." Pete said. "I guess it's all so different from what we were doing on the Tac Team. We knew everyone; we knew the area...it just seemed so comfortable."

"You're right, Pete, it was comfortable and maybe that's why you're feeling a little awkward right now. But you'll get used to it, just like we did when we first worked together—that was different too but we thrived and succeeded. Give it a chance, partner."

Nodding, Pete replied, "You're right. I guess that I'm just not dialed in yet. I'm still getting used to new people and the bosses. I think that Mac had me spoiled."

Mac was Sgt. McNamara, the desk sergeant on the midnight shift at the 8th District. He was Pete's old boss and a personal friend who made sure that Pete and his now deceased partner, Joe O'Hara, were always taken care of. Pete looked at Mac as a father-figure; Mac treated Pete like the son that he never had.

Marilyn put her hand on Pete's shoulder, "Mac's the best, Pete, no doubt about it. And, he's still going to be there for us on and off the job. C'mon, partner, let's go to work."

They made their way up to their unit. *Gotta get my head in the game.*

~ 3 ~

Susan O'Hara

"Good sermon today, Father." Mass had just ended and Father Mike, pastor at Queen of Martyrs Catholic Church, was greeting parishioners as they exited the church.

"Thanks, Susan," said the priest as he shook her hand. "It's always good to get feedback on my homily; it makes all my work seem worthwhile. How are you and the boys doing?"

Susan O'Hara was the widow of Joe O'Hara, Pete Shannon's long-time partner. Joe had been killed in the line of duty by a vicious thug who had been committing home invasions on the South Side. Pete and Joe had confronted him in a rail yard where he had held a woman hostage. In the exchange of gunfire, Joe and the bad guy had been killed.

"We're doing well, Father, thank you for asking. Our family and friends have been such a blessing; the boys still miss their daddy, but all the overnights at friends' homes and trips to movies and such have given them the attention that they crave."

"Good, I'm pleased to hear that people are still helping out, especially taking your four boys off your hands once in a while."

Susan sighed, "I am fortunate to have so many friends, and I confess that taking care of the four of them on my own is sometimes nerve racking. Every once in awhile I feel like I'm going crazy; I long for adult companionship. Am I wrong for feeling that way Father?"

"Of course not, you've lost your best friend and partner of ten years, someone that you shared your thoughts and conversations with—it's perfectly normal for you to miss that interaction. Why don't you go over to the parish activity center next door, we have coffee and donuts there after each mass? There's also a room set up for the kids, with supervision, so the boys can have their fun while you have a cup of coffee and meet some of your fellow parishioners."

Smiling, Susan said, "Thanks that sounds like a great idea. I really don't have anything planned for today, and I could use some adult conversation. See you later, Father."

Susan and the boys walked to the adjacent building and found a warm, welcoming room already occupied by many of her neighbors. She got the boys each a donut and some juice and then led them to the play area that had been set up for the children. Pouring herself a cup of coffee, she looked around for the cream and sugar. As she turned to walk the several steps to the counter where they were located, she bumped into a man carrying a tray of cookies.

"Oh my gosh...excuse me!" Too late, the tray and its contents hit the floor. "I am so sorry…." Susan immediately bent down helping to clean up the mess.

"Don't worry about it," said the man. "I'll take care of this. It could have been worse; it could have been hot coffee that I was carrying."

"I guess that you're right, anyway, sorry about making such a mess." They finished picking up the cookies and put them back on the tray.

"Three second rule?" asked Susan.

"What?"

"The three second rule…if you drop food on the floor but pick it up within three seconds you can still eat it. You've never heard of that one?"

"No," said the man with a grin, "I can't say that I have, but I guess that's a darn good rule of thumb. I'll have to remember that one."

Susan looked a little closer at the man now. He seemed to be about her age, 35, or possibly a few years older. Several inches taller than she was, with jet black hair and dark blue eyes, he was certainly attractive.

"My name is David…David Williams," he said, as he extended his hand toward her.

"Hi, David, I'm Susan O'Hara."

"Nice to meet you Susan, you are a talented woman."

Cocking her head to one side, she asked. "What do you mean?"

Smiling and pointing to her cup he said, "You didn't spill a drop of your coffee."

"Oh…well thanks, I guess."

She looked at his left hand holding the cookie tray—*no ring*.

Re-arranging the food on the tray, David said, "Well, let me get these cookies next door into the play area before the kids start a revolt."

"Are your children in there?" Susan asked.

"No, I don't have any kids. I volunteer at the parish coffee service once a month. Father Mike was looking for people to help out last year so I raised my hand; I've been doing it ever since. It's a small way for me to give back to the parish."

"That's great, David, but I've never seen you at Sunday mass before."

"That's because I usually go to mass on Saturday night, it's less crowded and it means that I can sleep in on Sundays."

"Sleeping in...I wonder what that's like," she said, as she closed her eyes trying to imagine such a luxury.

David laughed. "It's nice, Susan; I guess that I'm lucky to be able to do it," he replied, as he headed to the play area. "I'll talk with you later; it was a pleasure to meet you."

"Thanks, I just wish that it had been under less awkward circumstances. I'm such a klutz."

"Don't worry about it; I'm glad that we met."

He walked over to the children's room and disappeared. *What just happened?* She had made a fool of herself by knocking into this man and spilling the cookies, but in the process she had felt something stir inside. It had not yet been a year since Joe had died and here she was having feelings for another man. Or was she? *She was... she definitely was.* She felt attracted to him physically; just standing next to him was electric.

She went over to the counter and put cream and sugar in her coffee, her mind adrift about meeting David. Then it hit her...*this is wrong!* My husband would not approve. Yet she was torn, she was no longer married—she was a widow. Confusion ruled, what should she do? Was continuing to grieve her loss the right thing, or was this chance meeting a sign that she should start to move on?

David was coming out of the room and was walking in her direction. *What should I do? No time to think, here he is.*

"Time for me to go, Susan, I have a lunch date today with a friend. Again, it was a pleasure to meet you."

"Likewise...when are you here again?"

"I'm usually here the first Sunday of each month at the very least, sometimes I'm here more often. Will I see you again?"

"I hope so, David."

"Good, I look forward to it. He took her hand between both of his, "Good-bye."

"Bye."

He walked out and she felt it again—the attraction. Holding his hand had sent her heart fluttering, *Oh Lord, what am I doing? Joe, I'm sorry, honey.*

She gathered the boys and headed home. She needed some time to think things over. Today's experience came right out of left field. This was a first for her, the first time that she had felt something for someone other than her husband. She felt guilty; she felt as though she had sinned.

After she had put the boys in bed that night she prayed. *Father, help me...I'm lost. Guide me.*

~ 4 ~

On Their Own

Marilyn and Pete walked into the bullpen area of the Violent Crimes Unit. While most offices in the building were set up with individual cubicles, Lt. King, the Commanding Officer, disdained that arrangement. He said that it promoted individualism and invited people to make their own spaces. He liked to remind the detectives in his unit that they were there to work and solve cases, not hang pictures of their girlfriends and wives on the walls of their cubicle. Instead, the twelve people assigned to him were in the middle of a large space, a bullpen, if you will, each having their own identical government looking desk with no dividers or cubicles. It gave King the ability to simply glance out of his office window and see who was in and what they were doing. It was also much easier to get a person's attention if they were unable to hide in their own little space.

Being the newest members of the unit, Pete and Marilyn had their desks close to the lieutenant's office. It was somewhat uncomfortable at first, being this close to the boss, but as they got their routine down they learned that it was easy to control how much time that they spent in the office. Once the daily meeting at the beginning of the shift was over, most guys hit the streets to work on leads, conduct interviews, make court appearances, or just go out looking for their wanted subjects.

Marilyn went over to her desk; Pete hit the coffee pot that the unit kept going 24/7. He poured himself a cup just as King came out of his office.

"Alright, everybody, have a seat and let's get this day started. Our case load is starting to pick up, no doubt due in part to the weather getting warmer. That's no big deal; most of the violent crime is fairly simple to figure out. It's usually gang related, drug related, or both. Get a handle on the players and you'll spend less time clearing cases. Last period our clearance rate was down, that was due to our manpower compliment being down as well. We're back to full strength now with Benson and Shannon assigned here, so I expect the clearance rate to improve. Do I make myself clear?"

Most everyone nodded yes; a few said it out loud. King liked feedback; he told us as much by saying that he did not operate in a vacuum, didn't like talking to himself. Pete answered, "Yes sir!"

"Good," King continued. "Homicides are on the rise, again many of them due to gang activity. They all have guns and they aren't afraid to use them. I know that we're detectives, but I like stopping known gang-bangers and going through them. Even if they're not dirty it serves a purpose—they'll know that the cops are liable to stop them anytime, anywhere. It gives them pause, at least momentarily. If I see that your clearance rate is down a little, but see that you're making gun pinches and putting these creeps in jail, we're golden. Understood?"

"Yes sir."

"Good. Last night we had another robbery at Cub's Park. I still can't get used to night games at Wrigley Field, but anyway this is the third time this knuckle dragger has hit. He targets older folks walking back to their cars which are parked several streets away from the ball park. He's a black male, about 20 years old, 6'0, 165 pounds. He blends right in because he's wearing a Cubs hat so he looks like he's just another fan and lots of folks are on the streets during and after the game. He tells his victims that he has a gun while he keeps his hand in his pocket, so we're not really sure if he's actually armed or not. The Tac Team in the 19th District is going to saturate the area after each game. Most important, is that the District Commander is taking heat from the Mayor's office. If you've got leads in that area while there's a game being played, spend some time looking for him; if we can pinch this guy it will make us look good with the Old Man.

"The only other serious incident last night was a rape in the 8th District. A cleaning woman heading for the bus was accosted, beaten, and raped in a garage. A couple of kids trying to sneak a cigarette on their way to school in the morning found her. Seems they like to use the same garage where she was assaulted as their smoking parlor. It scared the heck out of them when they walked in and found her on the floor. She's over at Holy Cross Hospital in critical condition. The docs put her in a coma; she's got a skull fracture and swelling of the brain. The creep left her for dead after he took what he wanted.

"That's all I've got," King said, as he put his papers down. "Those of you with court dates make sure you get them on my office calendar. Also, I don't want to mention this again—jeans are not to be worn on duty. You are professionals, dress like it.

You don't have to wear a coat and tie, but slacks and a dress shirt or golf shirt is what I want to see. If you want to dress like a bum, find another unit. While you're working for me, your appearance will command respect. And make sure that you have your 'Star' on your belt next to your weapon. I don't want any of my people getting shot by another cop because they didn't know who you were. Clear?"

"Yes sir!"

"Good, see you this afternoon." He turned and went back to his office.

Some of the dicks headed toward the door, others went to their desks to make one or two more phone calls. Pete went to retrieve the file on the Cub's Park offender so that he would have the information handy in case he and Bens got up north.

Just then King stuck his head out of his office door, "Benson, Shannon…my office."

The pair dropped what they were doing and walked into King's office. He was seated behind his desk, which was immaculate. King was a former Marine, and he wasn't into all the individual honors and accolades, the "I love me wall" that most bosses want everyone to stare at and admire. The only things hanging on his wall were the Chicago Police Star and the Marine Corps logo. His son was presently serving in the Corps in the Middle East. He had the TV in his office turned on most days, tuned to the news to stay abreast of the war.

"Have a seat. Listen…I think that you've both had enough shadow time. You've ridden with each team; got a look at how each guy works—good and bad—it's time you stepped up and assumed your own case load. I want you to work that rape last night in Chicago Lawn." King tossed the file across his desk toward the two detectives. "Go over to the hospital and get with the doc handling the case and see what the prognosis for her recovery looks like. Then check with the district and the Crime Lab guys and review the evidence that we have thus far."

"Will do, sir," Pete replied.

They got up to leave, but Lt. King was not finished yet. "So tell me, can you handle this unit or not? Some guys that have been assigned here didn't last long, but the ones that stayed were able to do some of the best police work of their career. Think you can handle it?"

The pair stopped; Marilyn spoke up first. "Lew, I'm excited about it. I want to do my part, and pull my weight; I'm grateful for the opportunity to be assigned to a unit like this."

"Sounds like b.s., but I'll take you at your word, Benson. What about you, Shannon, can you handle it?"

Pete didn't want to get off on the wrong foot with this guy, but he didn't want to blow smoke at him either. "It's all new, Lew, and I'll tell you the truth, I'm not quite comfortable with it yet, but I'm going to give it my all. If it doesn't work for me, you'll be the first to know, sir."

"You're right about that, Shannon—I will be the first to know. I appreciate your candor; the worst thing that you can do is to try to fool me. I don't like people that aren't honest with me. This gig isn't a good fit for everyone, if you turn out to be one of those for whom it doesn't work, it's no big deal. We'll get you into a unit that's more suited to your style. I'm not here to cause you problems, but I am here to solve crimes and to get the most out of each one of my people. My door is always open if you have questions, but remember, I'm not your confessor. I don't like crybabies. Clear?"

"Yes sir."

"Okay, get out of here and get busy." He followed them to the door and closed it behind them.

They walked out to the parking lot and found their unmarked squad. After checking behind and underneath the seats for any weapons or contraband that may have been overlooked by the previous shift, they loaded their gear and set out for Holy Cross Hospital.

"Man, King's a straight shooter isn't he?" Bens asked.

"That's an understatement," Pete said, as he pulled out of the lot onto 35th Street, "but in a way it makes him a lot easier to work for. You never have to guess where he's coming from, and if you do your job he'll have your back. I guess that he epitomizes the Marine Corps slogan, 'No better friend; no worse enemy'."

"Yeah, I'd hate to ever cross that guy."

They headed west to the Dan Ryan Expressway, where it intersects with 35th Street. The huge, hulking shell of White Sox Park loomed in the background as they headed down the southbound ramp of the freeway. Now named U.S. Cellular Field, it replaced the iconic Comiskey Park, where legendary stars like Minnie Minoso, Nellie Fox, and Luis Aparicio played and later became Hall of Famers.

Marlene turned and asked, "How do you want to handle this, Pete? My thoughts are that we get as much as we can from the folks at the hospital, then hit the District and look at their paperwork from the incident."

"Yeah, that's a good start. Then we can call the Lab guys and see what they came up with before we head over to the victim's residence and talk with the family."

"Sounds good, partner," Marilyn said while giving Pete a playful tap on the arm. "C'mon, Pete, you've got to love this job! Move on, brother, we're not beat cops anymore; we're on to bigger and better things."

"Yeah, yeah…you're right. I need to get my head on straight and be thinking ahead more. I guess that it will work out. In the meantime I want to say a little prayer for the woman who was assaulted. I hope that she makes it."

"Amen."

~ 5 ~

The Plan

He had been following her for a week now, stalking her, recording in his mind her habits, her travel routes, and times. He knew her schedule, knew when she left for work and when she returned. She took the Pulaski Avenue bus to the train that took her downtown. She got off and travelled the rest of the way on foot to an office building on Wabash Avenue. She was another one—part of the many cleaning crews that inhabited the high rises at night, ridding them of the waste and debris left by the privileged people that occupied them during the work day.

He formulated his plan; she was vulnerable before she got to the bus stop near her home, and when she was walking to the office building downtown. He had scouted both areas well. The downtown area seemed to be the better of the two locations. The time of night, 11:30 pm, was ideal—most office workers were long gone by then. But what was more attractive than the time, was the overhead train that ran on an elevated structure above Wabash Avenue.

The "El," as it was referred to by Chicagoans, would easily mask any noise that she might make. It was the third busiest rail system in the country and it operated around the clock. He scoured the area along the route that she would take once she got off the train. He found several alleyways between the buildings, as well as a large alcove at the entrance to a vacant warehouse. Either of them would work but the alcove looked best. He had picked the lock to the burglar bars on the warehouse entry door and surveyed the immediate area. There was a space just inside the doorway that would be ideal for what he needed to do.

The whole process—the planning and the thrill of watching someone without their knowledge—it all added to the excitement of the "hunt." This one was more attractive than the last one, younger too. She would be well worth the risk, and she would bear the brunt of the punishment that he must inflict on those who had rejected him. She would pay, and he would take pleasure in her suffering and pain.

~ 6 ~

Holy Cross Hospital

Pete pulled the unmarked squad into the ER area where official vehicles were allowed to park. "Bens, do you want to do the interviews and I'll do the paper?"

"Sure," she replied, as they walked toward the triage area. Holy Cross Hospital was located in the Marquette Park neighborhood on Chicago's southwest side. Twenty years ago this area was home to a variety of ethnic enclaves, featuring specialty stores and restaurants that catered to each of the diverse cultures. Lithuanians, Polish, German, and Irish families all had their niches carved out in this serene middle class chunk of the city. It was not unusual to have "blood soup" for lunch at a Lithuanian restaurant on 69th Street, and then have a beer after work at an Irish Pub on 67th Street. But the area had changed; it was now inhabited mostly by Hispanics, people of Middle Eastern origin, and African Americans. The crime rate was on the way up, causing many retired folks to move out of the area and into the south suburbs.

They walked into the ER and Marilyn identified herself and Pete to the desk staff, advising them of the reason for their visit. A few minutes later they were escorted into the doctors' area where they were introduced to an attractive female physician. "Good morning, Detectives, I'm Dr. Bennet, how may I help you?"

"I'm Detective Benson and this is my partner, Detective Shannon. We're here to inquire about the condition of Maria Gonzalez. She was assaulted and raped last night as she was on her way to work. Is she conscious, and if so, may we have a word with her?"

The doctor's face took on a more serious look. "I was the one who examined her when she came in early this morning; what a mess. She's suffering from massive head trauma in both her face and the back of her head, the latter wound being the more serious of the two. She lost a substantial amount of blood."

She turned and went over to the computer screen at the nurses' station and pulled up Maria's information. "I did what I could to stop the bleeding and repair the wounds, but I could tell even before we got her x-rayed that she would likely have brain complications. The x-rays verified my diagnosis; she had internal hemorrhaging causing the brain to swell. She was also suffering from a skull fracture. We induced a coma and cut into her skull to relieve the swelling. We still need to do a CT scan on her. I'm positive that we'll need to repair or remove any hematomas that most probably have occurred, and there is likely to be a contusion or two as well. I'm not certain how all of this will affect her cognition, but chances are that she will have some type of disability as a result. Our neurological department will take over once she's released from ICU."

"Doctor, do you have any sense of what may have caused the

injuries?"

She leaned on the counter and turned the screen back toward the nurse on duty. "I'm not sure...the facial injury seems to be consistent with a very hard punch to the face, but the blow to the back of the skull had to be caused by something very hard...a pipe or rock possibly." She looked in Pete's direction. "Her prognosis is not good at all. She's in extremely critical condition, and if the swelling doesn't subside we won't be able to determine if she's suffered any permanent damage."

Marilyn was busy taking notes; she looked up and asked the doctor, "What about a rape kit? Did you take any swabs?"

"I did, although frankly, that was way down on my list of priorities. But since she was brought in totally naked from the waist down, I assumed that you would want that done."

"Good," Bens commented, "that DNA sample might be all we'll have to find the cretin who did this to her, especially if she's unable to speak."

"You said that she's in intensive care Doc?" Pete asked.

"Yes, and she's had some family members here already. Most of them don't speak English, except for her sister. She was the one who gave me most of the information that I have for the chart."

"Is the sister's last name the same—Gonzalez?"

Dr. Bennet leaned over and turned the computer screen back around again so that she could read the chart. "No, the sister's name is Modesta Alverez. She lives at the same address."

"Since we may be dealing with some language issues here, is it alright if I get some ID info from your chart?"

The doctor nodded her approval and Pete moved behind the desk and began to copy down what was relevant from the computer screen. Finishing with their questions they asked Dr. Bennet to take them to the victim's sister. "I can't leave right now," she replied, "but I think that she's in the cafeteria. She asked me where it was located just a few minutes before you two arrived. She should be fairly easy to spot; she's wearing a bright yellow tee shirt with Hubbard High School written across the front."

Marilyn shook the doctor's hand and they headed for the cafeteria. "Thank you so much for your help, doctor." She gave her a business card with their phone number. "If you can think of anything else that we haven't covered, please contact us at that number."

"I'll do that; I hope that you find the sick individual that did this to her. It's so unfair; according to her sister she's a hard-working woman, devoted to her family. She didn't deserve this."

"We'll do our very best," Bens offered. "Thanks again."

They left the ER and headed toward the cafeteria. "She's in critical condition, Marilyn; it may be a long time before we're able to interview her."

"I know."

They walked down the steps to the entrance of the cafeteria. White coats and surgical scrubs filled the room, like white blood cells on a slide upon the stage of a microscope. It was getting close to the lunch hour, and the staff of the hospital was obviously anxious to recharge their batteries. They surveyed the sea of tables and spotted a woman wearing a yellow tee shirt sitting, alone in a corner.

"That's got to be her, Pete…yes; I see the Hubbard High writing."

They made their way over to the table. "Miss Alvarez?

"Yes?"

They introduced themselves. "May we sit down?"

"We're here to find out what happened to your sister. Dr. Bennet told us that you are Maria's sister." Bens reached across the table and took one of the woman's hands in her own. "Ma'am, we're truly sorry for what happened to Maria. My partner and I have been assigned to find whomever it is that did this to her. Is there anything that you can tell us…anything that your sister may have told you about what happened?"

The woman was in obvious emotional pain; her eyes red from tears of grief and sorrow. She looked at the two detectives with a blank stare through two orbs of disbelief. "Why…? Maria is a good mother and wife. She works hard every day, morning and night, never taking time for herself. Who would do such a thing to her?" She took her hand from Marilyn and grasped her own hands together so tightly that her normally brown hands began to turn white around the knuckles.

Pete searched for some words of comfort, but came up short. Who would do such a thing to an obviously loving woman, adored by her family? I know that the Lord has plans for us all, and that all things work together for good, but what good could come from this?

Marilyn moved her chair closer to Modesta's and put her arm around the woman's shoulders. "I don't have the answers to your questions, only the Father knows why and who. But with your help we can try to find some reasons. Were you able to speak with your sister at all?"

"No, when I got here she was in the emergency room. People were running all over the place; it seemed like everyone was working on her. I saw her head and face—blood was everywhere. At first I thought that she was dead!" She buried her face in her hands. "I prayed and prayed that she would be okay, but I never got to talk with her. I think that the doctor said she was unconscious when she came in here."

"Okay, Modesta…okay, she's in good hands." Marilyn whispered, and then drew her close, hugging her for a moment. "We're going to go over to the police station and look at the report made by the officer who found her. We know that two boys discovered her inside the garage; they may have some information that will be useful."

Modesta sat up and wiped her eyes with a napkin from the table. "Here's my card," said Marilyn. "I will be in touch with you shortly. In the meantime if you have any new information, please call me."

The woman looked at the card. "Okay, detective. I will pray that God will help you find this man."

"Thank you, Modesta; Pete and I will pray that Maria is healed."

They said their good-byes and made their way back to the car. "This is going to be a tough case, partner."

"I know," said Bens. "But I just feel something inside about this one…like we're going to be involved in a huge case here. I don't think that Maria is this guy's first or last victim. I think that he's got a taste in his mouth right now of power and domination, and that he wants some more. It's more about the power than the sexual act itself."

They pulled out of the hospital lot and headed toward the 8th

District. "I hope you're wrong, partner, but your instincts have been right on in the past."

Like it or not, they were now fully involved in one of the biggest cases on the Violent Crimes squad. Pete had no choice but to get his head fully in the game. If not, Lt. King would have it on a platter.

~ 7 ~

Chicago Lawn, the 8th District

They pulled their car into the lot behind the station on 63rd Street. "Just like old times, eh, partner?"

Marilyn smiled at him. "Yeah, we worked some pretty decent cases here, Pete; lots of good memories."

"You're right; we made some great arrests here. I guess that's what I miss the most, the good times that we had."

They headed into the station through the rear entrance. "And don't forget the people. Except for Rosato, we made some wonderful friends at this station."

"I know," said Pete.

Rosato was Sal, "The Hammer," Rosato. He turned out to be a

rogue cop who had tried to kill Pete. He was subsequently convicted of attempted murder and was stabbed to death in prison by another inmate shortly after beginning his sentence.

"I guess that I miss seeing Mac every day, but at least we're still friends; we talk every week on the phone."

The two detectives walked up to the desk area that was manned by the day shift desk sergeant, Sgt. Mike Castro. He had been their temporary supervisor on midnights while Sgt. McNamara recovered from a heart attack. In the short time that they had worked for him, they had developed a great relationship. "Sgt. Castro, how are you, brother?"

Castro looked up from a report that he was preparing, "Shannon…Benson…how the heck are you guys?" He reached over the top of the desk and shook their hands. "What brings you two back, detective work too challenging?" He joked.

"No," Marilyn replied. "Actually we're here to investigate the rape that occurred in the district last night."

"Oh, yeah," said Castro. "That was a vicious one. Whoever did it really whacked her good, the two kids who found her thought that she was dead. Have you been to the hospital yet? How is she?"

Marilyn told Castro about their interview with the doctor and the victim's sister. "So what we need to do now, Sarge, is to review the preliminary report and get what info we can before we go over to the house and speak with the family."

"Good luck there," said Castro, as he shuffled through some papers. "Unless you're a Spanish speaker you won't get many answers. If I were you I'd concentrate on the two kids who found her in the garage. I'm not sure of exactly when she lost consciousness, but I thought that I read that she uttered something."

"Oh, I hadn't heard that," remarked Marilyn. "Thanks for the tip."

They said goodbyes to Castro and headed over to the Review Office where the reports are filed and later categorized according to the offense. Finding the stack of case reports from the previous day, they located the rape case and made copies for themselves and then headed to the break room for a cup of coffee. They sat down with their drinks and went over the report.

"Pete, both of the boys who found her are eighth graders. I would think that they'd make pretty decent witnesses... have a pretty good eye for detail. What do you think?"

"Maybe.... They were intent on sneaking a cigarette in there, so when they walked in and saw the victim they must have almost jumped out of their skin."

"Yeah, I know," she said, "but the report states that she uttered or moaned something like, 'the eye,' or 'my eye,' or something about an eye. That means that they didn't just turn and run out of there."

He thought about it for a second. "Good point, Bens. Let's hit their homes after school's out and talk with them. At the very least we can get some follow up on things that may have been overlooked in the initial report—like how much she was wearing, how her clothes were arranged or thrown about; things that might not seem important now, but may be later on."

"Now you're thinking like an investigator, partner." Marilyn finished her coffee then threw her cup in the trash. "Let's get some chow while we still have the chance and brainstorm this thing over lunch. What do you think?"

"I think that's a great idea. Hey, isn't Joe working the day shift today?"

Joe was Officer Joe Murphy, Marilyn's boyfriend, who was a beat officer in the 8th District. He had been a Chicago Police Detective, but had left the job for a couple of years before returning to work this year. His wife, Pat, had been killed in an auto accident and afterward Joe had lost the desire to be a cop. He had worked in a friend's business, keeping himself so occupied that he had all but lost contact with his former friends and colleagues. That all changed when he and Bens met at a barbeque at Pete and Beth's home. Since then, he and Marilyn had been inseparable.

"Yes, he's on days working a one-man car on the west side of the district."

"Do you want to hook up with him for lunch?"

They were back to their car by now. "No, Pete, I'd rather not."

"Why? Are you two having problems?"

"No, we're good," she answered, as they closed the car doors and buckled up. "I just don't want to start mixing business with pleasure. Besides, I don't know what lunch time that he's been assigned."

Pete wondered if that was the truth or not. It seemed that as long as they were in Joe's area it wouldn't hurt to have a sandwich together and just say hi, but he wasn't going to press the issue. "Okay, what are you hungry for today?"

"I need greens, Pete; I'm not getting enough veggies in my diet. Let's go get a salad."

Pete pulled out on to 63rd Street and headed west. "Greens it is. Say, are you training for another contest, Miss Illinois?"

"No, I'm just trying to maintain a good diet. This new assignment seems to have us sitting down a lot, much more than when we were working the beat. I don't want to put on any extra tonnage. Besides, I still have to get my run in after work."

He teased her and said, "Well if you could get your lazy butt out of bed early in the morning like I do, you'd have your run in already."

"Don't even start that with me, Pete Shannon," she joked, "you're the early guy; I'm the late one. I can't seem to get in bed in time to get the sleep that I need to get up early. I'm working on it though."

"Well, make sure that you can keep up with me, partner. I don't want to have to wait on you if we have to chase after someone."

She feigned looking offended and said, "You little...that's the last thing you ever have to worry about with me!"

"Whoa, partner, take it easy!" He laughed and gave her a hug as they walked into the restaurant. "I know that I can depend on you, Bens. I was just kidding around. I'm grateful that you are my partner...I feel blessed."

They got a table in the corner where they could watch the door and just about everything else going on in the restaurant. It's something that all cops do. They feel uncomfortable if they can't keep their eye on people that come and go. If something happens they want to be on top of it. The worse thing for a cop at meal time is to have his back facing the door. Watch one the next time that you see an officer come into a place to eat—he'll be checking out the seats that afford the best view of the door.

They placed their order, and then Marilyn turned to Pete with a frown on her face. "Pete, I lied to you when I said things were fine with me and Joe."

"What?"

"I didn't want to have lunch with him today because we're in the midst of a little spat."

"Oh," Pete took a sip of water. "Want to share with me?"

"He's been having stomach pains and not eating well as a result. I've been urging him to see a doctor but he's been reluctant to go for some reason. Last night we were out for a late dinner and he barely finished half of his meal. Things got kind of heated and we left the restaurant mad at each other. He dropped me off at home and I didn't even kiss him good night."

"I'm sorry to hear that, Bens, but Joe's a big boy. He'll see the light and get himself checked out."

"I hope that you're right; I'm worried about him. Anyway, I told you before that I would always be up front with you…I'm sorry that I lied."

Pete reached across the table and squeezed her hand. "Don't worry about it. I'm glad that you told me; I'll put Joe on my prayer list."

"Thanks, partner. Joe has really been a positive factor in my life in the short time that we've been dating. I don't want anything to happen to him."

Their food arrived; Pete blessed the meal and they started laying their blueprint for the upcoming investigation.

~ 8 ~

Time for Advice

"Where are the boys?" Beth asked, as she let Susan in the door while carrying Pete, Jr.; Susan closed it after herself and followed Beth inside.

"They're home; my parents came over today so that I could get out and do some visiting and shopping. What a blessing they are...."

"C'mon, Susan, let's have a cup of coffee and talk." Beth said, as she led the way to the kitchen.

Susan took little Pete from Beth so that Beth could prepare a fresh pot of coffee. They spent the next five minutes talking about the baby, Susan snuggling him the entire time. Beth poured them each a cup of coffee.

"Let me put this little guy down for a nap, then you and I can visit." A couple of minutes later Beth reappeared in the kitchen. "So tell me, Susan, are things any better...is the hurt going away any?"

Taking a sip of her drink, Susan played with the cup for a moment, looking into the murky liquid as if the answer might be found there. "That's what I wanted to talk to you about, Beth. I still miss Joe tremendously, especially at the end of the day, but something happened recently that has me confused and feeling somewhat guilty."

Furrowing her brow, Beth asked, "What do you mean?"

"Well, after Mass this past Sunday I was talking with Father Mike. I told him that I really missed being around adults and having grown up conversations. He suggested that I go next door to the Parish Activity Center for coffee; he said it would be good for me to meet some other parishioners."

"Pete and I have done that a couple of times," said Beth. "It's a nice little get together and a perfect way to meet some of the people that we see at Mass each Sunday."

"You're right, it is great, plus the kids can have a snack and play in the recreation area."

Beth got up from the table and poured herself a refill. "Can I get you some more?"

"No thanks."

Sitting back down, Beth asked her friend, "So what went wrong, why are you feeling guilty about having coffee after mass?"

"It's not about the coffee." Susan went on to explain to Beth about meeting David. "I guess that I was just so stunned that I had felt something toward this stranger, except that he didn't seem like a stranger. He was warm and sincere, and I felt…well…an attraction…."

"An attraction? You mean as in a romantic attraction?"

"Yes—that's why I'm confused, and, frankly, a little guilty about the whole thing. I feel like I'm being dishonorable, like I should be mourning and not even entertaining thoughts like that. Am I wrong, Beth; am I out of line?"

She took Susan's hand. "I don't know for sure, I'm hardly one to say what's right and wrong after all of the mistakes that I've made in my own life. But I do know that you are a strong, devoted, and loving mother. You were faithful to your husband, and you are most certainly dedicated to your children. My sense is that if this accidental meeting took place, and, of all places at the church, then perhaps there's a message there somewhere. Maybe it's the Father telling you that it's okay to get back to normal—to be back among people and not spend your days at home with the kids in mourning."

"What about the guilt?" Susan asked, raising her eyebrows, begging for an answer that would justify her feelings.

"I don't know how long that will last, or if it's even appropriate," said Beth. "I think that guilt is different with each person and each circumstance. I know that I am still feeling some guilt for what I did to Pete. I don't think that I will ever completely forgive myself for being unfaithful…but I'm working on it—hard—and praying about it every day."

"What do you think I should do? Should I go back and see him again?"

Beth let go of Susan's hand and took another drink of her coffee. "That's your choice. But listen, you haven't done anything wrong, Susan. You talked with a man for a couple of minutes; you don't even know him. I think that if he interests you then you should speak with him again. You're at church for goodness sake, it's not like you're meeting him at a bar."

"When you put it in that context it doesn't seem so bad," sighed Susan.

"It's not bad; go have a cup of coffee with him while the kids are playing. I don't think that there's any harm in that."

Susan got up from the table and brought her cup over to the sink. "Let me sneak in little Pete's room and give him a kiss before I leave." A minute later the two friends walked to the front door.

"Beth, I feel so much better. Thank you for your wise counsel and understanding. You have always been such a dear friend."

They hugged each other and then Beth opened the door. "You're welcome. I'm glad that I was able to say something that comforted you. Just know that I will be praying for you and the boys."

"Thanks, Beth, I appreciate your prayers. Please stop by when you can, the boys would love to see little Pete."

"I will. God bless you."

"Bye."

Susan got in her car and drove to the shopping center close to her home. She still needed to get some grocery shopping done, and it was much easier when she didn't have the little ones with her. On the way there she thought about her conversation with Beth. Meeting David seemed perfectly logical and innocent. *Why am I feeling so guilty about this?* She pulled into the lot and walked into the supermarket, determined to push the guilt from her mind. She would see David again, how wrong could it be?

~ 9 ~

The Diagnosis

"So what's the verdict, Doc, what's my problem?" Shifting in his seat, his muscles tensed as if expecting to be struck a blow, Joe stared at his oncologist. He had been dreading this visit since yesterday when Dr. Baker had called, and was told by the doctor that he was reluctant to discuss the results of the tests over the phone. Sure, he had been experiencing pain in his stomach for several months, but it had happened before so he brushed it off as probably just gas or spicy food. He enjoyed those "Chicago style" hot dogs with sport peppers. But when he had noticed blood in the toilet a week ago, he knew that he could no longer delay getting checked out. Although this recent development concerned him, he didn't want Marilyn to know anything about it. Just last night they had argued about it. She was insistent upon him going for an examination. Joe knew that she was right, that he needed to be looked at, but he didn't want to alarm her unless it was absolutely necessary. That's why he didn't tell her that he had indeed already been to a doctor.

Grabbing a file from the corner of his desk, the doctor sat down. "Joe, how are you feeling today?"

"Not bad…a little nervous right now."

"Well I must tell you that before we even ran the tests and did the MRI I already had a suspicion of what your problem was, but I didn't want to speculate until I was absolutely sure."

This is serious. Joe was feeling anxious now, beads of sweat starting to surface on his forehead and not liking the demeanor of the doctor—he was all business—no playful bantering or remarks. The doctor opened the folder that he had been holding.

"Joe, you've got colon cancer. When you told me that you were having stomach problems and that you had blood in your stool, I immediately thought colorectal cancer. The blood, along with your cramping, constipation, and weight loss…they're all classic symptoms of the disease."

Cancer…! Joe couldn't believe what he was hearing. How could this be happening? It can't be real…Dear Lord, let me wake up and find that this is all just a bad dream….

The doctor continued. "Your family history doesn't reflect that the disease is prevalent, but since colon cancer is the third most common type of cancer in the United States, it's not that unlikely that you would develop it. The good news is that the death rate from colon cancer has declined steadily, especially when detected early, but in your case, Joe, we didn't catch it in the very early stage so we're going to have to treat it aggressively."

"What do you mean by aggressively, doc?"

"Well, you've got what we call Stage I, the cancer has begun to spread but it's still in the inner lining—that's good. My treatment protocol usually involves chemotherapy to begin with, that will hopefully destroy the cancer cells that have metastasized. If I don't see the progress that I'm hoping for, I may add radiation therapy as well."

"What does that mean, doc, metastasized? "

"Cells that have spread, we want to kill them as well as shrink the tumor. Then I'd like to re-evaluate you first, but my sense is that we may wind up operating to remove the tumor and any surrounding affected tissue."

Trying to catch his breath after the onslaught of bad news that had rolled over him like a huge boulder hurtling downhill, Joe sat straighter in his chair, trying to force feed air into his lungs. More sweat popped out on his forehead, like acne on a teenager, and he began to feel a little faint. Trying to maintain his air of confidence, yet still absorb every word that the doctor was saying, he asked, "What are my chances here…I mean, am I going to die?"

"Joe, this is not a death sentence; far from it. Although I would have liked to have caught this thing sooner, the fact is that it's still somewhat early and you have a great chance of beating it. You're in good overall health, you're young and vibrant, and from what little I know about you thus far you're a man of faith. People that believe in God—those that pray—for some reason seem to experience better recovery rates. There's nothing scientific in my hypothesis, mind you, but that's been my observation."

"So when do we begin, doc?"

"Yesterday."

"What?"

"Just kidding, Joe, but we need to begin ASAP and take the battle to the cancer. The longer we wait, the harder it will be to defeat this enemy. I want to begin chemo on you right away."

A million ideas began running through his head: Marilyn, the job, his family. Joe responded, "Okay, can you get me in tomorrow?"

"Yes, in the afternoon. Come in around two and my staff will prep you on the first of four sessions this week." The doctor handed a couple brochures to Joe. "In the meantime, here's some literature that you'll need to familiarize yourself with what to expect in the short term while you're undergoing treatment. The first week will be tough to get used to, but I'm positive that you can handle it."

Joe reached across the desk and took the pamphlets, and at that moment somehow found some inner strength. "Doc, I like the way that you described the treatment. You likened it to a battle…to defeating an enemy. That's been a metaphor for my life recently. I've had some challenges, some demons that I've had to fight. If I just put this disease in that context I think that I can prevail."

The doctor stood and extended his hand to him. "Now you're talking, Joe. That's exactly the attitude that a patient needs to assume. Being a fighter is much better than being a complainer and a victim. I like the phrase, 'Be a victor, not a victim.' Your demeanor throughout this entire battle will be paramount in your recovery."

Feeling somewhat unsteady on his feet, but recognizing that he had many reasons to live—the most important one being Marilyn—he grabbed the doctor's hand to shake it before leaving. "Thanks for your honesty, sir. As you know I'm a cop, and we trust our partners with our lives. You are now my partner in this medical struggle and I am putting my life in your hands. I promise to do my part if you'll do yours."

The doctor shook his hand, "Joe, I promise you that together we will battle this adversary and win."

Turning to leave, Joe said, "I believe you, doc. I'm scared as hell right now but I'm ready to fight. I'll see you tomorrow, sir, God bless you."

"Thanks, Joe. I'm optimistic that we will be victorious."

Joe didn't even remember leaving the hospital and getting into his car. Before he knew it he was at Queen of Martyrs Church, not able to even remember having driven there. Getting out and walking into the familiar and comforting surroundings, he made his way to the front and knelt in the first pew. He looked at the figure of Jesus on the cross; reflecting on the pain and suffering that He went through so that we would enjoy eternal life. *Lord, I know that my pain will never equal yours, but I pray that you will strengthen me for the upcoming battle. Please don't let me despair; comfort me when I feel like quitting. Fill me with your Holy Spirit and help me defeat this devil within me. Hear me Lord, please....*

~ 10 ~

Billy Callahan

They arrived at the address listed on the initial case report. The house was a typical Chicago brick bungalow; thousands of them were built in the 1950's, and hundreds of typical city workers have lived in them ever since. They were each built on small lots, 25 by 100 feet, separated by a walkway, which in Chicago is referred to as a "gangway." The houses are so close to each other that it was not unusual to hear one's neighbors' conversations, as well as other usually private activities, during the summer when all of the windows were open on warm evenings.

Billy Callahan was a white male, thirteen years old; he had been the one that made the call to 9-1-1. The beat car had met him and his friend at the convenience store and the officer then drove to the crime scene with the boys in the back seat. On the way, they told the officer that the victim had mumbled something, causing him to immediately request an ambulance meet him at the scene. Once they arrived, the officer determined that the woman was indeed still alive, and several minutes later she was on her way to the hospital.

Luckily, the responding officer was an old-timer who knew the importance of protecting a crime scene. He interviewed the boys, got their identifying information, and then sent them on their way. The officer then guarded the garage until the Mobile Crime Lab arrived to process the area.

Pete was also keenly aware of the importance of evidence and routinely limited the number of people that he allowed in and out of a crime scene. Strange as it may seem, even though cops have seen hundreds of dead bodies throughout their careers, they seem to have a morbid fascination with seeing the next one. The problem is that the more people that enter the area to take a look at the victim, the more trace evidence that is brought into and taken from the scene.

The two detectives walked up the front steps and rang the doorbell. An attractive woman with red hair and nails to match answered, "Hello, may I help you?"

They presented their ID's to the woman who then let them into her home. "I guess that you're here about Billy finding that woman this morning," she said, as she offered them a seat.

"Yes ma'am," Marilyn replied.

"How is she, did she make it?"

"Actually she's still alive but in a coma; she has some brain damage and some swelling. The doctors want to keep her in a coma until they can control the swelling and repair some of the damage."

Lighting a cigarette and taking a long drag that seemed to last forever, the woman blew out the smoke which quickly drifted toward the two detectives. Her hand went to cover her mouth, as if to stop any more from escaping, and then blurted out, "Oh, I'm sorry, do you mind?"

"It's your house, ma'am," Pete replied. After looking at both of them she decided that they were non-smokers and put it out.

Marilyn readied her notepad and asked, "Are you Billy's mother?"

"Yes, I'm Kathy Callahan, his mom. His dad's at work; he's a firefighter."

"Mrs. Callahan...."

"You can call me Kathy."

"Ok...Kathy, what has your son told you about what he and his friend saw this morning at that garage near school?"

Flicking the ashes of her now unlit cigarette, the woman answered. "First of all he told me that he and Jose were sneaking a cigarette, that's why they were in there. I told him that his dad was going to take care of him tomorrow morning when he gets off duty. We don't allow him to smoke, he's just a kid."

"Kathy, we're not too concerned about why Billy was there, but we are definitely interested in knowing as much as he can remember about what he saw. Is Billy home from school?"

Glancing toward the staircase, the woman replied. "He's upstairs in his room probably playing his video games. That kid's addicted to them—probably plays them four or five hours a day. Want me to get him?"

"Yes ma'am."

Without moving from the couch, the woman screamed. "Billy!

Come down here!"

A few seconds later, a skinny boy with close cropped hair appeared at the bottom of the stairs. "What do you want, ma?"

"The police want to ask you some more questions about this morning, come in here and sit down," the woman said, as she motioned for Billy to sit next to her on the sofa.

The boy did as he was told and immediately took a seat next to his mother on the couch. He started wringing his hands, and it was hard to tell if he was more concerned with the police being at his home or with sitting next to his mom.

"Billy," started Marilyn, "at the moment that you and Jose walked into that garage, what exactly did you see?"

He hesitated for a moment, "We didn't really see nuthin at first," he looked at his mom, "because we were going to smoke a cigarette. But then we saw the lady on the floor." He looked at her again. "She didn't have any clothes on from her waist down."

"What else?"

"Well, Jose wanted to take a closer look, and then we saw that there was a lot of blood under her head and it looked like somebody smacked her pretty hard in the face."

Pete was writing notes while Marilyn asked Billy the questions.

"Billy, you and Jose go to that garage fairly often, don't you?"

"Yeah...kind of."

"Did anything look different to you...other than the lady on the floor?"

"No, not really. I mean we just go in there and share one quick smoke," Billy looked down at the floor, "and then we have to get to school."

"So...." Marilyn was about to ask another question when Billy interrupted.

"Wait, I just remembered," the boy said with a grin, "it was a little darker in there this time."

"What do you mean?"

Billy leaned forward. "The side window was covered, so I guess that's why we didn't see her right away. There was like a piece of steel or something leaned up against it, so it made it a lot darker."

"Good, Billy, that's a big help. What else can you remember about it? Is there anything that you didn't tell the officer?"

Now Billy was beginning to wring his hands again. Looking down at the floor he spoke, "There's one thing that we didn't tell him."

Benson leaned forward in her chair. "What Billy, what didn't you tell him?"

The boy looked at his mother, and then quickly averted his eyes downward. "Well...when we moved in closer to take a look at the lady, Jose touched her."

"Billy!" the boy's mother shouted.

"How, Billy, how did he touch her?" Marilyn asked.

Keeping his head down, Billy answered, "In her private area."

With that answer his mother jumped up from her seat. "What?"

"Mom, it was Jose, not me!" Billy cowered. "I didn't touch her at all. Anyway when he touched her, that's when she moaned and said something about her eye, or his eye, or something like that. It scared Jose so much when she said it, that he fell over backwards and then we both ran out of there to the store so we could call 9-1-1."

Her hands on her hips, Billy's mother stared at him. "Billy, you didn't tell me anything about that, why not?"

"I was scared, mom; I knew it was wrong."

Pointing her finger right in her son's face, she said, "You are grounded mister. Officers are you finished with him?"

Marilyn wanted to keep Billy on their side and didn't want him to think that the police were mad at him as well. "Billy, it's okay. You didn't do anything wrong, your friend was the one who touched her—right?"

"Yeah, I only looked at her."

"Good. Is there anything else that you can remember?"

He thought for a moment and then replied. "No ma'am, just that the window was covered. That's the only thing that was different."

"Did you see where the woman's clothes were?"

"No ma'am, to tell you the truth we never even thought about that."

Marilyn stood up. "Okay, Billy, that's all we have for now. We appreciate your help. Whoever hurt this lady has to be stopped."

"You get back up to your room, mister," his mother ordered. Billy turned and did as he was told while Pete and Marilyn prepared to leave. But before they left Pete wanted to ensure that Billy didn't take too much heat from his parents.

"Mrs. Callahan, I can appreciate the fact that you're upset with your son for smoking. I'm sure that you and your husband will discipline him appropriately, but I also want you to know that we appreciate the fact that Billy was cooperative and forthright with us. Our job is so much easier when witnesses come forward. I'd like you to praise your son for being a good citizen and reporting a crime. Unfortunately there are too many people today that refuse to cooperate and supply important information."

She shook her head. "I guess you're right. I'm just so mad that he was sneaking around."

"Kathy," Marilyn said, "you've got a good kid there. That information about the window being covered could really help us out with this case. Go easy on him."

"I will. I just don't want him to get involved with some of the punks around here that are up to no good. This used to be a good neighborhood to raise a family. Now, I see a lot of things going on that scare me. That's why I don't say too much about him spending time with the video games. At least I know where he's at and that he's safe."

"Thanks again, Mrs. Callahan," said Pete, as they exited and walked down the stairs. They climbed into their car and looked at one another.

Pete spoke first. "I say we go over to that garage and see what was covering that window."

"I agree," said Marilyn. "In fact, I say that we inventory it as evidence—it could have our guy's prints on it."

Pete pulled away from the curb and headed to the crime scene.

"You know, you're getting to be quite the investigator, Detective Benson."

"Thanks for the compliment, but I'll feel more like a detective when we catch this scumbag."

"Amen to that."

~ 11 ~

Bad Feelings

They recovered the evidence that Billy had described from the garage. It turned out to be a piece of sheet metal that had rested on the window sill. Hopefully their guy had placed it there to darken the interior and prevent anyone who may have seen him take the woman inside from observing him while he brutalized his victim. The detectives preserved it for prints, placed it in the trunk of their vehicle, and then headed back to the office to catch up on their paperwork.

Once they arrived, Marilyn worked on transcribing the statements from the Billy Callahan interview, while Pete filled out the necessary forms to maintain the chain of evidence relating to the piece of metal. He notified the police courier that they had property to go to the lab, and then started working on their Daily Activity Report. Every detective completed a "Daily." It was one of the ways in which each detective accounted for their time each shift.

While they were still involved with the reports, Lt. King walked into the squad area. It was close to quitting time; most of the squad was present and consumed with files. King stood just outside of his office and shouted a command, "Listen up!"

That was their cue to drop everything and focus on the boss. Typing ceased; phones were hung up. King ran a hand over his brush cut hair, and then placed both hands on his hips. "I just got through seeing the 'Old Man'. He's taking heat from City Hall about this cave dweller whose been robbing the old folks at Wrigley Field. The Mayor wants this idiot stopped right now, so since you all know what rolls downhill, here are our new marching orders."

Everyone leaned forward waiting to hear how this new information was going to impact their lives.

"The Chief wants a full court press on this guy. We're to drop what we can for the time being and focus on Cub's Park. Geraci and Carone…you'll be working backup."

Gerry Geraci and Phil Carone had been detectives for seven years, the last two of which had seen them working as partners in King's unit. Known to everyone as the "Italian Stallions," because of their love of women and constant display of gold jewelry, they were often the butt of jokes and pranks.

Geraci spoke up while raising his hand at the same time. "Boss, I thought that we had the paper on this case. What gives?"

"Take it easy big man; you still have the case.

Shannon…Benson…."

"Yes, sir."

"You'll be working as decoys on this one. I've arranged for the undercover unit to outfit you with some appropriate senior citizen clothing and wigs. The plan is this: you'll be dropped off at the ball park by Geraci and Carone who will be driving the surveillance van. You'll both leave the park around the seventh inning. And you'll both wear a wire so that we can monitor your location and hear your conversation. "

Bens and Pete looked at each other and smiled. But when they looked over at the Stallions, it was obvious that they didn't appear to be very pleased with the plan.

"You guys work out whatever code words you need to signal each other when this guy strikes, but this is the game plan for the near future until we grab this fool."

Carone stood up and asked a question. "Boss, why can't we just saturate the area with all of our guys instead of doing this UC thing?"

Biting his lip, King answered. "Carone, have you ever taken a good look at our cars?"

"Yes sir."

"Do you think that they look like cop cars?"

"Yeah, boss, but...."

"That's the reason why we're doing what we're doing. If we start throwing a heavier presence around the park we'll spook this guy. Benson and Shannon are the only team on the squad that has a female, that's why they draw the UC straw. Now, any problems with that?"

His shoulders drooping, Carone sat back down. "No, sir, I just thought that me and Phil could catch this guy if you gave us some time."

"I'm sure that you could but we don't have time. Tomorrow both teams work the afternoon shift. I'll have the motor pool bring the surveillance van and park it out back. I've already talked with the Tech guys; I've got two transmitters and receivers on the way to the unit, along with two cell phones programmed to the same channel. They'll be here in the morning. Shannon, you and your partner stop downstairs at the Undercover Unit and get your props for this gig. They're expecting you."

"Yes sir."

"Any other questions?" No one had any; King walked back into his office.

Bens rolled her chair over to Pete's desk. "Wow, what do you think, Pete?"

"I think that this is a pretty sweet deal for us, but I don't think that the Stallions are feeling the same way."

"Yeah." Bens lowered her voice. "I think that we should go over and see what's up with these guys."

"Okay." Pete grabbed his notebook and they walked over to their squad mates' desks. "You guys want to talk about a plan?"

Geraci spun around in his chair so that his back was to them. That spoke volumes. Carone wasn't as subtle. "Who do you two think you are? You're still wet behind the freakin' ears and you want to steal our case? You got balls."

Pete couldn't believe what he was hearing. "Hey, listen, Carone," said Pete, "let's get one thing straight here. We knew nothing about this UC deal until just now. We're not trying to steal anything from anyone."

"Yeah, right. You two are glory hounds, man. I seen you on TV on that kidnapping case...big friggin' camera hogs."

Marilyn was steamed, the color creeping up her neck filling her cheeks with the color of war paint. She put both hands on Carone's desk, leaned over and put her face just inches from his.

"Hold on a second, my friend. The last thing that we want to do is work someone else's case. Pete and I have our hands full with our own case load. As far as the undercover assignment...I hope that it ends quickly because now our own leads will be getting cold."

Carone rolled backward on his chair for some breathing room, his eyes opened wide in fear of this woman's wrath being directed his way.

Marilyn continued. "And one more thing...you saw us on TV alright—just after we were both almost killed by some steroid fueled psycho. We've earned everything that we have, pal, no one's handed us any gifts. If you can't deal with what's happening, that sounds like a personal problem to me—go see the Chaplain."

King walked out of his office toward the four detectives. "Is there a problem here?"

"No sir," Pete said, smiling broadly. "Just working on the plan and what our trouble code will be."

"Good, before you hit the street tomorrow I want an OPS plan on my desk. Geraci, I want that from you, understood?"

"Yes, sir, you'll have it."

King walked out of the squad area and into the hallway.

"Alright, heroes," said Carone. "We'll make this thing work, but I'm not happy about it."

"That's too bad," said Bens. "But if it makes you feel any better, we're not exactly jumping up and down for joy either."

They made their way back over to their own desks. "Man, I can't believe those two guys."

Pete sat down. "Listen, let's just finish our paper and then check in with the UC office and get what we need for our disguises. Tomorrow's a new day. Maybe those two hot heads will have cooled down a little by then."

"Okay, partner," said Marilyn. "Or should I say, geezer?"

~ 12 ~

The Next Day

Pete finished up his morning run and then headed into Xav's for a session with the weights. Living next to the campus of St. Xavier University was convenient. As a graduate of the school he was able to maintain his membership at the gym, which allowed him to keep in touch with his many friends and colleagues. Father Mike, the pastor at Queen of Martyrs Catholic Church, was also a member. Pete was hoping to see him there this morning. Some of their best moments together had been spent running and working out.

He got busy with his exercise routine; today was chest and triceps. His philosophy about the importance of staying fit was simple, his job as a cop demanded that he be able to handle any challenges that he might face. The stress of police work could sometimes be overwhelming. Many of his colleagues suffered heart attacks and developed other health problems because they didn't maintain a fitness program. Having attended a street survival seminar toward the beginning of his police career, gave him the opportunity to speak with several officers who had been involved in critical incidents. They told him that one of the big reasons for their survival had been their physical conditioning. That was all that Pete needed to hear; from that point forward he made exercise a part of each day.

He was about twenty minutes into his session when he spotted Father Mike walk in. "Father, how are you today?"

Father Mike was a great friend. He had been close to Pete and Beth when their marriage was about to go off the tracks. Pete sought his advice on all things spiritual; he was an important part of his life.

"I'm good, Pete, thanks. Looks like you're already into it so I guess that I'll get changed and head out for a run on my own."

"I would have called you, Father, but I didn't know until late yesterday that I would be working afternoons for awhile."

"Big case?" He asked.

"Kind of...." Pete filled him in on the robbery suspect at Wrigley Field.

"Wow, Pete, that's exciting stuff. I sometimes envy you and Marilyn, working on cases like that. It's like some of the stuff that's on TV."

"It's a good case, Father. The Mayor wants this guy grabbed before he hurts someone, not to mention the bad PR that it could bring to Cubs Park."

"Well you two be careful out there, Pete, no telling what this idiot might do when you confront him. I'll pray for your safety."

"Thanks, Father, I'll return the favor."

"You're a good man, Pete. Let's get together for a run Saturday morning…call me."

"Will do, brother." The priest disappeared into the locker room and Pete finished up with his workout so that he could get home and spend some time with Beth and little Pete.

Twenty minutes later he was walking into the back door of his house. "What's for lunch, babe?"

Beth and the baby were in the kitchen. She was cleaning some bottles while the little guy reclined in his baby seat watching his mommy.

"I've got some leftovers from last night. I can heat them up and put a salad together; how does that sound?"

"Sounds terrific," he said, giving her a big hug and a kiss. "Did I ever tell you how much I love you?"

Grinning, she replied, "No, never. Let me hear it."

"I love you, Beth Shannon." And he meant it. The last year of their marriage had been the worst ever, yet strangely it had also been the best. Their faith had been tested and challenged like never before. His partner had been murdered, he had been wounded by of all people—a fellow cop, and their whole life seemed to be spiraling downward. He had seen Satan at work, doing his best to sink his claws into Pete and drag him down into the never ending fire. But his faith and trust in the Father had redeemed him.

Beth had experienced her own struggles. She had to confess her one-time infidelity to Pete, and then endure their agreed to separation. And then…the horror of the shootings. Amidst all of that, the demons that had haunted her for so long—infidelity and addiction—finally caused her to face reality. And when she was able to be honest with herself and with Pete, they found that the Holy Spirit had strengthened them and they were blessed with their son, Pete, Jr.

Pete grabbed a quick shower and then played with the baby while Beth prepared their lunch. "So, what's the story on these two guys...Geraci and Carone?" Beth asked, as she cut up some lettuce. "Why are they mad at you and Marilyn?"

"I'm not sure, honey, but they may think that perhaps we're trying to steal their case, or at least kiss in on it." He put little Pete back into his baby seat on the table. "Of course, they're wrong, but there's no doubt that it's a high visibility case that potentially will get someone an award or maybe a favor granted. But to tell you the truth, Bens and I would be happy to just concentrate on the rape case that we've been working. That case is going to suffer if we can't put our entire focus on it."

Beth brought the plates over to the table and set them down.

"Beth, why don't you bless the meal?"

"Okay." They held each other's hands and she began.... "Dear Father, we thank you for this meal and for this day. We are grateful for all of your blessings, especially our beautiful son, Pete, Jr. May your light continue to shine upon our family; we bless your name and pray that your son, our Lord and Savior Jesus Christ, will walk with us this day and every day. In Jesus' name we pray...Amen."

"Amen," he joined. "The Stallions think...."

Beth looked up, "The Stallions?"

Smiling, Pete said, "Oh yeah, that's the nickname for Geraci and Carone in the unit. I guess they're a couple of skirt chasers who adorn themselves with lots of gold jewelry. Anyway, they accused us of being publicity hounds as the reason for wanting to work their case."

"That's ridiculous," Beth said.

"You're right. We didn't even know that we were on the case until the same moment that they found out. Bens got ticked off; you should have seen her, honey. She got right in Carone's face and let him have it...told him that if he had a problem with it that he should go see the Chaplain. It was priceless."

"Marilyn's a tough cookie," replied Beth. "They're messing with the wrong gal when they mess with her. But, Pete, this thing worries me somewhat. Last night you said that you and Bens would be out as decoys and the other two guys would be your back up."

"Yes, that's the plan."

Putting down her fork, Beth began to shake her head, "Pete, remember what happened with Rosato? He got mad and tried to kill you. What happens if these guys want to get even and decide that they don't want to back you up? What if they let something bad happen?"

"I don't think that they would do that, babe; Rosato was just a bad cop, but I guess that you can't ever rule anything out. Marilyn and I will be super cautious, regardless. Besides, if we lock this guy up it's still their case and they'll get credit for the clear up."

"More coffee?" She got up to pour herself a refill.

"No thanks."

"Pete, I'm still going to say my prayer to St. Michael every day, and I hope that you are doing the same."

St. Michael the Archangel was the patron saint of police officers. It had been Pete's practice for years to say a quick prayer to him before each shift. He was convinced that St. Michael had saved his life on at least one occasion.

"I never forget, babe; I say that prayer every day."

"Good, I'm going to put the baby down for a nap."

"Now that's a plan; I think that I'll join you both. An old guy like me needs more rest than you younger folks."

"Pete, don't play that role around me," she said, jokingly. "I like you just the way you are. Wait until you get into your undercover assignment at work before you turn into a 'senior'."

"Okay, babe." This assignment was going to be very interesting

~ 13 ~

Under the "EL"

She was there, leaving at exactly 11:30 pm just like clockwork. She exited her apartment on Kedzie Avenue to catch the bus on 59th Street that would take her to the El train. She lived on a busy thoroughfare which made it much too risky for him to try to grab her there. His scouting trips, the ones where he had followed her to work, had convinced him that taking her downtown was the best plan.

He watched her board the bus and then pulled out onto Kedzie to start his own journey to the Loop. It would have been easier to get on the bus with her, except that he had done that once already. Chances are that she would get suspicious, not many passengers this time of night. No, driving himself downtown was even smarter. He would beat her there and then be able to prepare for her—everything would be perfect.

He headed northbound toward the Stevenson Expressway, which would carry him quickly to the Loop. From there he would head east to his chosen spot where he would await her arrival. Parking downtown was always a headache during the day, but at night the regulations were relaxed and there were plenty of spaces available. Parking on the street was no problem. He found a space on Wabash Avenue, just a block away from the location where he intended to punish this one.

He had made good time getting here. He looked at his watch—still about 15 minutes to spare before she would be walking down the street. Plenty of time to check the building, he thought, getting out of his car.

On the way to the location he looked at the businesses—everything's closed—perfect. He stopped at the burglar gate at the entrance to the building that he had scouted for the attack. *Something's wrong here....* The padlock that he had previously left open and hanging for appearance sake had been moved. He pushed open one side of the gate and went inside. It was dark; he stopped momentarily allowing his eyes to adjust. He heard something. Walking around the corner of the alcove where the main entrance doors were located, he saw a figure lying on the ground, asleep...snoring.

He crept forward and noticed that it was apparently one of the many homeless people who seek refuge from the night once the business people leave to go home. Kicking the man hard in the side, he shouted, "Hey, you, get up...get up. Get outta here!"

Propping himself up on one elbow while trying to process what was happening the man squinted his eyes to see who this intruder was. "You the cops?"

"Never mind who I am. Get outta here before I kick your ass."

The vagrant was used to getting rousted by the police; it was part of the game. "Hey, man, I got no place to sleep. I ain't hurtin' nobody."

Kicking him again, only harder this time, the man commanded, "I said get outta here—now!"

That struck a chord with the homeless man. He had become able to read people pretty well, having lived on the street the past couple of months. *This guy was bad news, better listen to what he says.* "Okay, okay. Just let me get my sleepin' bag and I'll be gone."

"No, leave it."

Something told him that this was not the time to argue. The homeless man stood up and made his way to the burglar gate, his rib cage aching from the rude wake up tactic employed by this intruder. He stepped outside and turned to walk down the street, giving a final look of defiance to the stranger. A chill went through him as he stared into the man's eyes. He turned and walked away quickly, thinking that he was lucky to have survived this encounter.

Watching the vagrant leave he checked his watch, *I still have time.* He found the padlock on the floor and put it back on the burglar gate. He partially closed the gates and moved into an alcove just down the street where he could watch his victim approach.

***

It had been another long trip downtown for Martyna Gorski. Being an immigrant meant that there were few well paying jobs available to her, but she had her green card and soon she would take her test that would finally make her a U.S. citizen. Although she loved her native Poland and the beauty of her family's farm, life there was harsh with little promise of success.

When her mother died from tuberculosis, her father decided that there was no future for his daughter there. He sold the family farm and most of their belongings and left for America. Martyna had been working with the cleaning service for three years, and had saved enough money to start college in the Fall.

She got off the bus and began walking down Wabash Avenue toward the huge building where she had been cleaning offices for the past year. She recalled her first few months in America, how everything was so different from her own country. The buildings were on top of each other, the highest floors seeming to float in the clouds, thousands of people on the streets constantly moving from one place to another. The pace of each day was so fast that she had often times longed to go home to Poland. But there were many good things as well. The abundance of everything...food, clothes, electronics...the stores were filled with things that she had only seen in magazines.

She often daydreamed about owning many of those things and about meeting someone who might one day be her husband. She had a boyfriend back home, but he was poor like her and had skills that were only suitable for farming. Jan was a tall, handsome boy who would have made a good husband someday. But now her expectations were much higher, she wanted someone who was educated, someone who would be a professional—not a farmer. It was difficult to say good bye to him, but she knew it was for the best.

The wheels screeched on the train track above, sparks flying over the sides as it made the turn on the elevated structure to head south on Wabash. Her first few days working downtown had been like working on a different planet. The sights and sounds assaulted her senses, frightening her more often than not. The El Train was one of those things that used to scare her, as it travelled high above the street encircling downtown Chicago. Now she hardly paid it any mind at all.

She was just one block from her building now; she brought her purse up in front of her. Opening it as she walked, she began to rummage through the contents looking for her work ID that would allow her to enter the building after hours. As she pulled it out, she felt something strike the back of her head. Her balance gone, she felt her legs buckle, but someone caught her before she fell onto the sidewalk. *Someone is carrying me...saving me.* Dizzy, yet still conscious, and suddenly grasping the notion that something was terribly wrong, she heard a scraping sound and saw a metal gate being opened and then shut.

Darkness filled her soul, as well as the inside of whatever building she had been carried into. Only a faint sliver of light sliced through the thick blanket of black. Falling to the ground, she put her hand down to try and catch herself and felt some type of blanket. Recovering slightly, she saw a man bend over her. "What do you want...who...?"

She saw the fist too late to do anything about it. Stars of pain danced in front of her eyes. Trying to resist, but realizing that she was no match for the man's strength, she turned into herself. Drifting off, her body unable to respond to the synapses firing inside of her brain that told her to fight back, her thoughts instead carried her back home.... Back to her parents' farm in Poland...back where she had always been safe. Almost unconscious, yet aware that this man was about to take a gift from her that she had been saving only for a future husband, she willed herself to sleep. She prayed that when she awoke she would find that it had all been just a bad dream.

***

This one was better than the last one…younger, stronger, and attractive. She was definitely in need of punishment. He felt good; his plan had worked well, except for the homeless guy. His choice of locations had been perfect. He would continue to find others who would feel his strength and fury. He would dominate them and make them sorry…. He was in total control.

~ 14 ~

I Need To See You

Yesterday, Joe had cleared his time off with the Watch Commander on the day shift. His boss had been reluctant to grant a sick day to someone a day prior until Joe told him in confidence that he needed to get his first chemo treatment. The captain's tone changed immediately after that information, and he wished Joe good luck.

Now he was faced with a dilemma—to tell Marilyn what was going on, or try to keep it under his hat for as long as possible. She was expecting him to be at work today. If she showed up at the station with Pete on business and discovered that he was on sick leave, he would have to explain his absence to her somehow. But it had already been bothering him that he had kept from her the fact that he had been to the doctor. Should he compound the problem by not telling her the truth? Probably not; he decided to call her.

***

"...8, 9, 10. Good job, Marilyn." Kim racked the weights, setting the bar back on the uprights. "That's it girl, we're done, good workout today."

Marilyn sat up on the weight bench and wiped the sweat from her brow. "Yeah baby, it's good to get in a workout when I'm feeling a little more energized. Those evening workouts don't seem to produce the same results as the morning ones do."

The two women gathered up their gym bags and headed out toward their cars in the parking lot. "So how long are you going to be on days?"

"I'm not really sure," said Marilyn. "This UC thing could end in one night or run for several weeks. It depends on the creep that we're looking for."

"Well I hope that you're on days for as long as possible. I hate working out alone."

"Can't you get one of the guys from the firehouse to workout with you once in a while?"

"Are you kidding me?" Kim laughed. "Those guys couldn't hang with me; they'd be on disability if they went through one of my workouts. Remember, they're firemen; they live on spaghetti and meatballs. Besides, they don't have the drive and ambition to stay in shape that you do. You challenge me."

"Alright, wonder woman." Marilyn said, as she opened the door to her car. "I'll leave a message on your machine tonight to let you know if we grabbed this nut or not. If he's still on the loose tomorrow, we'll hit the gym again."

"Okay, Marilyn. Be careful tonight. From what you've explained, I don't know if you should be more wary of the stickup guy or your backup."

"I know; I'll be watching them both. Take care."

Marilyn drove toward home, her thoughts turning to Joe. With her on nights and Joe on days it would be almost impossible to get together, unless one of their days off coincided. But until the stickup man was captured, she wasn't even sure that she'd have a day off. Their last night out together still bothered her. Their disagreement about whether or not Joe should visit the doctor had put a damper on their evening...one of the few times that had ever occurred. Things had been good between them both. They had found each other at a time in each of their lives when they both really needed someone. Joe had been in the dumps for two years since his wife's death, quitting the Department and working at a shirt shop seventy to eighty hours per week. Immersing himself in work allowed him to forget about his grief.

For Marilyn, meeting Joe had proven to be a godsend. After several bad choices in men, and risky behavior that included several one night stands, she had rediscovered her faith. Pete and Beth had played a huge role in her reawakening. Her partner's Christian example sparked a new excitement in her; she wanted what Joe had—a powerful love of God and a desire to spread His word through role modeling and good deeds.

Joe proved to be a decent man who promised to take it slow with their relationship. So far things had gone well and her feelings for him had begun to take on a new dimension. It was now beyond friendship, it was a deep affection...love.

I should call him. Driving past St. Christina's Church, which was only a few minutes from her home, she dialed Joe's number.

"Hello…."

"Hi, Joe, it's Marilyn. Are you busy?"

"No, I'm not." *I guess that I need to tell her.* "Marilyn, I'm off from work today."

"You are…why didn't you say something?"

"Well…I guess that I should have…listen, can I meet you somewhere?"

She pulled into her parking spot in front of her building. "I just got home from the gym and haven't eaten yet; do you want to get brunch somewhere?"

"Uh…not really. Can I just come over to your place right now? I need to see you…it's important."

She didn't like the sound of his voice. Something wasn't right here. "Joe, are you okay? What's wrong, honey?"

"I need to tell you something, Marilyn, not on the phone and not at some restaurant. Can I come over?"

"Yes, Joe, yes. I'll put on some coffee…see you in ten minutes or so?"

"I'm on the way."

"Okay…sweetheart, I love you."

The phone went dead. Her mind raced, thinking what this urgent news might possibly be about. Whatever it was, she decided that it had to be something bad. Why else would he need to say it to her directly rather than over the phone? She unlocked her apartment door and dropped her workout bag by the closet. She went into the kitchen and put on a pot of coffee. She freshened up in the bathroom, and as the coffee finished brewing the doorbell rang. Opening the door she saw Joe and quickly wrapped him in her arms. "Honey, what is it...what's the matter?"

Returning her embrace, Joe said, "I'm sorry to alarm you, but I've been thinking about our relationship, especially how our last date ended."

Marilyn took him by the hand and led him into her apartment. "I know...it's been bothering me too, but, Joe, please, just tell me what's going on?"

Joe put his hands in his pockets and told her, "I haven't been honest with you."

"What do you mean?"

"You've been telling me that I need to see a doctor, and I've been telling you that I didn't want to. I lied, Mar; I did go to the doctor."

"That's okay, honey...is that all that's bothering you?"

"Let's sit down at the table." They grabbed chairs next to each other and Joe took her hand and looked into her eyes, "The doctor told me yesterday that I have cancer."

Her eyes tearing and lips quivering, Marilyn cried, "No...oh Joe, no...how...why...?"

Holding her he continued. "He said that it's colon cancer and it has to be treated immediately. That's why I'm on sick leave today; my first chemo treatment is this afternoon."

Sobbing loudly, her body trembling, she felt like her whole world was collapsing. They had become so close, and the future looked so bright….

Joe explained in detail everything that the doctor had told him as they sat face to face holding each other's hands. While tears rolled down Marilyn's cheeks, he reached over to wipe them away. For some reason he felt some inner strength building inside of him as he spoke with her.

Marilyn got up to grab a tissue from the counter. Wiping her tears she sat back down. "Joe, we'll get through this…together. I know that it's clichéd to say, but we've only just begun. I think that God has good things in store for us, and that this challenge is meant to strengthen our love. Joe, this doesn't change one thing for us—it only makes me love you more."

"Thanks, I'm relieved to hear you say that. You may be right, Mar. This illness may strengthen our love. I'm determined to fight this thing and win. I've prayed about it and I think that He's heard me and reinforced my resolve. I have too much to live for to let this get the better of me. If this is indeed a test from the Father, then I expect to pass it with flying colors."

She leaned over and kissed him gently on the lips. "My dear Joe, you do have much to live for…'we' have much to live for. I'll help you get through this; and with God's help we'll defeat this devil that's invaded your body."

Now that she knew, relief washed over him like a spring rain. Her strength and love would only help him win this battle. "Thanks, honey, you are a big reason that I need to be victorious."

"You will be," she said, taking his hand, "Let's pray….

Dear Father, we glorify you and thank you for your love. We pray that you will strengthen your child, Joe, as he undergoes the chemo therapy treatments. Give him courage and faith to endure the difficult days ahead. May his suffering only bring him closer to you, and may our love for you, and for each other, give him comfort and rest. In Jesus' name we pray, Amen."

~ 15 ~

The Sleeping Bag

The homeless man was concerned. *Getting a little cooler now, a storm must be moving in.* A slight drizzle began to fall; he needed to find a place to sleep and stay dry. *Damn that guy!* The vacant office building that he had picked for the night had been perfect; no one had yet discovered it. The gates had been locked when he checked it several times before, but yesterday he saw that the padlock had been opened and the lock set back in place so that it appeared that the gates were secured. He pulled them apart, checked inside, and found it to be ideal for spending the night. He then put the gates back the way that he had found them so that no one would bother him.

The homeless man may have been down on his luck, but he still had the ability to think clearly. *Who was that guy, and why did he kick me out?* He wasn't a cop or a guard—he wore no uniform. *And why didn't he let me get my sleeping bag?* Living on the street the past several months was tough enough. To be able to stay warm at night was important.

The more he thought about it, the more strongly he felt about going back...at least to retrieve his bag. He headed back to the building and saw that the burglar bars were closed again; the lock was back in place. He walked by, not stopping for fear that the stranger might still be inside. He waited a few minutes and then re-traced his steps back to the entrance. Stopping to listen for a moment he heard nothing. It was getting late, the night shift people had all made it downtown by now and were in their buildings. There was hardly any movement on the street—no cops in sight.

Removing the lock he re-hung it on the bars, and as quietly as he could, he pulled them open. Slowly he moved toward the alcove that he had earlier claimed as his own. It was probably too risky to sleep here now, at least for tonight, but he needed that sleeping bag. Creeping along, as his eyes adjusted to the murky interior, he turned the corner. *Damn, someone's already here and is using my bag.*

He moved toward the figure on the ground and was about to impart the same painful lesson that the stranger had taught him, when he suddenly realized something was wrong. *It was a woman...and she was half naked!*

Startled momentarily, but transfixed by the sight, he stood motionless, frozen while contemplating what to do next. He had seen plenty on the street since becoming homeless, but this was a first. Concerned that he might be wrongly accused of having something to do with whatever happened here, he turned and ran to the gate. Hastily pulling the gates apart, and mindless of the noise they made as they scraped along the ground, he quickly departed. As he turned the corner he came face to face with a cruising squad car.

"Hey you...**STOP!**"

~ 16 ~

Two Geezers

The news from Joe had been a shock, like a bomb dropped on top of what had looked like a firm foundation for a long-lasting relationship. What made it worse was being torn between her duty to Pete to work the undercover assignment tonight, and her desire to be with Joe. But Joe was more pragmatic about things and had made the decision for her. He had assured her that the first treatment wasn't as bad as some of the others will be, and he told her that he appreciated her offer of support. He convinced her that she needed to fulfill her obligation to the squad, and try to catch the guy who had been ripping off the old folks at the ballgames.

Still, Marilyn felt terrible, and after Joe left she took time to pray and read her Bible. She found solace in Psalm 41:3, "The Lord will sustain him on his sickbed and restore him from his bed of illness." She had to put her trust in God; she desperately wanted Joe to pull through this, and she was determined that she would put her faith in His will.

She gathered her duty bag that regularly accompanied her on each tour; it contained all the things that she might need. Even though she couldn't carry all of them on her person they were always close enough to retrieve…ballistic vest, extra box of ammo, spare magazines, extra handcuffs, flex cuffs, baton, gloves, flashlights, and extra batteries. Pete had taught her that it was better to always have too much gear than too little. Making her way to her car she spotted her neighbor, Leslie, waving to her.

"Hi, Marilyn!"

Leslie had inexplicably come into her life at a point in time when Marilyn needed a friend and confidant. Broken and questioning her faith, she had spent time with Leslie who patiently listened and then laid the groundwork for Marilyn to re-establish her relationship with God. They had been good friends and confidants ever since, sharing hours of conversation over coffee.

"Oh, hi, Les." Marilyn opened the trunk of her vehicle and set her bag inside.

Knowing her friend rather well by now, Leslie asked, "Is anything wrong, you look worried?"

Closing the trunk, Marilyn replied. "I just got some terrible news from my boyfriend, Joe…he told me that he has cancer." Bringing a tissue to her eyes, Marilyn continued, "Les, please put him on your prayer list. I'm worried about him; he was doing so well, finally putting his wife's death behind him and getting on with his life. And now this…."

Leslie walked over and hugged her friend. "My dear Marilyn, I will indeed put him on my list, and my congregation will pray for his full recovery. But I'm equally concerned for you. You'll be on the list as well."

"Thank you; you are a treasured friend who always seems to appear when I am in need. I'm on my way to work right now so I can't talk, but let's have coffee if we can tomorrow."

"Okay. You call me, but make sure that Joe doesn't need you before you call."

"I will. Bye, Leslie"

She pulled out of the complex and headed toward 35th Street. Listening to country music while she drove was usually her habit, but today her thoughts turned to Joe and what he might be going through during his treatment. She decided that this quiet time was perfectly suited for prayer. Before she knew it, she had arrived at Police Headquarters. She retrieved her gear and went up to her unit. Walking into the office she spotted Geraci and Carone sitting at their desks, working on Italian beef sandwiches and fries, and washing them down with diet sodas. Geraci saw Marilyn heading to her desk and remarked, "Well, if it isn't the TV star…ready for makeup and wardrobe?"

Marilyn wasn't in the mood for confrontation right now. Rather than anger toward him, she felt pity. How could one person find it so easy to be mean and confrontational on a regular basis? She set her bag down and sat at her desk where she began filling out the forms she needed to check out her UC props. She finished quickly and then took the elevator down to the Undercover Unit in the basement where she would pick them up. As she walked into the office, she found that Pete was already there and in the process of collecting his disguise for their role as senior citizens.

"Hi, partner, God been good to you today?"

"Pete…." She took him by the hand and led him out into the

hallway. She blurted the news out, "Joe has cancer."

Pete's smile disappeared instantly, and with a furrowed brow he said, "Oh, no…Mar, I'm so sorry to hear that."

Marilyn quickly filled him in on the details that Joe had related to her. "I feel so sad for him; he's been upbeat and happy since he's been back on the job, and he's dealt with his grief and guilt so well. I feel like I've been kicked in the chest by a team of mules, our relationship had been progressing nicely and now this…."

"So why are you at work, Bens?"

"Joe convinced me that my place was here, working this new case with you. Besides, I think that after we talked and prayed about it yesterday he feels strongly that God is testing him. He wants to beat this thing and not allow it to disrupt his life."

Shaking his head Pete replied, "Joe's an amazing guy who's been through some tough times. I don't know what further test he needs, but I'm positive that he'll pull through this one. I'll be praying for him."

"Thanks, Pete, that's all that we can do right now. He's in for a battle."

"Yes, but what about you? Are you going to be okay, especially tonight? I need to know that your head is going to be in the game, that you're focused on what we have to do."

Hands on her hips, Marilyn responded. "I'll be fine, believe me. I know that Joe doesn't want any sympathy or special treatment; he wants life to go on normally—that's what I want also. Let's get our props and get back upstairs and gear up."

"Okay, partner, let's dedicate our work tonight to Joe and his treatment." They gathered their accessories and made it back up to the office.

Lt. King was waiting for them at their desks.

"I know that you two were worried about your rape case going cold while I had you assigned to the ballpark, but I think that you can forget about that for now."

Puzzled by what their boss had just told them, Marilyn asked, "What's up, are we off the case?"

"It's still your case but it looks like a beat car in the 1st District grabbed the guy last night. They caught him running out of a vacant building down on Wabash Avenue, and when they took him back to the scene they found another victim."

"Assaulted and raped?" Pete asked.

"Yeah, looks like the same M.O., the guy cracked her on the back of the head then brought her inside the building and raped her."

"Is she alive?"

King walked over to his office and grabbed a report. "She's hurt, but not as bad as the first woman. They were able to do a quick interview with her before the docs had them leave. Tomorrow I want you to touch base and do a final report on this so that we can clear it."

"Okay, boss, will do."

King went back to his office, leaving Pete and Marilyn somewhat stunned. "Wow, I never thought this guy would be so easy to grab. That beat car sure got lucky."

Pete rubbed his chin trying to analyze this new information. "Something's not right here, Bens. We hardly had any info or leads on the first victim, and now he hits for the second time and gets caught in the act? We need to check this out."

"You're right," she replied. "Let's see what happens tonight. If we don't get this idiot at Wrigley Field, we'll come in early tomorrow and go over the case report and try to interview the victim."

"Agreed."

They went to their respective locker rooms and changed into their disguises. Pete's included baggy pants, short sleeve shirt and sweater vest, gray wig, and coke bottle glasses. Marilyn had to contend with a baggy polyester pants suit, gray wig, scarf, and an oversize purse. After their ensemble was complete, they emerged from their dressing rooms and took one look at each other. They burst out laughing at how funny they looked.

Hearing the commotion, Lt. King came out of his office. "Who are you two old coots, and what have you done with my detectives?"

Geraci and Carone were taken by a fit of laughter as well. "I hope the TV cameras are out tonight," yelled Carone.

Strangely enough the curious sight of Pete and Marilyn dressed as old timers had a bonding effect on all of them. King looked at his troops. *Maybe this thing will work out after all.*

~ 17 ~

Mac

Locking the door behind him, Joe threw his car keys on the counter and headed for the couch. Fatigue had begun to sweep over him, just like the doctor had advised that it would. *The first skirmish is over, now I've got to prepare for the next one.* If this was the worst of what chemo would throw at him then he knew that he could prevail, but something told him that the constant infusion of toxins into his body would begin to take its toll at some point.

He had a little pain around the injection site and felt a little nauseous, but other than that he just felt tired. He went to the fridge and grabbed a bottle of water. *Got to stay hydrated.* His plan was to just chill out the rest of the day and conserve his energy for tomorrow. He wanted to work a normal shift for as long as possible. He was no martyr, and he didn't want people to pity him.

He turned on the TV and was about to lay down on the couch

to watch the Cubs and White Sox play the first game of the three game "Cross-town Series." Each year both Chicago Major League baseball teams, the Cubs who play on the north side, and the White Sox on the south, play each other to determine who is the better team and who has bragging rights for the season. The game was about to begin when the doorbell rang. *Who could that be?* He wasn't expecting anyone and he knew that Marilyn was working nights. He opened the door to find Sgt. Mac standing there.

Extending his hand, the police veteran said, "Joe, how are you my friend?"

"Mac…uh…I'm fine. What are you doing here?"

Mac was a 30 year police officer who was the midnight watch desk sergeant. Mac and his wife, Shirley, had been married 35 years and they both spent their days babysitting their two grandchildren for their daughter, Tina. With his seniority he could work any shift he wanted but he chose to work mids to be with his wife and grandbabies. Mac was well respected throughout the department for his character and strength. It was not unusual to find him helping his fellow officers, both on duty and off.

"Can I come in, or are you going to leave me standing out here on the porch?"

"No, I'm sorry, Mac, come on in. I'm just surprised to see you. Can I get you something to drink?"

"No, nothing for me."

Mac walked in and followed Joe into the family room. "Have a seat, Mac, what can I do for you?"

Seated on a chair across from Joe, Mac leaned forward. "Joe, I know that we don't know each other all that well, but what I do know about you, other than speaking with you that day at Pete and Beth's barbeque, I learned from both of them and from Marilyn. I know that you are a good man, and a damn good cop who's had his share of personal tragedy. Since Pete and Marilyn became partners, I've grown fond of her and I've admired her work ethic and character."

Joe took a drink from his water bottle still trying to wash the metal taste of chemo from his mouth, while he listened intently to what Mac had to say.

"Marilyn called me today and filled me in on what you're facing. I guess that I don't need to tell you that she's very distraught."

"Mac, I didn't mean for this thing to become public knowledge, I just...."

"I know...Marilyn told me this confidentially. But she let me know about you for a good reason—she's trying to get as many people to pray for you as she can. I'm no saint but I talk with the Lord every day, and believe it or not sometimes He even talks back. I came here tonight just to let you know that you're not alone, that there will be plenty of folks helping you get through this fight. I had a brother go through what you're facing; I know what your life will be like in the short term. Let your friends help you, Joe. Let them pray *for you* and pray *with you*, and don't be shy about asking for a few favors from them—even at work. I know that you're not on my watch, but I've got more time in the 8th District than anyone which means that I have some clout. If you need some time off or need to get off the street for awhile, let me know and we'll work it out."

His hand covering his mouth, and tears welling in his eyes, he was surprised to hear this offer from a man who he hardly knew, but who nonetheless was a brother in blue. Maybe it was the side effects from the chemo, but his emotions were like a roller coaster ride, uncontrollable highs and lows that left him breathless.

"Mac, I don't know what to say, except, thank you, brother."

"You don't need to say anything, Joe. I'm here because you need a support system while you battle this demon. I know…we lifted up prayers for my brother every day. Some days were worse than others; you'll find that happening with your treatment as well. But I just wanted to give you a little moral support. Even though the first day isn't as bad as most people expect it will be, it's still a good idea to go through each treatment with someone. Now…what can I do for you tonight; can I get you anything or take care of something around the house for you?"

"You've already done it, Mac, by just being here and lending your support. What I really need is to lay down for the rest of the night; I'm on an early car tomorrow."

"Okay, I can take a hint; I'll be on my way." He set a slip of paper on the coffee table. "Here's my contact info. You can get me 24/7, and you know where I'm at most every night. Listen, Joe, I realize that I'm not family, at least not by blood, but we're part of the 'Police Brotherhood'. I'm here for you whenever you need me…okay?"

Joe stood up and walked over to Mac. The two men hugged each other and then Mac headed toward the door.

"I'll let you rest, son. I'll be praying for you to get through the treatments with as few side effects as possible."

Joe opened the door for him to leave. "Mac, thanks so much

for coming over. Your visit has been just what I needed tonight."

"Good, and by the way, don't blame Marilyn for this. I decided to come on my own."

"It's okay; it was a good decision on your part."

He walked down the stairs and out to the street where his car was parked. Joe closed the door and then lay down on the couch. Closing his eyes he offered up a prayer of thanksgiving….

Thank you for this day, Father, for dear friends and fellow Christians, for your strength in guiding me through this first treatment, and most of all, for your love. I pray that this ordeal will bring me closer to you. Fill me with your Spirit of hope and courage that I may be victorious. In Jesus' name I pray…Amen.

Joe was asleep just as the first inning of the Cubs/White Sox game was set to begin.

~ 18 ~

The Ballgame

"They got the better end of the deal," said Geraci, after they had dropped Pete and Marilyn off at the game.

"Yeah, this sucks…it's our case, and here we sit in this friggin' van while they watch one of the best games of the season." Carone grabbed a cannoli from the box of bakery goodies that he had brought along as he shared his displeasure with his partner. "We would have grabbed this guy anyway, ya know? He's a freakin' numbskull thinkin' he can rip people off in Streeterville and get away with it. That's like me and you goin' through the projects, stickin' people up, and thinkn' no one's gonna notice."

Streeterville was a close knit north side community founded in the 1880s, that in addition to being home to Wrigley Field, boasted upscale restaurants, shops, and theatres. It was also home to Northwestern University and the Museum of Contemporary Art. It enjoyed a relatively low crime rate.

"We've got some time to kill here," Geraci offered. "Let's get a couple of dogs and some fries from one of the street vendors."

"Good idea," laughed Carone. "Hey isn't that what you're supposed to do when you're at a ballgame, eat hotdogs?"

"Yep, go on over to that Vienna cart on Waveland and Clark, I heard that he takes care of cops."

Geraci headed the van in that direction and then parked partially on the sidewalk so that he was almost right on top of the hot dog cart. One of the uniformed officers saw the van park illegally and quickly came over to chew this obnoxious driver a new one. That is, until he saw the portly duo and recognized one of them as Geraci. He waved and went back to his foot post.

Carone got out, making sure that he had his hand held police radio with him just in case the guy failed to notice his police star and gun on his belt. That was entirely possible, given the excess flesh that rested on top of his police gear, sometimes obscuring it from view, like a perfect fold of extra skin designed just for that purpose. It all depended on how many pastries he had eaten the day before. The bottom line was that he wanted there to be no confusion as to who he was. Ambling up to the cart he nodded to the man and said, "Hey, what's up? Good crowd tonight…hope that we don't have any trouble. You okay?"

The vendor eyed him suspiciously, but quickly figured out that this small talk was a prelude to having "the arm" put on him for some free food. "Yeah, officer, everything's good. You hungry?"

Trying to seem disinterested, Geraci answered "Uh…sure, why not…let me have four dogs with everything, two cokes, and two bags of chips."

"Comin' right up, officer." Grudgingly, the vendor prepared the food the cop had ordered. Although he didn't like what was going on, he figured it was the price of doing business in Chicago. Everybody had their hand out—cops, city inspectors, code officers—they all had to get their share. He completed the order and handed the cardboard tray to the cop.

"Thanks, man...we'll keep an eye on you tonight. See ya later." Geraci carried his ill-gotten gains back to the van.

The cart vendor watched him walk away. That one was pretty bold, he never even asked if he owed me anything...just took it and left.

Geraci hopped back in and shut the door. "Let's find a hole somewhere so we can listen to the game. I don't want to be bothered by anybody till it's time to go to work."

Carone drove a few blocks west and found a quiet spot in a parking lot where the two could hide out while Pete and Marilyn were inside.

***

It was the end of the seventh inning, the agreed upon point when Pete and Marilyn would leave the ballpark and begin to walk the neighborhoods surrounding Wrigley. This would give them a good hour to make themselves a target if their bad guy was indeed still out hunting for victims. They had discussed beforehand with Geraci and Carone what the code word would be if they were accosted by the robber. If either Pete or Marilyn were to utter the code, it was Geraci and Carone's job to get there as quickly as they could—it meant that they were in trouble. Unable to find a code that everyone liked, Marilyn finally put her foot down and said, "We'll use,' St. Michael'."

"That's nutty," Carone said.

But Marilyn quickly added, "That's my point exactly. "It's coming completely out of left field—St. Michael will mean nothing to the stick up guy—but to me and Pete, he's our protector—it's perfect."

"Whatever…" sighed Carone.

Pete and Marilyn made their way to the exit; just before leaving they activated their transmitters. "Testing, testing…Geraci…Carone…you copy?" They would be wearing transmitters rather than transceivers so that their backup didn't accidentally transmit a message to them and blow their cover. If they needed to reach their backup they would use a cell phone with a push to talk feature and a dedicated direct channel.

Back in the van the Stallions had slipped into a food-induced coma after having filled their bellies with hot dogs, chips, and Italian pastries. With a soothing, tropical-like Lake Michigan breeze blowing in through the window of the vehicle, and the ballgame playing on the radio, the rotund duo slept like two infants who had just finished their cereal bottles and had been put to bed for the night.

"Try yours, Bens, mine must not be working."

"Testing, 1, 2, 3, 4….testing, Benson to Carone or Geraci…."

No reply on the cell. Frustrated with the plan hitting a snag right from the beginning, Pete looked at the cell phone to see if he had missed a call. "They were supposed to call and tell us that they were receiving our commo. Do you think I should call them?"

"No, give it a couple of minutes. We know that it works; we

tested it before they dropped us off. Maybe they're in a bad cell or something. Let's just start walking and talking to each other, maybe they'll pick up our chatter and call."

The two headed away from the park, across Addison Avenue and then South on Sheffield, a street with an assortment of brownstones and apartment buildings. Pete had added an Irish walking stick to his costume. It had supposedly belonged to a great uncle and had been in his family for years.

"Hey, slow down, partner, did you forget that I'm an old man?" Marilyn had moved out ahead of Pete and had to be reeled back in. "We've got to make this look believable, Bens, that's why I brought this stick, to slow me down."

She adjusted her pace and said, "Sorry, the stick was probably a good idea, Pete, plus it makes you appear a bit more vulnerable."

Raising his senior prop, Pete said, "Yeah, but if this guy hits us he's in for a shock. I've got the stick, and my 9mm is in the small of my back under my sweater. I've got a pair of flex cuffs in my sock."

Laughing, Marilyn responded, "Pete, you never cease to amaze me."

They plodded along the street, shuffling like two old people who might topple over at any second, and came to the intersection. "Let's go left here," said Pete. "We'll walk under the EL tracks to the next corner, and then I'm going to call those two guys on the cell. This is ridiculous."

They walked arm in arm, and to the casual observer they were just another elderly couple strolling down the sidewalk. But as they crossed under the elevated transit structure, they were startled by a man who jumped out from behind one of the pillars that serve to support the mammoth structure.

"Hold it, mutha…gimme yo' wallet—quick!" Blocking their path, and with a hand in his pocket, there was no mistaking what this guy was after. "I got a gun, man, give it up quick 'foe you get hurt."

Realizing that they were in a bad way, Pete tried his best to send his backup the pieces of the puzzle that they needed to swoop down on this guy. He raised his cane and pointed to the man's hat, "That a Cub's hat you're wearing? They're looking good tonight, brother, but I think the Sox are going to win it this year."

Stepping closer to the undercover cops, the man said, "Don't talk no shit, man, just give me yo' wallet!"

Pete kept up the banter. "We're lost, my friend, we came here from the South Side on the El; we're looking for the station, is it around here somewhere?"

Glancing around quickly, and shifting his weight nervously from one foot to the other, the robber cried out, "You stupid old man, you fixin' to get shot if you don't give me dat wallet right now!"

Marilyn grabbed Pete's arm with both hands in an effort to buy time by diverting the man's attention to her. "Don't hurt us, sir, we're old—we have no money. St. Michael is our friend; St. Michael is the one who protects us, St Michael…."

His eyes opened wide in disbelief at what Marilyn was saying, he blurted, "What you talkin' bout woman—you crazy or somethin'?"

As the thug took his eyes off of Pete to momentarily focus on Marilyn, Pete made his move. With both hands he brought the walking stick down on top of the Cubs hat. The man collapsed in a heap, like a scarecrow without its stick. The two dicks quickly cuffed him; Marilyn found the gun in the man's pocket. Taking a close look at it, she said, "It's not real, Pete; it's a pellet pistol." She handed it over to Pete.

Pete took a quick look. "Yeah, but if he would have pointed it at us I would have shot him first and then worried later about whether or not it was real."

They had their prisoner secured with a pair of flex cuffs. Now it was time to try to contact their supposed backup. Pete looked at Marilyn…"St. Michael is our friend? Is that what you said?"

"Yes. I couldn't think of anything else, and to tell you the truth it was kind of a prayer as I said it rather than a signal. Almost like a chant."

"It worked, Bens; he was here tonight backing us up when our earthly partners failed us."

"I've said that prayer every day since you taught it to me, Pete," she said with a broad smile, "and just like you I'm convinced that he's with us on every shift."

Taking in a deep cleansing breath, Pete replied, "He's here alright and I think that he knew that we needed him."

Pete pulled out the phone and hit the push to talk button. "Geraci…Carone, this is Shannon. Are you guys copying us?

Carone stirred in the van. He looked over at his partner who was dead to the world. Suddenly it hit him…. *Holy shit we fell asleep!* He grabbed the phone, "Pete, this Carone, where are you guys?"

Looking at Marilyn and shaking his head, he answered. "Come down Sheffield and make a left. We're right under the

EL tracks. Hustle up we've got a prisoner."

"10-4, be there in a sec. Just so you know, we had some commo problems, must be the area we're in."

Geraci was waking up, the phone conversation having disturbed his nap. "We're screwed, man," said Carone, "they're on the street with a prisoner—we missed the whole gig. Floor this damn thing."

While they waited for their partners to pick them up, Pete retrieved his walking stick from the ground where he had dropped it after striking the bad guy. "Wait till I tell my sister, Lisa, and her four kids about this one. They'll each want to carry the stick to school for show and tell."

Marilyn looked at her partner. "Pete I guess that walking stick was meant to be kept in your family for a reason. The luck of the Irish saved us tonight."

"That and St. Michael."

~ 19 ~

Early Morning

Having showered and dressed, Joe poured a cup of coffee and turned on the news to see which team had won the ballgame last night. He had slept well, having been fatigued from the chemo treatment as well as the anxiety that accompanied not knowing what to expect. He felt reassured that at least in the short term he could weather this storm and not allow it to have too much of an impact on his daily routine. Taking a sip from his cup, he heard the doorbell ring.

He opened the door to find Marilyn standing there in her running clothes, looking almost angelic, with a light film of sweat causing her skin to glow in the soft backlight of early morning sunlight. She came in and wrapped him in her arms, kissing him at the same time. "How was it, honey? How do you feel?"

With a chuckle, he said, "What are you doing here…it's six in the morning. Didn't you work last night?"

"Yes...and we caught the guy that was ripping off the old folks!"

"You did? That's great!"

Giving him some breathing room, she took his hand and they both walked into the kitchen and sat down. "I'll fill you in later on the details Joe, it's unbelievable how it went down. But right now I want to hear about your treatment."

Joe filled her in on the details, as well as the visit from Mac.

Marilyn took his face in her hands. "Don't be mad that I told him, honey. I only wanted to get more people to pray for you; I didn't expect that he would visit you."

Kissing her on the cheek, Joe replied. "No, no, I'm not mad, don't worry about that. In fact, his visit really helped. After he left I kind of mellowed out...felt at peace with things."

She smiled. "Great! I've got to finish up my run and get to work. Lt. King told us that our rapist was grabbed by the 1st District, but there's something not quite right with this one. Pete and I are going to interview the guy today and see if he looks good for our case. For some reason it doesn't add up."

Marilyn got up to leave and gave Joe a big hug. Kissing him gently, she said, "Joe, honey, I love you very much. I was worried about you all night, wondering how you were. Just know that I'm thinking about you constantly and praying that all of this will work out for the best. You're such a gift...."

"Thank you, I love you too. That's the reason why I have to beat this thing." Letting herself out the front door she called back to him. "Have a great day, honey. I'll call you after work...love you."

Joe went back into the kitchen feeling very good about his life. Even though a potentially deadly disease had attacked him, he knew that the Father was very much in his life. Marilyn was the best thing that had happened to him since his wife's death. He now had so much to live for…again.

He finished up his coffee while the TV news show reported on an undercover team of police officers who had been working the baseball game last night. They had arrested an armed robber who had been victimizing old people; the Mayor and Police Superintendent would be holding a press conference later in the day.

~ 20 ~

King's Dilemma

Lt. King had called Geraci and Carone early and told them to be in the office by nine. He had been notified by the Chief of Detectives that the Mayor wanted to hold a press conference this morning to announce the arrest of the ballpark stickup man. King was to provide the two dicks that would stand in the background as props. King wasn't much interested in these types of things himself, but he couldn't blame the Mayor for wanting to put on a dog and pony show. He had been taking flak from neighborhood and senior groups while this guy was operating. Now that his police department had caught the guy responsible for so much bad PR, it was SOP for the top politician of the city to make himself look good again. This would be just another one of those hurry up and wait moments that cops learn to put up with from the pols that run the show.

He debated about whether or not to have Shannon and Benson attend as well, but he thought that the Stallions would appreciate being in the limelight, especially since they actually had the paper on the case. Nevertheless, he would make sure that he told his newest detectives that they had performed well. They didn't appear to need the ego boosting that Geraci and Carone seemed to crave. From what he knew of the facts surrounding last night's arrest, everything had gone according to plan. And aside from the bad guy suffering a head wound from being hit on the head with a cane, which seemed very apropos since he had been victimizing old folks, it was a rather routine arrest. At least that's what Geraci had told him over the phone.

In any event the Old Man would be happy, the files would be cleared, and King would wait for the next crisis to emerge that would try to swallow him up like a leviathan from the depths of the ocean. The case that Shannon and Benson would clear this morning clearly had had the potential to develop into that next crisis, were it not for a couple of alert street cops nabbing the guy. Rape cases were inflammatory issues that the news media loved to grab hold of, especially if they could paint the victims as already being victimized by society simply because of their status. It was their way of wielding power and causing social change. They seemed to enjoy making the Mayor sweat. The fact that the women were immigrants who worked manual labor jobs would make for good copy. Had this guy continued with his crime spree, the Mayor would have had his hands around someone's throat, squeezing until his cops either caught someone or somebody got transferred. Either way, the emperor's appetite would need to be sated.

Hopefully this case would be resolved this morning after his two detectives sorted things out and had this guy charged with both counts.

***

Sgt. Amy Grey set her coffee cup down and clicked on her Department email account. Being in the Media Relations Unit of the Chicago PD was a job that she relished. Her task was to always put the Department first, ensuring that little, if any bad press at all, made it to the media. She did her best to put out any fires before they became raging infernos. If she was able to get hold of an issue early, she could generally make sure that it was buried, or at least minimize its impact. Her boss, the Superintendant of Police, expected her to advise him of any potential mine fields that he might have to navigate, and to prepare him with plenty of information to mitigate any issues that she was unable to defuse.

She ran through her always full mailbox as quickly as she could, deleting requests for appointments with her boss by anyone that did not hold any sway with the community. Then she brought up an email from an anonymous source that included a picture attachment. *Better see the photo before I hit delete.*

"Anonymous" had sent an apparent camera phone picture. The photo showed two men asleep in the front seat of a van amid discarded hot dog wrappers, empty bags of potato chips, and other debris. The sender sent the following text to accompany the photo:

2 cops sleep on job cubs park. this where tax money goes

Amy took a closer look at the two men in the photo. *Uh oh...these two might be in King's unit.*

Years ago, Lt. King had been Amy's field training officer after she had graduated from the police academy. It had been her goal to wear the same Star that her father had worn when he was on the job. Her first assignment was the Englewood District on the South Side; what street skills she hadn't learned from her dad, were provided by King. In those early years, while she was learning her trade, her children, Bella and Aidan, would beg her to entertain them with stories about bad guys. She was more than happy to accommodate them; it reminded her of when she was a child and her father had held her spellbound with tales of larger-than-life cons and scammers as the family sat at the dinner table.

They had kept in touch ever since. Amy had attended King's Unit Christmas Party last year and was introduced to all of the members. She particularly remembered Geraci and Carone because of the gaudy gold jewelry that they each wore, and because Geraci came on to her. The two cops in the photo were wearing the very same adornments that were indelibly etched in her mind after that night.

Amy was well aware of the UC Operation at the ballgame last night, as well as the press conference scheduled for this morning. Keying King's number in the phone, she got him on the second ring. "Jerry, it's Amy. I need to give you a heads up on something."

***

Pete and Marilyn arrived at the 1st District where their subject was still being housed. They had asked that he be held over and not taken to the County Jail until they had a chance to interview him and then confer with the Assistant State's Attorney assigned to the case. They had him brought into an interview room where they could question him without any distractions.

Shackled like a bear that wrestles all-comers in the circus sideshows, he wore a belly chain and leg irons. The lockup officer hooked the pseudo-demon to the handcuff ring on the wall and said, "Come get me when you're finished."

Pete decided that the man didn't really look like a vicious thug, but appearances are sometimes deceiving. And Pete's gut instinct immediately told him that this guy was not who they were looking for. Cops generally are very adept and sizing up people and situations. Their gut instincts are usually right on. They had decided on the ride over that Pete would conduct the interview and Marilyn would do the paper.

Pete flashed his ID and said, "I'm Detective Shannon; this is my partner, Detective Benson. We're here to talk about why you were arrested. The report indicates that your name is Mark Bradley, you're 45 years old, born and raised in Chicago, single, unemployed…that correct so far?"

The man nodded, "Yes sir, that's me."

"There's no home address listed here…you homeless?"

He sighed, "Yes sir. I've been on the street for a couple o' months…couldn't pay my rent so the landlord had me thrown out. The sheriff showed up one day and evicted me; put all my stuff out on the curb…most of it was stolen before I could do anything about it."

Pete was beginning to get a much stronger sense now that this guy most certainly was not good for the rapes. "What happened with your job, Mark? Were you fired?"

"No, not fired. The man struggled to stand and search his pockets—"Hey, you guys got a cigarette?"

"Sorry, brother, neither of us smokes."

The man sank down in his chair like a balloon that had sprung a slow leak. "I worked at a small tool and die shop over on State and Archer—they went belly up—just ran out of money. I couldn't find another job, didn't have any savings either, that's why I got behind on the rent. I'm not lazy officer; I'm a good worker. Heck, I never missed a day of work at the shop, my boss loved me. There just ain't no jobs nowhere."

Pete glanced over at Marilyn who was shaking her head as if in agreement with his unspoken assessment that this guy was not who they were looking for.

"Mark, tell me what happened the other night. Why did the police arrest you?"

The man related what happened that night with the stranger. His whole demeanor and background gave no indication that what he was saying was anything but truthful.

"So you never touched the woman, you had absolutely no idea that she was even there?"

His chains scraping against the table top as he tried to gesture with his hands, he answered. "No sir. In fact, it scared the hell outta me when I saw it was a half naked lady! I just wanted to get my sleeping bag back. Soon as I seen her, I knew I had to get outta there before the cops tried to pin it on me."

"I believe you, Mark," Pete assured him. "Now what I need from you is everything that you can recall about the stranger who you say you saw that night. What did he look like, how old was he, his clothing, anything at all that you can remember…."

Looking up toward the ceiling for a moment, the prisoner

began. "Now remember, officer, I didn't see 'em very long and it was dark in there too. Maybe he was 30 or 35, with black hair, 'bout my height.…"

"Good. What else…what did he wear?"

Hesitating, the man grimaced. "I don't really remember, I mean, I guess just regular clothes."

"Okay, brother, but just concentrate for a minute and take your time. Close your eyes and go back to that night. What stands out in your mind about the guy, anything out of the ordinary, or did anything…maybe…scare you?"

Banging his restraints on the table top as he brought his hands down, the man responded. "Yeah! When I was getting out of there I tried to give him a hard look, you know…kind o' trying to scare 'em? I mean, you know how it is on the street; you can't let anybody know you're scared. Well, it didn't work. I looked in his eyes—he was evil, real mean—and one of his eyes was like, I don't know, like off to one side. Almost like he was lookin' in two directions at once. I've never seen the devil but if I had to imagine what he looked like it would be that guy."

Yes! Pete was now certain that this was not their man. The only thing this poor guy was guilty of was being in the wrong place at the wrong time. Whoever handled the case that night did a shoddy job of putting the facts together.

"Okay, Mark, you've been a big help. I'm convinced that you are not responsible for what happened to that woman, but I need to talk to the prosecutor and convince him. It's going to take a couple of days, but we'll get you released. I need you to submit to a DNA test; will that be okay?"

"Sure, anything to get me outta this jam I'm in. But to tell ya the truth, it's kinda nice to have three meals and a safe place to sleep."

"Okay, brother; enjoy your stay while you can. Pete leaned over and handed his card to the man. "Here's my contact information. I need to know where you'll be once you get released. Give me a call, reverse the charges if you have to, I may need you to testify in the future. Will you do that?"

"Oh, yes sir. Do you think that you could help me out a little...maybe a few bucks for food or whatever?"

"I'll put a twenty in your property envelope right now. Call me when you get released and I'll see what else I can do."

"Okay, officer; you're a good man, sir."

"You're welcome, brother, and I'll say a prayer for you. I think that your best days are still ahead of you and that the Lord has plans for you."

"I hope you're right, sir. I don't think things can get any worse for me."

They signaled for the lockup to take the prisoner back to his cell. Once he was gone Pete and Marilyn had a chance to talk. Marilyn spoke first. "Pete, that's not our guy, he wouldn't hurt a fly. Plus, he came up with the same key descriptor that the first victim revealed—the lazy eye."

"I know, Bens, the poor guy got railroaded, but we're going to make it right. The good news is that our bad guy is becoming less of a mystery. I know that we don't have much, but we finally have someone whose actually seen him and talked to him."

"Exactly, now we need to talk with the woman who was the victim in this last attack and see what pieces that she can add to the puzzle."

Preparing to leave, Pete's cell phone rang. He took it out and looked at the caller ID—it was Lt. King.

"Hello, sir, what's up?"

"Are you two still at the jail?"

"Just leaving, sir."

"Good, the guy you're talking to is not our guy."

"How do you know?"

"Because another woman was raped last night on the South Side."

~ 21 ~

Claudia Sanchez

Stepping off the bus on Cicero Avenue a little less gingerly than normal, her thoughts focused on sleep. Her crew had finally finished with their task of cleaning the huge auditorium in the downtown building where she worked, but it had been exhausting. Now she could rest and prepare for her class in the morning at Daley College.

Since arriving in Chicago from her home in Puerto Rico just over two years ago, Claudia had focused on her education. She had moved in with her aunt and uncle to save money for school. Her plan was to graduate with a two year degree from the city college system, and then attend the University of Illinois. Her ambition was to become a lawyer, and she set her mind on that goal, determined to do whatever she had to in order to accomplish it.

Working the afternoon shift while attending school during the day left little time for much else. But Claudia was intent on getting a college education, something that no one in her family in Puerto Rico had yet to accomplish. The time spent cleaning offices downtown only served to reinforce her plan. She couldn't imagine working like this for the rest of her life.

She slowly began her trek home, a short four block walk from the bus stop. Her uncle used to pick her up each night after she got off the bus, but last month he had suffered a heart attack and her aunt insisted that he get a full night's rest so that he could recover and return to his own job. She didn't like having to walk home alone at this time of night, but she had no other choice.

She walked one block north on Cicero Avenue, which was a main thoroughfare. The sodium vapor street lamps, installed throughout the city as a means to prevent crime, took back the night and made most of the city streets as bright as day. It was only the last three blocks, through the not as well illuminated neighborhood, where she felt somewhat uneasy. She turned off Cicero onto the side street and suddenly felt the hairs stand up on the back of her neck. Taking a quick glance over her shoulder, she caught movement. *A man with....* Trying to duck out of the way, she was hit with a glancing blow on the side of her head. Staggering, trying to maintain a solid hold on her footing, she felt a kick to her midsection. Her equilibrium compromised, she collapsed on the ground, the wind knocked out of her. Trying her best to breathe, the phantom took her by her arms and dragged her from the walkway.

Gasping for air, panicked that she would suffocate, she was helpless in her ability to confront her attacker who appeared to materialize out of the thick, humid night air. So desperate for a life-saving breath was she that it hardly mattered when her clothes were being viciously ripped from her lower body.

Seconds later—relief—she felt her lungs fill with the invisible, yet life-giving oxygen of the Chicago night. But that deliverance only served to allow her to comprehend the terror of the moment. The violation was brief, but just long enough for her to regain her senses and fuel an outraged response.

Quickly deciding that her life was precious, and that she had too much to look forward to, she erupted like a volcano that had been asleep for ages. With a rage and anger that seemed to emanate from deep within her soul, she screamed. "No! No! Nooo...!" Fighting back, she raked her nails across the stranger's face, trying her best to attack his eyes. *Something about them...one's not right.* She focused on it, trying to gouge it out, and perhaps leave him with an indelible scar, that like her, he would bear forever.

Her fury surprised the attacker, as did her strength. She managed to get to her feet, kicking and clawing her way out to the sidewalk and into the public domain, while the predator did his best to drag her back to his lair. Just then a car turned off of Cicero Avenue, its headlights like a beam of justice, illuminating the life and death struggle. Startled by the sight in front of him on the sidewalk, the driver screeched to a stop.

The light and sound of the vehicle snapped him quickly back to reality. The attacker released her, angry that he had not been able to dominate her completely, disappointed that she was able to inflict harm, albeit minor. But he couldn't risk the possibility of more people seeing him. He hurriedly fled back into the crevasse between the buildings, disappearing into the shadows as swiftly as a glass of beer in an alcoholic's hand.

A middle aged couple emerged from the vehicle. "Miss, are you okay?"

The man looked at his wife, "Christine, call 9-1-1."

~ 22 ~

Coffee Service

Susan tried her best to concentrate on the Mass, but between the boys fidgeting and her anxiety about hoping to see David at the coffee service afterward, she was having difficulty focusing on the ritual. She found her mind wandering during Father Mike's homily, questioning whether or not she should even be doing this. Last night she had a hard time sleeping. She tossed and turned, conflicted about her attraction to this man. She had only met him once, but for some reason she was drawn to him. *Was it Satan trying to tempt her?* But what could be wrong? She was no longer a married woman, and David was a single man. Even Beth agreed with her on that point.

She prayed that the Lord would guide her and help her to make the right decision. Before she knew it, the Mass was over and she and the boys were making their way to the church exit. Father Mike was outside, as usual, greeting the parishioners. "Good morning, Susan."

"Good morning, Father."

"How are things with you and the boys?"

"Oh, we're fine. It's been a good week. We're going next door to have some coffee and donuts."

"Good. Have you met any other parishioners?"

She didn't know how much she should tell the priest. "Yes, your suggestion was a good one, Father. It's been wonderful to be able to interact with new people."

"Good. I knew that it would lift your spirits. Enjoy your day."

"Thank you, Father."

Susan and the boys walked the short distance next door to the Activity Center and went inside. *I hope that he's here.* She quickly scanned the area by the tables where the drinks and pastries were served. Then, as she saw David walking out of the kitchen, her body relaxed with the knowledge that he was there. She prepared a plate of snacks for the boys. "Here you go, take them into the other room—have fun."

"Susan! Good to see you," he said, smiling.

Her stomach twisted into knots, the excitement getting the best of her. She couldn't believe her reaction to just his simple greeting.

"Hi, David, we're here for more of your superb hospitality."

David set the two coffee urns down that he had carried from the kitchen. He took Susan's right hand between both of his own and warmly and shook it. "I was wondering if you'd be able to make it here again. I can imagine that your schedule must be hectic with four little ones. Is your husband here with you this morning?"

With a downward glance, she replied. "Uh...no, I'm a widow, David."

With a tone of sorrow in his voice he replied, "Oh, Susan, I'm sorry to hear that. I hope that I wasn't out of line asking that question. I didn't mean to cause you any pain."

"No, David, that's quite alright. My husband was a police officer; he was killed in the line of duty."

"I'm so sorry for your loss, may God rest his soul. You must be very proud of him, he was a hero."

Nodding, Susan said, "Thank you. He was a good man; we miss him very much."

Other parishioners were now filling the room, causing David to have to return to his volunteer duties. He gathered up a few empty cups and opened a couple more juice containers.

"Susan, I don't mean to brush you off but it's getting busy here. I'd like to talk with you some more...get to know you a little better. I hope that you don't take this the wrong way, but would you like to have coffee some morning or go out for lunch sometime?"

Her heart reacting to his invitation, doubling its rate, she answered. "I'd love to, David."

He took out his wallet and handed a business card to her. "Here's my card; think about when you would like to have coffee and then give me a call."

She took it with her left hand, and reached instantly with her right hand to hold his. "Thank you, David. I will definitely call you."

He squeezed her hand and smiled broadly at her, his white teeth framed on either side by dimples. "Great, I look forward to hearing from you. Now it's back to work for me. You and the boys have a great day!"

He walked back into the kitchen while she stood staring at the doorway where he had just disappeared. Her palms were sweating. She looked down at the hand that held his business card to find that she had unknowingly squeezed her fist, crumpling the card. She placed it on the table in front of her and carefully smoothed it out. With trembling hands she brought the card up to read it:

David Williams
Consultant / Freelance Writer
(312) 434-3775

Susan went into the playroom to gather the boys, feeling a bit unsteady. She was experiencing emotions that had been absent in her life for some time. She felt like a school girl with a teenage crush on her grade school teacher. She was excited about having been asked out on a date, yet there was some trepidation that perhaps she was doing something wrong by accepting. She was in unchartered waters, not knowing whether to proceed, or to tell him that she had made a mistake and that she wasn't quite ready yet to go out with anyone.

"C'mon, boys, it's time to go. I have to run a couple of errands and then fix lunch." They piled into the car and Susan headed for the market.

"Mommy, who was that man you were talking to?" Joey, her nine year old asked, as he buckled his seatbelt.

"His name is David. He volunteers at the coffee service."

"Does he like you?"

She turned around to look at her little boy. "Joey...! He's just a friend that I know from church." *Had Joey picked up on something?*

~ 23 ~

Consequences

"Pete, what's up? What did Lt. King want?"

They were back in their vehicle and headed toward HQ. "He said that the guy in the lockup is not our guy."

Looking puzzled, Marilyn asked, "How could he know that?"

Pete headed toward the Dan Ryan Expressway that would take them back to HQ. "He said that another rape occurred last night. It looks like our guy is still on the loose."

"Holy cow, Pete; this case is taking on a life of its own…we may have a serial rapist on our hands. I knew that homeless guy was not who we're looking for."

He dropped down on the freeway and immediately got into the far left lane, trying to make it to the office as quickly as possible. "You're right, Bens; we're definitely involved in something big here. But I sense that there's something else on King's mind. He said to get back to the office, ASAP."

"That doesn't sound good," she said. "Do you think that he's not happy with something we've done?"

Shrugging his shoulders, Pete said, "He didn't elaborate, just said to get back quickly."

They pulled into the parking lot fifteen minutes later and made their way upstairs. King was seated at his desk and Pete and Marilyn went right in. "You wanted to see us, sir?"

"Have a seat," he said, as he got up to close his office door. There were only a few guys in the squad area at this time of the day, but King obviously didn't want his conversation to be overheard. He sat back down at his desk and picked up the case file on the arrest at the ballpark. Dropping it down on his desk on the edge closest to the two detectives he said, "Is there anything that you want to tell me about this arrest last night?"

Marilyn and Pete looked at each other. Pete replied, "Sir, it's all in the report. The subject is definitely the guy that pulled the other stickups. His physical and clothing match all the other reports; is there a problem?"

"Who made the arrest?"

Now Marilyn answered, "Sir, this guy confronted us as we were walking through the neighborhood—he demanded Pete's wallet. We reacted, Pete cracked him with his cane, and then we cuffed him and found the weapon."

"I know that much," said King. "What I don't know is what role your backup—Carone and Geraci—played in all of this."

Pete didn't like the way this was unfolding. He knew that his boss must somehow know about the lack of communication last night between the two teams. Pete decided that he needed to be straightforward with Lt. King. He took a deep breath, then letting it out, he began. "We had a bit of a problem last night with our equipment. For some reason Carone and Geraci weren't picking up our signal. I finally contacted them using the cell phone."

"When…? When did you contact them?"

"Right after we arrested the offender, sir."

King got up from his desk and paced behind his chair. "So what you're telling me is that you two didn't see or hear from them until you had already made the arrest?"

"Yes, sir," replied Marilyn.

"Did they explain why it took them so long to resolve the problem—why they were unavailable to back you up?"

Marilyn sensed that the boss knew something that they didn't, but she also knew that this was definitely not the time to be anything but truthful about what happened. "Lt. King, we never discussed with them what the problem was. To be honest, Pete and I were pretty mad about not being able to raise them. But since it all worked out in the end and no one got hurt, we thought it was best to leave it alone."

King raised both arms palms up; with a shrug he asked, "So neither of you has a clue as to why they weren't' there to help out?"

Pete and Marilyn shook their heads. "Uh, uh."

King grabbed a sheet of paper and slid it across to his two detectives. "That's the reason!"

Pete picked it up and held it so that he and Marilyn could both see it. The photo showed their backup team asleep in the van.

"Wow," was all that Marilyn could offer.

"Boss, we had no idea," said Pete.

"Well now you know. I have the two of them on their way back here from City Hall. They were supposed to be standing in the background while the Mayor and Superintendent gave a press conference on the arrest. I can't risk that now in case whoever took that photo might see them and make a stink about two cops being asleep on the job."

Taking the photo back from Pete, King cautioned them. "I don't want this information to leave this room, understood?"

"Yes, sir."

"I'll handle this matter myself, but I want you both to know that you did a great job last night; you'll be getting credit for the arrest and clear up. What I need for you to do right now is to get your butts down to City Hall for the press conference. Try not to get involved in any interviews, but if you must say anything stick to the facts of the case—say nothing about Geraci and Carone. Understood?"

"Yes, sir."

"On the way down there, I want you to review the case report on last night's rape," he said, as he handed them the report. "It's definitely the same guy, the good news is that the victim was not seriously injured and she got a good look at this creep as well. There are also two other eyeball witnesses that were in a car and saw the guy. Get back here as quickly as you can, this thing is reaching a flashpoint."

"Will do, sir." They got up and left the office, going directly to their car.

"I'd hate to be in Carone's and Geraci's shoes right now," said

Pete, as he dropped back down on the Interstate.

"Copy that, partner. I could swear that I saw some steam coming out of King's ears."

"Yeah, they're in for a whipping for sure," said Pete. "I feel kind of sorry for them, even though they left us in the lurch."

"Pete, you're a softie—they could have gotten us killed by sleeping on the job."

"Yeah, I know, Bens, but those two have fragile egos. I hope they can survive the trip to the woodshed."

Pulling up to City Hall, Pete parked in one of the "Police Personnel Only" parking spots. He threw their blue light up on the dashboard and hung the mike cord around the rearview mirror. They hurried inside and showed their police ID to bypass the security checkpoints and then made their way to the elevator that would take them upstairs to the Mayor's Office. Little did they know, but just a few minutes prior to their arrival, Geraci and Carone had ridden the same elevator down. They had no idea why Lt. King had ordered them back to the office, but their gut instinct told them that it couldn't be anything good. Their instinct would prove to be correct.

~ 24 ~

Interviews

Pete and Marilyn finished at City Hall as quickly as they could, and then made their way back to the office. Lt. King was waiting for them and signaled through the glass for them to come in.

"Any problems?" He asked.

"No, sir," Pete replied. "Sgt. Grey told us that all that she wanted us to do was stand behind the Mayor and the Superintendent. She said that we weren't there to answer any questions."

King motioned for them to sit. "Good, I don't need any more headaches. Geraci and Carone will be gone from the squad for at least 30 days, effective immediately, so we're going to be short handed. OPR (Office of Professional Review) will be reviewing my request to send them back to uniform duty."

Taken aback by the swift, decisive action taken by their boss, Pete figured that it was best not to pursue the subject any further. If King wanted to reveal any more details, he would probably do it when he was ready.

"Okay…let's get down to business," said King, as he stood behind his desk with his arms crossed. "I've sent another team to interview your second victim, Martyna Gorski. Before you two get upset about someone else working your case let me explain. These incidents have the potential to cause a whole lot of bad PR for the Department, which means that the Mayor will catch flak because of it. We need to quickly get a handle on whoever is committing these rapes before the media gets hold of it and causes a panic."

Marilyn leaned in and said, "Sir, our first victim is still in the hospital. We haven't been able to interview her."

"I know that, Benson, I've been reviewing the file while you were downtown. We have to get these interviews done, that's why I sent a team over to Gorski's. For the rest of the shift you two will concentrate on interviewing the latest victim…what's her name?"

"Sanchez," Pete replied, quickly.

"Right, Claudia Sanchez. Get her information and then sit down with the two eyeballs. Tomorrow morning we'll all put our heads together and plot our course. We've got to tie the commonalities together, come up with a profile, a good physical on this guy, and then work from that point forward."

"Any questions?"

"No sir," the partners replied in unison.

"Good, hit the bricks; let's see if we can't clamp down on this creep before he strikes again."

***

Pete and Marilyn walked up the steps of the two flat and rang the doorbell marked, "Sanchez." The apartment was on the second floor of a clean and well maintained building. The neighborhood was mostly Hispanic working class folks—big families with plenty of kids running around.

A voice came over the speaker, "Who is it?"

"Police Department, we'd like to speak with Claudia Sanchez."

"Come up," came the reply, as the door buzzed allowing them to enter. They walked up to the second floor landing where they were met by a woman who identified herself as the victim's aunt.

"How are you, officers? Please, come in."

They were ushered into a living room decorated in floral patterns and bright colored hues. The walls and tables contained an assortment of religious symbols and icons, making it feel more like a chapel rather than a residence. Seated on the couch was a man who was introduced as the woman's husband.

Pete and Marilyn introduced themselves and showed their police IDs; the woman glanced at them and then directed the detectives to have a seat.

Taking a dish towel that had been draped over her shoulder and wiping her already dry hands, the woman asked, "Did you catch the man who did this to our Claudia?"

Marilyn answered, "No ma'am, that's why we're here. We'd like to have a word with Claudia so that we can see if there is any additional information that she can provide that will help us arrest the man responsible."

The woman got up from the couch. "Let me get her, she's on the back porch studying her schoolwork. The doctor told her not to go to work for a couple of days."

A minute later the young woman appeared. Dressed in shorts and a White Sox tee shirt, she was very attractive. With her long, straight hair, lean and fit figure, and cocoa complexion, she could have easily been a model. And despite having been involved in a brutal attack, she was surprisingly bereft of any scars or marks, at least none that were visible.

"Hello, officers," she said, timidly.

"Hi, Claudia," said Marilyn. "Please sit down; let's talk about what happened last night."

She took a seat on the couch with her aunt and uncle. Pete opened his notebook and prepared to take notes while Marilyn led the interview. She walked the victim through her activities leading up to the point where she got off the bus, and then asked the woman to relate what happened next.

With a quick glance toward her aunt, the girl began. "I had just turned off of Cicero and was walking on our street just a few blocks away from home. I had a feeling that someone was following me, so I turned around…that's when I saw this man. Before I knew what was happening, I saw something that I think looked like a white sock. He swung it at me and I tried to duck away, but it hit me on the side of the head. Something hard was inside."

"Did you fall down at that point, Claudia?"

"No," she said, shaking her head. "He didn't really hit me as hard as he probably wanted to because I was kind of ducking out of the way, but as I was bent over he kicked me in the stomach—it knocked the wind out of me and I almost passed out."

"But you never lost consciousness?" Marilyn interrupted.

With her arms between her legs she squeezed them tightly together, as if this gesture might erase the events of last night, and replied. "No, I never blacked out but it took me a while to catch my breath. In the meantime he had taken off my pants and was raping me."

"Oh, honey…." Claudia's aunt and uncle were obviously becoming uncomfortable as she was describing the actual event. She hadn't told them much detail about what had happened; they were hearing it for the first time. Her aunt had tears in her eyes; her uncle sat in silence, staring straight ahead.

The two women hugged. "It's okay, Auntie…it's okay." The woman's aunt reached over on the end table and grabbed a crucifix, holding it to her bosom she began to mumble some prayers in Spanish. Claudia finished describing her ordeal, maintaining her composure, but looking down at the floor while she spoke.

Marilyn moved forward in her chair. "Claudia, we think that this man has attacked a couple of other women. It's important that you do your very best to give me a detailed description of this guy, especially anything that stands out about him or that you remember more clearly than anything else."

Without hesitation the woman answered. "His right eye."

Confirming her suspicions about the offender, but not wanting to lead the victim, Marilyn asked another question. "What about his eye? Why does that stand out for you?"

Looking at Marilyn, and sitting much straighter now, the woman replied. "Because it was off to one side...you know...it wasn't normal like everyone's eyes. When I caught my breath and fought to get away from him, I tried to gouge it out with my nails," she said, while thrusting her arm out and making a poking gesture with her hand. "I think that I hurt him because he jumped back and put his hand to his face. It gave me time to get up and try to get back out to the sidewalk—that's when the car stopped."

Smiling at the woman, Marilyn continued. "Claudia, that's excellent information; it will help us a great deal. Is there anything else...anything that stands out?"

"No, not really. But he was strong...in good shape, you know? I don't know how important it is; it sounds kind of crazy."

"That could be important, Claudia. We'll definitely bring that up with the other victims; maybe they noticed it as well. You are a brave woman. I would have never suspected that you were attacked last night, you seem so composed and confident."

"Thanks, I think that it's because I'm mad as hell about what happened. I've worked so hard; made so many sacrifices.... I'm not going to let some low-life stop me from making a success of my life."

"Good for you," Marilyn replied. Looking around the room, she added, "You are obviously a family with a strong connection to your faith. Your guardian angel must have been with you last night."

With a smile the woman replied. "Funny that you should say that officer. We are a Catholic family. In Puerto Rico the nuns taught us that everyone has a guardian angel that will protect them from evil. From the moment that I step off of the bus each night, I say a prayer that my guardian angel will be with me until I'm safely in the door. He saved me last night."

"Amen to that," said Marilyn.

The two detectives finished up the interview and left their business card with the family. Once inside their vehicle they headed toward the address of the couple who were in the car that witnessed the attack. On the way they discussed Claudia's information.

"This guy has definitely got a problem with his right eye. That makes two victims that have mentioned it. I'd be surprised if the Gorski woman didn't notice it as well." Pete pulled up to the address on the case report where the older couple lived.

"Yeah, that's going to be a big help for sure," said Marilyn. "What do you make of her comment about the guy being strong and in good shape?"

"I don't know, Bens. That one came out of left field, but it could turn out to be as important as the guy having a lazy eye. Maybe he tries to compensate for the eye imperfection with getting his body in perfect shape. I guess that we'll find out in the morning when we go over all the statements and get a better idea about our guy."

They got out of their car and walked up to the front door of the residence. "You want to do the paper on this one partner?"

"Sure," said Marilyn. "I trust you. I'm sure that you'll ask all the right questions, you don't seem to have any doubt about your abilities, not like you did last week. I think that you've got the hang of this detective thing."

"You're right, partner; it's beginning to feel natural...like this is what we're cut out to do."

Pete rang the doorbell and then looked over at his partner while they waited. "Detectives Shannon and Benson, who would have ever imagined?"

~ 25 ~

Coffee for Two

On the drive to the coffee shop Susan had second thoughts about meeting David. She was going back and forth in her mind about whether or not she was doing the right thing. Her mother had come over to babysit the boys. Susan hadn't told her the truth about where she was going…but she hadn't lied either. Though certainly not a child anymore, she still felt like she was acting like one who was cleverly deceiving her parents. She didn't feel comfortable telling her mother that she was meeting a man for coffee, a date, so she simply told her that she was going to the mall. The part that she was completely truthful about was that she needed some time away.

Ever since her husband's death, she had spent most of her days in the house with the boys. The weeks following Joe's death were a blur, time ceased to exist; there was only the constant hurt, even though people were stopping by the house trying to console her. The visits eventually slowed to a trickle and then stopped. She was left alone with her children and her thoughts. Lately, the cold reality of it all struck her like a sudden dip in a tub of ice water—she was a single mother with four kids, no job, and no real skills.

Although she had a college degree she had never worked. For the sake of their children, she and her husband had made a pact that he would be the bread winner; she would be a stay at home mom. They both agreed that it was important that the children be raised by their parents, not sent off to child care. The last nine years had seen their plan work successfully. Now that was all gone...Joe was dead and Susan needed to think about the future.

She parked her car and went inside the mall. Dozens of people wandered about, some hand in hand, paired off, each half equaling a whole. It struck her that she never really noticed the couples before, never paid any mind to the dynamics of two people becoming one. She still had a few minutes to spare before the appointed time. As she walked past the various stores on her way to the coffee shop, she looked at her reflection in the massive windows that afforded a mirror-like image of those who dared to take a look. She was certainly not glamorous, but she knew that she was attractive. Her husband, Joe, had always maintained a fitness program; his job demanded that he be in shape. He kept Susan involved in exercise as well, both of them taking long walks and bike rides together. Their weekend getaways with the kids always involved walking and hiking. And although she had given birth to four children, she made it a point to lose the "baby weight" after each one was born. She walked every day and maintained a healthy diet. Her slim figure was the result of all that hard work.

She had prayed about this day, knowing that sooner or later

she would have to start over. She certainly wasn't looking for someone to replace her husband; no one could ever do that. But she was expecting to resume a normal life. She longed for the companionship, the partnership, the sharing, and the loving that she had enjoyed with Joe. She missed the simple touches and smells—the things that two people in love hardly realize they're doing until that dreadful moment in time when those unassuming pleasures no longer existed.

Was she being selfish? She stopped just before turning the corner to the food court. *Do I continue, or am I going down the wrong road? Dear Lord, please guide me....* Confused, she turned to leave and as she did she walked right into David's arms.

"Susan, am I late?" David grabbed her, steadying her so that she wouldn't fall. "It's eleven o'clock; I'm right on time," he said as he glanced at his watch. "You weren't' leaving, were you?"

Embarrassed by her indecision, she couldn't leave now. Was this perhaps another sign that she should follow through with her decision to meet with David?

"Uh...hi, David, it seems that bumping into you is becoming the norm for me, I'm sorry."

Letting her go, he said, "No problem...I'm getting used to it. Shall we get a cup of coffee or have you changed your mind?"

Smiling, Susan replied. "Yes, I could use some coffee right now."

They walked into the coffee shop; David tending to the coffee, while Susan chose a table by the window. Bringing the two coffees to the table, he placed her cup in front of her. "Here you are...cream and sugar, correct?"

"Yes, how did you know?"

"I watched you at the Activity Center, "he said, as he sat down, "I have an eye for detail. It comes with the territory."

"Thank you," she said, sampling the coffee. "David, I have a confession to make. I *was* getting ready to leave when I bumped into you. I was torn about whether I should be doing this…thinking that I'm selfish…wanting something that perhaps I should be waiting for and not rushing into."

Puzzled, he asked. "Exactly what is it that you're doing that you think is wrong, Susan? Having coffee with someone that you met at church doesn't strike me as something that you should be indecisive or guilty about."

"I know, it sounds silly when I hear you put it in that context. But when I run it through my mind, I come up with different reasons for just waiting a bit longer before I begin seeing someone. Waiting for what I'm not quite sure of, but I guess that I'm just confused about my role in life right now. Like what am I supposed to be doing?"

David patiently listened to her while he sipped his coffee. When she finished he put his cup down and folded his hands on the table in front of him. "Susan, I can't say that I know what you're going through. Losing a loved one is a life-changing event that impacts people differently; it's one of the most stressful things that can happen to someone. Some move past it successfully, others are scarred forever and have a difficult time dealing with it and moving forward. May I share something with you?"

"Yes, please do." Susan sat back in her chair and drank her coffee while David spoke. "I come from a military family. My Father was in the Army, a career soldier, and my mother was a stay at home mom. My dad was killed in the Viet Nam War when I was eighteen years old. It was devastating for both of us when we lost him, he was our whole life; it sounds corny to say, but our world revolved around him."

"No, David, it hardly sounds corny; it sounds natural."

Susan focused on his face while he spoke; she could see his sorrow and feel his pain even though the event that he was describing happened decades ago.

He continued. "My mother never remarried. And it never really struck me as anything out of the ordinary; I just figured that she hadn't met anyone that interested her. Two years ago she died, but before she passed away we spent many hours together, talking about things that we'd never, ever discussed. One of the things that she told me about was her remorse for not having remarried. She said that during the first several years after my dad's death, she felt that if she began dating it would disrespect his memory. In her mind the proper thing to do was to wait—give her heart time to heal and then begin to see other men. But she kept putting it off, finding excuses not to date, and before she knew it she was an old woman, having neither the desire nor the ability to look for a partner. She told me that she regretted not having shared the rest of her life with someone. She felt that she missed out on what could have been many happy years. And with me being away most of the time in the Army, she said that she felt very much alone."

"You have no siblings, David?" Susan asked, while taking another sip of coffee.

"No, I'm an only child."

Setting her coffee down on the table, Susan was beginning to feel much better about being here with David. "Tell me if I'm being too nosy David, but have you ever married?"

"You're doing fine, Susan," he said, with a smile, "that's why we're here today—to talk and get to know each other. No, I've never been married. I was engaged about ten years ago, but several months into it she wanted me to agree to leave the military once we were married. She said that she didn't want to have a long distance marriage. I naturally couldn't agree to anything like that. Besides, my career was important and I wasn't about to throw away what would eventually be a government pension and other benefits."

Grinning, Susan remarked, "What a mistake she made! She probably didn't realize what she was doing."

"I don't know what she was thinking," replied David. "Plenty of people in the military are married and accept whatever difficulties come along with that situation. It's not unlike any other occupation; every job has its good and bad points."

Susan had finished her coffee and David quickly grabbed her cup. "I'll get us a refill." He went to the counter and Susan watched him, thinking what a gentle man he was.

David returned with the two coffees and Susan asked another question. "So now you're retired…your business card says that you're a consultant and a writer?"

"Yes, I retired several years ago. I didn't want to get involved in a conventional job after I left the service; you know the 9-5 office routine, so I decided to contract my services as a type of consulting business. I write opinions and articles about military matters for the Defense Department and other government entities. In my spare time I like to write fiction novels—mostly Christian based."

Bringing her cup to her mouth, Susan said, "You are a talented man, David, I'm impressed."

"No need to be impressed, Susan. Frankly, I do those things because I enjoy doing them and I'm too young to be sitting idly every day." His elbows on the table and his chin resting on both of his hands, he said, "We've talked too much about me. Tell me about Susan."

Feeling her face flush, she replied, "I don't have much to tell, David; I'm just a Mom and a wife…I mean I was a wife."

"Exactly," he said. "That's what I want to hear about. I will share this with you…after our first meeting at church I asked Father Mike about you."

Sitting upright, she responded, "You did?"

"Yes. Don't be upset, some of my military habits are firmly ingrained—I can't shake them. Anyway, I just wanted to know if he knew anything about you. Father briefly explained what happened with Joe and he went on to tell me what a loving, dedicated family woman you are."

With a quizzical look she asked him, "But you asked me on our second meeting if my husband was with me."

"I know, I just wanted to see what you would say, how you would react to the question. If you would have become upset, that would have been my cue to go no further; you handled it well."

"So I passed the first test?"

"If you want to call it that…yes, you passed. So please, tell me more about Susan."

Before they realized it, two hours had passed and they were both hungry.

"Susan, if you're not sick of my company yet may I buy you lunch?"

Deep inside she wasn't as hungry for anything to eat as much as she was for his company. She was thoroughly enjoying being with this man; he was compassionate, kind and intelligent, she wasn't ready for it to end.

"David, I can't see myself ever being tired of your company, you're fascinating. Yes, let's get lunch."

A while later she was back in her car headed home. *What a great day; God's been good to me.* If her meeting David was indeed ordained by the Father, it was truly a blessing. She felt energized and excited for the first time in many months. She thought about what David had said about his mother and how she regretted not remarrying. It was just what she needed to hear. She decided to no longer live in the past, but rather to plan for the future—for herself and her boys.

~ 26 ~

The Matrix

On the way into work Marilyn needed to make a quick stop. She swung by Joe's house and saw that his car was still in the driveway. She quickly pulled in, parked behind it, and went to the front door. As she was about to ring the bell, the door opened.

"Hi, honey, surprised to see me?"

Startled by the sight of his girlfriend, Joe dropped his keys. "Uh…yeah." He bent down to retrieve them. "We talked on the phone last night; I didn't expect to see you this morning."

"Good, I don't like being predictable." She stepped inside, pushing Joe backwards out of the doorway. She took his face in her hands and kissed him long and passionately.

Breathless, Joe asked, "What was that all about?"

"That's my therapy—it counteracts the chemo. Did it work?"

Smiling, and with a laugh, Joe replied, "Heck yeah, if that's what I can expect after each chemo treatment, sign me up for another."

"Joe, all kidding aside, I'm really worried about you and I feel terrible that we can't spend more time together."

"It's okay, Marilyn, I'll be fine. We knew that our jobs would cause problems like this…we'll get through it."

Putting her head on his shoulder and holding him tightly, she said, "Joe, I love you so much…. I had to see you before I went to work today; I just had this urge."

He stroked her hair and said, "I'm glad that you stopped by, especially since you delivered your special therapy." He kissed her and opened the door. "C'mon, I've got to get to roll call sweetheart. Call me later and tell me your new strategy with the rape case."

Walking hand in hand out to their cars, Marilyn said, "I'll call you this afternoon. King's going to have us compare notes on our interviews and then we'll devise our next move. You be careful honey; I love you."

"I love you too."

Marilyn pulled out and headed to HQ, while Pete made his way to the station. He hadn't told her how he really felt.

***

Marilyn walked into the squad area. Pete was pouring his coffee and spotted her, "Mornin', partner, God been good to you today?"

"Oh, hi, Pete, yes, He has. I stopped by Joe's house on the way in."

"That was nice of you. How is he?"

She set her duty bag down by her desk and picked up her notes from the interviews. "I think that he's doing well, at least he looks and acts well. I don't really know what to expect from the chemo…I don't know how he's supposed to react."

"Well it's only been one treatment so far. I know that he's in good shape physically so his body should allow him to put up a good fight. I just worry about him once the treatments start to add up. What will the cumulative effect be?

They headed toward Lt. King's office for the meeting, and Marilyn took in a deep breath. "That's what worries me Pete. Sooner or later it's going to wear him down. What's going to happen to him on the street? Will he be able to handle himself?"

They stopped short of the office and Pete turned to her. "Just between you and me, I spoke with Mac last night. He's ready to take care of Joe any way that he can, whether it's an admin job or even giving him time off whenever he needs it."

"Thank God," she sighed. "Mac is the best!"

King stood up in his office and signaled the two teams to come inside. "Good morning!"

"Morning, sir!"

"Let's get started." He walked over to a white board that rested on a table against the wall. On it he had set up a matrix which plotted the three crimes—names, addresses ages, occupations, nationalities, and the time and locations of the rapes. Next to the white board was a map with stick pins, indicating similar information and a geographical plot of all the residences and crime scenes.

King had the master case file in his hands as he addressed his teams. "Look at the board…you can see that with the exception of the assault downtown, everything is centered in the 8th District. All three victims live there, two of them were assaulted close to their residences. If you look at the three locations where they live, you'll find that the second victim, the Gorski woman, lives on Kedzie Avenue near 59th Street. That location differs from the other two in that it's on a busy street. Our guy probably didn't want to risk grabbing her there—too much traffic. My guess is that he found out where she worked and looked for a spot there. Turns out he found a good one."

"You're right, boss," Marilyn added. "We interviewed the homeless guy who said that entrance to the abandoned building was perfect for what the offender had in mind."

King set the file down on his desk. "So what we know about our guy is that he's obsessed with cleaning ladies for some reason, and that they all live on the Southwest Side. They take public transportation to work, which is the midnight shift, and he hits them in the back of the head to immobilize them. One victim described it as something looking like a sock containing something very hard. What other common threads do we have?"

Pete jumped in, "Boss, I think that it's a good bet that our guy must live in the vicinity, he knows the area too well just to be passing through."

"Good point, Shannon."

"There's something wrong with the guy's right eye," added Marilyn. "Victims two and three quickly pointed that out, and although we have yet to interview the first one, the two boys that found her said that she muttered something about his eye."

"Right," said King. He put that up on the board. "What else?"

"The last victim said that he was strong—well built."

King looked over at the other team. "Did your victim say anything about the guy?"

Paul, a heavy set old-timer responded. "Yeah, our gal said that the guy had the eye problem, but she didn't say anything about his shape or strength. I think that she told us that she went into some kind of trance, so we didn't get a whole lot from her."

"Okay…we've got a few things to go on here, but nothing very solid in terms of who this guy might be. Shannon and Benson, I want you two to check the data base and see if we've got any sex offenders with that lazy eye characteristic, and then get a listing of recently released cons that live in that general area where the victims reside. From what we've got so far our guy looks like a white male, probably around 30 to 35 years of age, probably average height and weight but strong, and he's got a lazy right eye."

Pete sat up in his chair. "Boss, what about getting a Crime Lab guy to go visit the last two women, maybe they can remember enough for a composite of our guy?"

"We don't have much, but put in a request—maybe they can generate some type of image."

"Yes, sir."

"That's all I have for the time being." He looked over at Shannon and Benson. "Good interview on that guy that the 1st District busted, he's clearly not the one we're after. Make sure you follow through on the paperwork to get him released; we want to keep him on our side. He's probably our best witness right now."

"Already working on it, sir." Pete stood up and set his chair back against the wall.

King sat down at his desk. "Dismissed...get busy on your dailies and case summaries, I have to brief the Old Man this afternoon on our open cases."

Pete and Marilyn went back to their desks and started on their paperwork. Marilyn looked over at Pete. "This is the worst part of the job. The paper never seems to end."

"I know, partner, and depending on how long it takes for us to grab this creep, the file's going to grow like a weed on a rainy summer day."

"I'm afraid you're right," said Marilyn. "We need to check in with the Crime Lab and see what they've come up with. If they've got any good prints we'll need to run them through NCIC and the known offender list."

"Good one, Bens. Let's get on that after lunch. Maybe we'll catch a break and grab this guy before he hurts someone else."

"Amen to that...."

~ 27 ~

Joe's Surprise

The next couple of days saw a flurry of activity for Pete and Marilyn. They concentrated on all of the admin work that was needed to put their case together. First, they had all the case reports and investigative interviews serialized and put into the master file. Next, they followed up on the physical evidence at the Crime Lab. And there was good news to report. They spoke with the DNA section that had processed samples from all three victims—the samples were identical, proving that the same offender committed all three rapes. They found good news at the Fingerprint Section as well, there were two good prints found on the piece of metal at the scene of the first rape. Little Billy Callahan's memory proved to be extremely helpful to the case.

The lab had sent its composite specialist to sit down with Martyna Gorski and Claudia Sanchez. He came up with an image of the offender, and even though it was very non-specific, it nonetheless added another piece to the puzzle of who the attacker might be. Now it would be awhile before results came back from the search of the national data bases, comparing prints and DNA. In the meantime, the good news was that the creep had not struck again.

Pete looked over at Marilyn, who was packing up her gear to go home. "Looks like you're ready to head out."

"Yeah, that's enough for today. I'm meeting Kim at the gym right after work; I need to vent somehow."

"I hear ya. The flyers with the sketch should be done by late tomorrow. We can grab a handful and start hitting some of the businesses along the bus routes over in the 8th District. Maybe we'll get lucky and someone will recognize the guy."

"I hope so, Pete." Marilyn threw her bag over her shoulder. "Are you ready?"

"Yeah." They left the office together and made their way out to the parking lot, stopping at Pete's truck.

"Are you still going to dinner tonight with Joe?"

"I'm pretty sure…I'll call him on my way home from the gym. I haven't seen him in a couple of days; he said that the treatments have made him so tired that all he wants to do is sleep. I hope that he's okay."

Pete threw his bag in the rear of his truck. "Tell him I said hi and that Beth and I are praying for him."

"I will, Pete…see you tomorrow. Kiss the baby for me."

Marilyn turned out of the lot and headed for the Interstate. *Better call Joe after I'm finished with my workout to make sure that he's up to going out tonight.*

***

Joe looked at himself in the mirror. *Not too bad, only two little nicks.* He grabbed a septic pencil and used it to stop the bleeding. He cleaned all the hair out of the sink and then hopped in the shower. Getting himself wet, he instinctively reached for the shampoo bottle to begin his cleaning ritual which had always begun with washing his hair first. *Won't need any of this for awhile....* He put the bottle back on the ledge and grabbed a bar of soap.

As the water hit his now naked skull, it splashed off wildly like a heavy downpour on a city sidewalk. A few minutes later he stepped out of the shower; he dried himself and then looked at his reflection in the full length mirror on the door. *Must be dropping some weight too....* The chemo had left him nauseous and with a bad taste in his mouth; it had also left him with some canker sores inside which made eating uncomfortable. His appetite had diminished considerably since his diagnosis. As much as he would love to eat his favorite meal, a beef sandwich from Portillo's, the agony involved in doing so quickly dissuaded him from following through.

Marilyn had called earlier to confirm that they would be going out for dinner. Maybe something high in carbs would give him some energy. She was going to pick him up shortly; he was grateful for that. Driving the squad car around all day had worn him out. *Am I turning into a wimp?*

While he began to get dressed, he thought about the decision to shave his head. He had discussed it with his doctor who told him that many chemo patients decide to do that early on in treatment rather than wait for all of their hair to fall out. It's a form of acceptance of the disease that they suffer from. Some patients say that it strengthens their resolve, and that it becomes much easier for them to admit to others that they are sick. Losing weight was troubling though. He would have to ask his doctor about that, maybe get some type of medication. He couldn't afford to be tired and weak if he was going to continue to work the street.

He searched his closet for a baseball cap to wear. He found his White Sox baseball hat and promptly put it on. Looking in the dresser mirror: *Hmmm...not too horribly ugly.* He grabbed a bottle of water from the fridge and turned on the TV to watch the news. Ten minutes into the program the doorbell rang. *Lord, please don't let Marilyn freak out when she sees me.* He removed his cap and opened the door. Marilyn was standing on the porch.

"Joe...Joe...." She covered her face with her hands and quietly sobbed. He went out to her and wrapped her in an embrace.

"Honey, it's going to be okay. Don't cry...I don't look that bad, do I?"

Her body trembled and she buried her face in his neck, continuing to weep. The two stood silently on the porch that way for several minutes, not wanting to let go of each other. Finally, Joe put his arm around her and led her inside. Marilyn sat on the couch next to him sniffling and dabbing at her eyes with a tissue.

"Oh, Joe, I'm sorry. It's just that it was such a shock to see you like that—I wasn't ready for it. I guess that the serious implications of what you are going through finally hit home for me at that moment." Continuing to dry her tears, she said, "What prompted you to shave your head? I thought that you didn't want anyone to know."

"My hair had begun to fall out, not a lot, but I could see some on the pillow in the morning and I had a couple of bare patches beginning to form. And then in the shower, some would accumulate around the drain—I talked it over with my doctor and he told me that many of his patients decide to do it, they say that it's cathartic for them."

Marilyn took his hand in hers. "Joe, forgive me."

"For what?"

"For being so self-absorbed," she said, sternly. "I haven't focused enough on what you're facing, what a life and death struggle you're involved in. I need to get more involved in this battle honey; I need to hold you up."

Joe squeezed her hand. "Mar, you're fine. Your concern and your prayers have helped me more than you know."

"It's not enough," she said. "I need to be with you as much as I can; you shouldn't be going through this alone."

Joe took a drink of his water and screwed the top back on. "Listen, honey, things are still fine right now. Maybe I'll need a little more help from you in the future. Believe me; I'll let you know when that time comes. But right now I'm just grateful that you're in my life. After I beat this thing and find that you still love me, my prayers will have been answered."

Tilting her head quizzically, Marilyn asked, "What prayers?"

"I pray that not only will the Father help me be victorious in my struggle with cancer, but that He will somehow convince you to continue to love me."

Her eyes moist, she kissed him gently on the lips. "Joe, that prayer has already been answered. I couldn't love you any more, no matter what happens with this battle. I am a lucky woman to have the love of a strong, Christian man like you. I am blessed."

Joe returned the kiss. "Thank you, sweetheart, now let's go get something to eat and introduce the new bald guy to Chicago."

Standing together they walked hand in hand toward the door. "Lead the way, honey; I'm here with you always."

They had an enjoyable dinner, Joe not eating much but managing to get down some pasta and bread hoping that it would give him some energy for tomorrow's shift. He felt self-conscious about his lack of hair, but Marilyn reassured him that no one in the restaurant gave him a second glance. The real test would come tomorrow at work, when he saw people that he knew. Cops are tough critics.

She dropped him off at home. They didn't stay out very long since Joe was tired and needed to rest for tomorrow. On the way to her apartment Marilyn called her neighbor, Leslie.

"Hello...."

"Hi, Les, it's Marilyn."

"Oh, hi, how are you, Marilyn?"

"Okay, I guess. I hate to bother you, but can you come over to my place? I really need to talk."

"Of course."

"Good. I'm just around the corner; I'll be home in five minutes."

No sooner had she arrived home than Leslie was knocking on

her door. "C'mon in, Les."

She followed Marilyn into the kitchen; they both sat down at the table. "Leslie, you have been such a good friend and such an inspiration to me. Can I trouble you again with my thoughts?"

Smiling, her friend replied, "You're never any trouble, I enjoy our conversations."

"Thank you. I was out with Joe this evening; he's getting so weak, and he's shaved his head. I'm afraid that I didn't help matters any when I broke down after seeing him for the first time without any hair."

"Oh…did it seem to affect him…your reaction?"

"Not really," she said, shaking her head. "And that's my problem. Even though he has the disease, I'm the one that seems to be having a problem with it. He seems strong-willed and well adjusted while I just fall apart every time that I see him. What's wrong with me? Why can't I be his strength?"

Leslie leaned forward in her chair. "There's nothing wrong with you, Marilyn. Your reaction is perfectly normal. You see someone whom you love that's in pain and it hurts you. If you didn't react to that I would be questioning your feelings."

Nodding in affirmation, Marilyn asked, "What can I do? I feel like I don't spend enough time with him. He's all alone in that house when he's finished with work with no one to care for him. I'm working every day and still trying to do all the things that I need to do, and at the end of the day it seems like I have no time for him—plus he's tired from the cancer treatment."

Leslie looked directly at her friend. "What is it that you want to do?"

Marilyn shook her head. "I'm not sure, but I know that I need to do more. I've been thinking about asking him if I can move in with him. I never would have considered that if it weren't for his illness, Joe and I have discussed our faith. We both agreed that if we have a future together, that if our relationship should lead to marriage, we would wait to be together until God blessed our union."

Sitting upright, Leslie took in a deep breath. "Normally, I would say that moving in with someone is not a good idea. But I think that considering the circumstances, perhaps our Lord is sending you a message that Joe needs you. I know that you are both firm in your Christian faith; you believe that God ordained marriage so that a man and a woman would become one. Joe recognizes that—he and his late wife were perfect examples. But he needs you. Believe me, even though he may put up a strong front, he needs you. His treatment will only make his health deteriorate as the days go by. Have you discussed this with him?"

"No," she said, wringing her hands. "It's been in the back of my mind until now, but when I saw him tonight it was as if that thought immediately turned into a glaring neon sign that flashed—Joe needs you!"

"That sounds like a strong message to me. Let's pray about it before you make any decision. Maybe God will send you a clear sign."

"Okay."

Leslie folded her hands in prayer, closed her eyes and bowed her head.

"Dear Father God, please hear the prayers of your children as we come to you in need. We pray that you will strengthen Marilyn as she struggles with her decision to move in with your servant, Joseph, who suffers alone. Send her a sign that your blessing will be with her as she ministers to her loved one who is in need of her help. Father, you are our refuge and strength in times of trouble and despair. We know that all we need do is to seek your help and it will be given. You are a loving God, a shepherd who tends to his flock. When one is in trouble you rescue that lost soul and bring it back to the fold. Father, we pray that you will heal Joe, rescue him from the illness that has filled him. May your love shine on both your children, Marilyn and Joe, and may this cross that they bear bring them closer to you. In Jesus' name we pray, Amen."

"Amen," said Marilyn, as she opened her eyes and unfolded her hands.

"It's late" said Leslie, as she got up from the table. "Bill is out of town, and I need to get home and pack some lunches for my boys for school tomorrow. Thank you for calling me and asking me to pray with you. I have grown closer to the Lord through you, Marilyn. Your faith has strengthened me."

Opening the door, Marilyn replied, "That's strange. I'm the one who called on you for help, yet you're thanking me."

"Because I see the Lord at work in you—he favors you."

Leslie opened the door to leave. "The Father is a loving God; He won't give us more than He knows we can handle. You and Joe will have some tough times ahead, but you are blessed with the Holy Spirit—he will fill you with the grace and the fortitude that you'll need to get through this painful journey."

"God bless you, Leslie, you are Heaven sent."

"Good night, my friend."

~ 28 ~

The Dumpster

Where was he? She looked up and down the street, searching for his car. It was almost 12:30 am and she had been waiting over twenty minutes for him to arrive; she had called his cell phone—no answer. As much as she didn't want to take the bus home, she also didn't want to stand out in front of the building any longer either. Resigning herself to the long ride home, she walked around the corner to the bus stop and ten minutes later she was on her way, headed toward the southwest side.

Alicia never had a problem taking public transportation to her job downtown. It actually saved her a lot of money. She didn't have to worry about a car; her boyfriend would take her shopping and wherever else she needed to go, that is if he wasn't high. He was usually good about being where he was supposed to be, unless he had been drinking. *That must be what happened with him tonight.*

Last week she had asked him to start picking her up from work. The talk among the cleaning crews downtown was that there was some creep attacking women late at night. Her supervisor told her that three ladies had been attacked already as they had traveled to and from their jobs. Alicia didn't want to be on that list, so until the cops caught the guy, she wanted her boyfriend to drive her home. Not showing up or calling tonight, the first night that he was supposed to begin, was not a good start. She would raise hell with him tomorrow.

***

The stranger was more than ready for this one. He wouldn't make the same mistake with her as he had with the last girl. He had been caught up in the sexual act, not following his plan to make sure that these sluts had no chance to interfere with what he needed to do. She had been stronger than he had anticipated, recovering from his attack and countering with her own. *Bitch tried to gouge my eye out....* He would have loved to punish her further for not submitting completely, but the car that had stopped to see what was going on prevented him from doing so. That wouldn't happen again. He would be more aggressive, more dominant. *How dare they resist him?* Women were whores; only good for one thing—serving a man. Besides, they should be enjoying his good looks and toned body. Women should be fighting over one another to date him.

He watched her as she got off the bus—a little late tonight. Last night she had been 20 or 30 minutes earlier. Maybe she had worked overtime. He knew that she had a five block walk to her apartment, and that there were at least two good spots to grab her on the way. He drove ahead and parked his car inconspicuously among the others parked on the street and then set his plan in action.

The woman approached his hermitage at the mouth of the

Gripped by Fear 161

alley. He was just inside an enclosed dumpster area—it was perfect, with its tall fence that hid the refuse container from the public view. As she drew near, he saw that just like last night she had earplugs in her ear, apparently listening to music. *Stupid woman, you deserve this!* As she passed by, engaged in the entertainment the small electronic device provided for its users, he sprang from his position. Like a moth to a light, he went quickly to her swinging his weapon at the same time. She went down instantly, and like an animal that drags its capture into its lair, he roughly dragged her behind the fence. He tore her clothes off, leaving the gift of her womanhood exposed. *I'll teach you not to reject me....*

Several minutes later it was done. His plan had been executed flawlessly; he was proud of himself. Satisfied, he took a deep breath and quickly assessed his work. He was indeed a dominate force; no one could overcome his strength. Standing over her, like a bird of prey admiring its catch, he reached down among her belongings and grabbed her earphones and MP3 player. *This is what got you in trouble.* He put it in his pocket.

She started to stir. Opening her eyes just a slit, Alicia saw her attacker smiling as he looked down at her. Frightened, and not knowing what else to do, she decided it was best to do nothing—to just lay there. *Had the worst already happened?* Her head was pounding and she felt as if she were about to vomit, but she forced herself to lie still. *Please go away....*

The stranger gave her one last look. As he moved closer to her, she dared a quick glance with one eye at his face. She didn't know what the devil looked like, but she was certain that this man bore a close resemblance. There was evil in his eyes...and something wrong with one of them as well. Breathing deeply, recovering from the effort, the man pointed at her and said, "Next time I tell you what to do, you'd better do it, you worthless bitch!"

What is he saying?

The man turned and walked through the partially opened gate. Too scared to move, Alicia stayed on the ground a while longer until she was certain that he would not return. After several minutes had passed, she sat up and looked around for her purse and her clothes. It was then that she noticed a pool of blood where she had been laying. She dared not try to stand; she was dizzy and uncertain as to where she was. She struggled to get into her pants, her underwear now useless having been torn during the savage act. She could feel remnants of the stranger down there, like toxins oozing from an infected wound, but she needed to reclaim her modesty, needed to cover up. Finding her purse and locating her cell phone, she dialed 9-1-1.

"Chicago Police Emergency Operator, how may I help you?"

"I've been raped…please come."

~ 29 ~

Early Morning Call

Pete heard the phone ring just as he was about to go out for his run. He quickly grabbed it from its cradle on the kitchen wall while glancing at the clock which read 5:30 am. "Hello, this is Pete Shannon," he answered; knowing that it had to be work related this early in the morning.

"Pete, this is Lt. King. Your guy was busy last night; he attacked a woman in an alley on the southwest side again. She's over at Holy Cross now; the detailed officer at the hospital said that she's in pretty good shape considering that she lost a lot of blood and took 15 stitches to close a gash on the back of her head."

"Has anyone interviewed her yet?"

"No. The beat car that responded spoke with her briefly at the scene and got a quick physical description of the guy to put over the air in case he was still in the area. Beyond that, nothing."

Pete quickly scrubbed his plans for the run, knowing that he had to get to the hospital right away. While he spoke with King, he was already pouring a glass of juice and unpeeling a banana—it would have to do for his breakfast. He took a drink. "Mobile Crime Lab been notified, boss?"

"That's affirmative. Considering that it was early morning and that he raped her in a dumpster area, it should be a good crime scene. No one except the responding officer was there to contaminate it."

Pete finished his juice and swallowed a bite of banana. "I'll get there right away, sir, and I'll notify Benson and have her meet me at the hospital."

"Good. There's another problem, Shannon."

"What is it sir?"

"The newspaper had a reporter on the street last night with a police scanner. He heard the call and rolled on it, and then followed the ambulance to the hospital. I don't know how much they know about the incident, but if they connect all of the dots together we're in trouble. They'll make headlines that the Chief and Mayor will have fits about."

"I hear you, sir; I'm on the way."

"Good. By the way, I've already talked with the lab; there should be a composite specialist on the way to talk with her as well. Maybe we can dial down a little deeper on this guy and get a decent physical description to work with. Call me when you get a handle on this one."

"Will do."

Pete finished his hurried meal and hung up the phone. He quietly made his way back to the bedroom and got out of his running clothes, grabbed a fast shower, and quickly dressed. He went to the hall closet and retrieved his duty bag and was about to leave a note for Beth when she appeared in the kitchen with the baby.

"Pete? What's going on...it's so early?"

Going over to his wife and son he hugged and kissed them both and explained. "King just called. He said our rapist attacked another woman last night. I need to get to Holy Cross to interview her."

"That's terrible, babe. I hope that she can supply you with more information on this guy than the other women have; he needs to be stopped."

He headed toward the door to the garage. "King said that she was in pretty good shape. Hopefully she got a better look at our guy than the others have. Say a prayer that she can supply us with what we need to arrest him."

As little Pete smiled at his father, Beth said, "We'll pray to Michael for your safety and to the Father that he will help you and Marilyn in your investigation."

Looking at the two people that meant the world to him, he was frozen in the moment. He had always considered her to be attractive, but as she stood there holding his precious son in her arms, he was moved by it all. He was so blessed.... He went to them, wrapping his arms around them, feeling their warmth and basking in their glow of innocence and pure love. "Thanks. I love you both."

"Be careful, Pete."

He went into the garage and got into his truck. He pulled out of the garage and headed toward the hospital. On the way he phoned Marilyn and filled her in on the sketchy details that he had thus far. He arrived in short order and went immediately to the ER and was happy to see that his good friend, Dr. Grossman, was on duty.

He and Grossman had known each other for a couple of years. Pete had taken him to the firing range and eventually had cleared it so that Grossman could be a ride-along on a couple of Pete's shifts. They had developed a close relationship that was sealed forever when Grossman had operated on Pete's gunshot wound.

The doctor was working on a patient's chart when Pete walked in, "Hey, Doc!"

Looking up from his paperwork, the doctor spotted him, "Pete, good to see you my friend! You're up early."

The two shook hands and hugged. "God been good to you today, brother?" Pete asked.

"Every day, Pete."

"Good." The detective's smile disappeared as he asked the next question. "Did you treat a rape victim here tonight?"

"Yeah…." He walked over to the nurses' station and pulled a file. Flipping it open he read from the chart. "Alicia Johnson; she came in via ambulance around 1:30 this morning—nasty gash in the back of her head—showed signs of a concussion. I stitched her up, x-rayed her, did a rape kit, and then let her rest. Considering what she's been through she's in pretty decent shape. I'm going to keep her here today because of the concussion, but I don't expect that she'll have any complications."

"Can I speak with her?"

"Oh sure, she's lucid. Actually, it appears that she's angrier with her boyfriend than with the guy who attacked her. Seems he didn't pick her up at work downtown, so she had to take a bus." With a slight laugh, he said, "She blames him for the rape—she's a feisty gal. Apparently the guy took her iPod too; it had all of her favorite songs."

Pete smiled and turned to go into the treatment area.

"Hey, Pete, one more thing...."

Stopping to listen, he turned to face his friend.

"I don't know how important this is, but there was a guy from the paper here. He was talking with one of the paramedics who brought her in. One of the nurses overheard their conversation. I guess that you guys have had other women attacked, possibly by the same guy; at least the paramedic said so. When the reporter heard that, he was all over the guy firing questions at him like a Gatling gun. Anyway, the reporter figured the cops were trying to cover the whole thing up. You might want to watch your butt on this one."

Shaking his head, he knew that his friend was right. "Thanks for the heads up; Doc, sounds like the whole city's about to find out about our rapist whether we like it or not."

~ 30 ~

The Dinner

Susan had no choice in the matter now; her mother had come to babysit while she met David for dinner; she would need to finally tell her that she was dating. She would have to explain why she was all made up and wearing a dress—it certainly wasn't shopping attire. Finishing with her makeup, she walked into the family room where her mother was entertaining the four boys.

Here goes nothing.... "Okay, mom, the kids are fed; they should all be in bed by nine. There are snacks in the fridge and a movie rental that they can watch. I should be home around ten."

Eyeing her daughter's attire, Susan's mother asked, "I take it you're not going shopping."

"No, mom, I'm meeting a friend for dinner."

"Oh, do I know her?"

Fidgeting with her earrings, Susan replied, "Him...but no,

probably not?"

Her eyes opening wide, Susan's mother replied, "You're going on a date?"

"I guess you could call it that, Mom. I'm meeting someone from church."

Joey, her nine year old looked up from the police cars that he was playing with and chimed in, "Are you going out with David?"

Susan really didn't want to get into a discussion about this right now. In due time she would sit down with her mother and tell her about David, but right now she just wanted to get to the restaurant. "Yes, Joey, David and I are going to have dinner tonight."

"He's a nice man," replied little Joey. "He works at the church, Nana."

Susan grabbed her purse off the kitchen counter and headed toward the door to leave. Her mother followed close behind. "Susan, I hope that you know what you're doing. Don't you think that it's a little too soon to be dating?"

Not wanting to start her evening off on the wrong foot, she smiled at her mother. "Mom, don't worry, it's just dinner. I've been out with him once before…we had coffee and talked. He's a good man; he even asked Father Mike about me before he asked me out for coffee. Besides, I'm a grown woman, Mom; I know what I'm doing."

Kissing her on the cheek, her mother said, "I know, honey. I just don't want to see any more hurt in your life. Have a good time, dear."

She hugged her mother. "Thank you; I don't want any more

hurt either. I love you."

Twenty minutes later she was at the restaurant. She walked in and spoke with the hostess, who then led her to a table along a side wall where she saw that David was already seated. *In this soft light he looks even more handsome, if that's possible.* His blonde hair and blue eyes were accented by the navy blazer, white shirt, and blue tie that he wore. He stood when he saw her approach.

"Susan, hi, you look gorgeous." He grabbed her chair and helped her get seated. The waitress appeared with the menus and asked for their drink order.

"I'd like a glass of white wine, please."

David quickly added, "I'll have a diet soda."

A candle burned in the center of the table, it flickered ever so gently, casting an intimate glow on them both. Susan smoothed her dress and then folded her hands on the table in front of her. "David, won't you have a glass of wine with me, or am I drinking alone tonight?"

The waitress appeared with their drinks and a basket of warm dinner rolls, and then quickly disappeared.

David pondered the question before he answered. "I'm not a drinker, Susan; I haven't had a drop of alcohol in more than ten years. But I have no problem with you enjoying one."

Furrowing her brow, and taking a sip, she asked, "If I'm not being too personal, may I ask why?"

Lord, please let her be understanding. "Susan, I want to be perfectly frank with you. I don't want to hide anything; I particularly don't want to lie to you. I want you to get to know the real me, imperfections and all."

She couldn't imagine him having any from what she'd seen of him thus far.

"I'm an alcoholic. For many years I allowed alcohol to get the better of me, causing myself and others around me much humiliation and embarrassment. That could be another factor in why I've never been married—I don't know. But one day I finally got tired of who I was, and I prayed that God would take the compulsion to drink from me. I was just sick and tired of being sick and tired."

Pushing her glass of wine away, Susan said, "David, I'm sorry; I didn't know. I don't need this drink; in fact I rarely drink at all."

With the palms of his hands facing forward as if to stop her from pushing her glass away, David responded. "Susan, it's fine. You can finish your drink; believe me, it doesn't bother me anymore if people drink in front of me."

"I'd rather not; I'd feel uncomfortable doing it knowing that you don't drink." The waitress returned for their dinner order and Susan requested a glass of water to accompany the meal.

Leaning forward in a hushed tone, Susan told David, "I admire your strength. Not many people would be able to abstain from alcohol that long. Are you in Alcoholic Anonymous?"

Smiling, David replied. "It's okay, Susan, you don't have to whisper. I don't keep it a secret; I'm not ashamed of being a member of AA. I mean, I don't broadcast that I belong, but I'm not reluctant to discuss it either. In fact, belonging to the Fellowship has made me a much better person. And the people that I've met inside the rooms have proven to be some of the finest ever."

"I never would have guessed that about you. What else don't I know about you, David Williams?"

Dinner began arriving—salads first and then the entrees. "Well, I was born and raised in Chicago," said David. "I was an only child; I longed for brothers to play with, but realized that my parents weren't going to provide me with that companionship. So I made it a point to seek it at school and through the neighborhood. And I played on all of the sports teams—baseball, football, basketball, and hockey—no matter what the season I was involved in sports."

Taking a sip of her water, Susan commented. "I'll bet that you kept your folks busy with plenty of friends coming around constantly."

"Yes, there was a constant parade of kids at our house, and it wasn't unusual for me to ask Mom if she would set an extra place at the table for one or more of them." Pausing to take a drink, David asked, "Shall I go on, or are you bored yet?"

Susan smiled. "Please do, I'm enjoying listening to your story."

David continued. "I had scholarship offers to several colleges, but I felt drawn to military service; I enlisted in the Army and got my degree while serving.

Susan had hardly touched her meal. She rested her chin on her hands and stared at him while he related his past.

"Is your dinner okay?" David asked.

With a quick shake of her head as if to awaken herself, she said, "Yes, it's fine. I guess I'm just so spellbound listening to you that I completely forgot to eat."

They finished their meal and then lingered at the table a while longer over coffee. Susan looked at her watch and noticed that it was getting late. "As much as I hate to end this night, David, I must be going. I told my mother that I be back around ten."

"I understand, but now we've got a problem."

Surprised, Susan replied. "What problem, David?"

"We spent so much time on who I am, that now I need another date at least to learn more about you."

He came around to her side of the table and grabbed her chair, pulling it out so that she could stand. When she did, she quickly took his hand and said, "That will be no problem at all. I look forward to another night out with you."

He paid the bill and they walked out to the exit. "Where are you parked? I'll walk you to your car."

She led him to her vehicle, where they paused before Susan opened the door. "David, I can't tell you how much I've enjoyed this evening with you. It's been a long time since I've been out on a date, and I was really anxious about dinner tonight."

With a warm smile that she was now beginning to not only enjoy but to crave, David replied. "Susan, it's been my pleasure. I enjoy your company…who wouldn't enjoy being with a beautiful, intelligent woman? Are you sure that you'd like to do this again?"

"I'm positive, David."

He moved forward and hugged Susan warmly, kissing her on the cheek. Before he could let her go, Susan returned the kiss—on his lips. David closed his eyes momentarily then said, "I'll call you, Susan, have a safe trip home and tell the boys that I said hi."

Feeling a rush of emotions, her face flushed from the kiss and embrace, Susan got into her car and rolled down the window. "Thank you for everything tonight, David, it was fantastic."

They waved goodbye as she pulled out of the lot. On the drive home she went over the evening in her mind, thinking about how blessed she was. She had been worried that a woman in her position—a widow with four young children—might never expect to meet someone like David. Yet here she was, coming home from a wonderful dinner with a man who most women could only conjure up in their dreams.

For the first time since her husband's death, Susan's heart was filled with hope for her future, and that of her boys. *Father, I know that it is your will and not mine. But I pray that this relationship will be blessed by you, and that you will fill me with your Holy Spirit, that I might have the wisdom and courage to know if I am on the right path.*

~ 31 ~

Foot Chase

Pete and Marilyn finished at the hospital and made their way toward the 8th District station. They needed to review the original case report that the responding beat officer had completed, as well as contact the Crime Lab to see what evidence they had collected at the crime scene.

Pete turned down 63rd Street and headed west. "Why don't you take a quick look at the case report and I'll get the Lab on the phone. Then we can head over to the crime scene—I want to see for myself where this one occurred. Our guy certainly has no favorites when it comes to locations."

Marilyn turned to her partner with her notes in her hand. "You know, Pete, this is the first time that we know of where he's taken anything from his victims. Do you think that robbery has had any part in his motive?"

Shrugging his shoulders, Pete replied. "I'm not sure, but my first instinct would be to say no. Anyway, an IPod doesn't seem to be motivation enough for someone to do what this guy's been doing. Maybe he took it as a souvenir."

"Hey, while you're on the phone with the Lab, find out about the composite guy. See if he came up with anything different."

"Good idea, Bens."

"Hmmm...."

Pete looked over at his partner."Did you say something?"

"Just thinking...Pete, I know a Professor at the University of Illinois Chicago in the Psych Department, his name is Denny Wilson. He's studied serial crimes and written several papers on the subject. I used to talk with him about serial killers and psychos while I was there getting my MBA. I'm going to give him a call about this guy, maybe he can offer some kind of profile, or at least fill in some blanks that we're missing."

"Denny Wilson...I know that name. Isn't he the basketball coach?"

"He is," replied Marilyn. "He started out years ago at St. Xavier's, and then went to Chicago State before ending up at UIC. He's had several championship teams and now he's made the Flames into a high-profile NCAA power house."

Nodding, Pete answered. "Right, I remember reading that Denny and his partner—I think Bob Hall is his name—worked together to bring UIC into a Division I contender."

"Exactly, but he's also well known for his work in helping to capture several high profile rapists and murderers in the Chicagoland area."

"Units in the 8th District...Attention all units on City-Wide...we have a 10-1...a 10-1. Police Officer needs help... 63rd and Fairfield in front of St. Rita Church. Beat 8-1-7 calling for help...63rd and Fairfield...any units available to assist?"

"Pete, that's Joe," yelled Marilyn.

She grabbed the mike from the radio, "VCU 2-8 responding; anything further squad?"

"VCU 2-8, 10-4 on the assist...817's on foot chasing a robbery suspect...units in the area be advised VCU 2-8 is responding in plain clothes."

"10-4, squad."

Pete jammed on the brakes and cracked a u-bender, launching them in Joe's direction. With the precision of a NASCAR driver on a track in a crowded field of speeding race cars, he weaved through traffic and had them at the location in a matter of minutes. They spotted Joe's marked unit in front of the church, empty, with the driver's door standing open. A priest stood nearby and pointed down the street. Joe made a quick left in that direction and was halfway down the block when Marilyn yelled. "Stop!"

Brakes squealing and the smell of burning brake pads in the air, their car came to an abrupt halt, smoke billowing from the wheel wells. Marilyn threw open the door and rushed to a figure lying on the sidewalk. "Joe!"

The two detectives rushed to their friend and helped him sit up. Tears clouding her vision, Marilyn asked him, "What happened?"

By now several other police units had arrived on the scene. They canvassed the area for the wanted subject. Breathing heavily, sweat pouring down his face, Joe explained. "There was a lookout on a guy who just robbed a deli on 63rd Street. I spotted him as he crossed in front of St. Rita's. I yelled for him to stop but he took off running."

Joe hesitated momentarily to catch his breath and then continued. "I caught him about halfway down the block and I struggled to get him under control and cuff him, but I ran out of gas. He broke away, Mar; I couldn't go after him."

They heard the radio blaring from their unmarked unit. "All units…all units…slowdown at 63rd and Fairfield. Beat 8-1-8 advises subject in custody, officer located. Again…all units disregard the 10-1 at 63rd and Fairfield, everything's under control."

Pete knelt down next to his friend. "Joe, are you hurt, what do you need, brother?

"No, I'm not hurt, just exhausted. Pete, I've never had anything like this happen before. I was totally defenseless."

As they tended to their friend and colleague, the priest that had pointed them in the right direction approached and spoke to Joe. "I'm Father Rooney, are you going to be all right, officer? I've called for an ambulance."

"Thanks, Father. I think that I'll be okay, I'm just a little out of shape I guess."

Holding him like a mother cradles her sick child, Marilyn spoke up. "Joe, you're not out of shape—you're sick, honey, you have cancer. That chemo is sapping your strength."

Father Rooney added, "That explains the bald head. When I saw you jump from your car it struck me that you were too young to be bald. Why are you still out here chasing these outlaws, son, if you're ill?"

"That's a good question, Father." Marilyn was realizing that

Joe was more at risk than ever, being out on the street in his weakened condition. She would need to convince him to take that desk job that Mac had offered earlier.

The Fire Department ambulance arrived on the scene, as had the sector supervisor, Sgt. Mike Castro. They brought a stretcher over to where Joe sat on the sidewalk.

"I don't need that; I'll be fine, I just need to sit and rest for awhile."

"Nonsense," said Sgt. Castro. "Just go and get checked out. I'll make an IOD report for you on your injury, and we'll work on getting you assigned indoors for awhile. I've already had this discussion with Mac and the Watch Commander. We all appreciate your dedication, Joe, but we need to ensure that you'll recover from your illness. That's really what's important here."

Marilyn looked up at Castro. "Thanks, sarge, you're absolutely right." Castro was quickly becoming one her favorite supervisors on the job. He was the perfect role model; the quintessential cop.

They loaded Joe on the stretcher for the trip to the hospital, but before they placed him in the back of the ambulance, Pete had a request of the priest. "Father, can we say a quick prayer?"

"Of course. Dear Lord, we pray for healing for your servant. May your sacred hands touch his soul and his body that he might once again serve you as your warrior here on earth. Most loving heart of Jesus, bring him health in mind, body, and spirit, that he might lead others to you by his example. We ask in Jesus' name…Amen."

"Amen."

The paramedics loaded Joe in their vehicle, and Marilyn turned to Pete. "I'm going to ride with him to Holy Cross. I'll call you when I'm sure that he's okay."

Nodding his head in agreement, Pete told her, "I think that Joe will appreciate that. I haven't seen him in several weeks—he looks thinner—vulnerable."

Her eyes still moist, she answered in a whisper. "Pete, I'm scared. I think that I'm more worried about his cancer than he is. He seems to think that he can continue on as if he were suffering from a cold rather than a deadly disease."

"Joe's always been strong...always been fit," said Pete. "But I've never seen him like this. Talk with him, Bens; convince him to take that desk job. Tell him that no one will think less of him; I'm sure that he's worried about people thinking that he's slacking off."

"I will. Sorry to leave you with the paper and follow-up on our case. Tell King that I'll get back as quickly as I can."

She climbed in the back and took a seat on the bench next to the gurney. The paramedics had already hooked Joe up to an IV to replace his lost fluids.

"Don't worry, partner, King will understand—family comes first." Pete tapped Joe on his leg. "Rest my friend, take advantage of this time. It's a gift from God."

The ambulance pulled away and Pete went back to his vehicle. As he was about to put the car in gear to leave he stopped suddenly, closing his eyes to concentrate. *Was that who I think it was?* Recalling his arrival on the scene when Joe was lying on the ground, he was certain that he had seen St. Michael kneeling over Joe as if to shield him from any harm. *Was it real or imagined?* Regardless, it was the second time that God's

Principal Warrior had appeared to Pete—it was comforting.

His cell phone ringing quickly brought him back to reality. "Hello?"

"Pete...Lt. King here. Get back to the office—ASAP."

~ 32 ~

Geraci

On the drive back to Headquarters Pete tried to analyze Lt. King's phone call. It reeked of bad news, but whether it concerned the two detectives, or someone else, he just couldn't figure out. Parking his vehicle in the unit's assigned spot, he noticed that his all of his colleagues' vehicles were also parked in the lot. *Must be a big meeting….*

Pete went upstairs and walked into the office. He was met with a deafening silence, and a squad area completely devoid of any activity. All of his fellow detectives were seated at their desks, conspicuously doing nothing. Strangely, there was a palpable sense of sadness that hung in the air, smothering the normally good-natured ribbing that went on among his fellow dicks. Pete threw his notebook on his own desk and walked over to King's office where he spotted Reverend Dean sitting in a chair by the file cabinet. Dean was the Police Chaplain for the Chicago PD, and had been a spiritual mentor and friend to Pete for the past couple years.

He hesitated in the doorway until King gave him permission to enter. "What's up, boss?"

King pointed to a chair next to Reverend Dean. "Take a seat. I know that you and the Chaplain know each other, he's here at my request to speak with the squad."

This is bad…. Pete leaned forward in his chair, puzzled as to why the Chaplain would be here."

"There's no good way to say this, Shannon—Gerry Geraci is dead."

"What?"

King took a deep breath. "He shot himself with his duty weapon sometime yesterday; Carone found him. Apparently he was to have picked up his mother and take her on some errands. When he failed to show, she got worried and called Carone. She knew that Carone and her son have keys to each other's homes. He drove over and rang the bell for several minutes, but got no response. He used his key to get in and found Geraci on the kitchen floor."

Slumping down in his chair, Pete hung his head. "Why…how…couldn't we have stopped it somehow?"

"No one had a clue," said King. "He didn't say a word to his family or his partner about what was going on in his head, but he left a note."

"What did it say?"

King swung his chair around so that his back was facing Pete and the Chaplain. Reverend Dean answered. "He had been drinking, Pete; he wasn't thinking clearly. It looks like he wrote the note after becoming intoxicated, it rambles, but basically he was upset over being suspended and reassigned back to uniform. He didn't want to face his family and friends for fear that they would consider him a failure. He was very proud of his position as a detective, and he felt like he had damaged his career beyond repair."

Pete slumped forward in his chair, his head in his hands, trying to stifle a sob. "No…he was no failure—he was a good cop."

"We all know that, Pete." Putting his hand on his friend's shoulder, Dean continued. "He mentioned you and Marilyn in the note, said that he didn't blame you two. He apologized for that night at the ballpark…said he was wrong for not being there to back you up."

Lt. King swung his chair back around, a tear clearly visible running down his cheek. "Listen, Shannon, don't blame yourself for any of this. You and Benson went above and beyond the call making the arrest that night. The fact that you never mentioned that Geraci and Carone dropped the ball, didn't go unnoticed by anyone on the squad; they admire you two. If anyone has a part in any of this, it's me—I was probably too harsh in my discipline of them."

"Lew, we'll talk about that later," said Dean, as he stood up. "Right now I'd like for all of us to go out to the squad area so that I can say a few words to the men."

"Okay, Reverend."

Dean spent about fifteen minutes with the members of the unit, trying to explain an unexplainable horror. Police officers are trained to take a life, unfortunately that also gives them the means to take their own. All Dean could do was to reinforce the importance of being supportive of each other; talking problems out, rather than keeping them bottled up inside.

When he finished, Pete took him aside. "Dean, I'm worried about King. I get the sense that he's blaming himself for Geraci's death."

"I know. I've talked with him about it. Deep down he knows that he did his job; he did what he needed to do. But he also knows that he couldn't let their behavior go unchecked—they were definitely wrong."

"So what are we going to do, Dean? I think that we need to keep an eye on him."

Nodding, he answered. "You're right, Pete, it's a critical time for the lieutenant right now. But he's a smart man; he's been through a lot in the Corps and here on the job. He knows what he needs to do. We've already set up a couple of sessions together just to talk things over."

Breathing a sigh of relief, Pete said, "That great. No need for this tragedy to claim more people. Speaking of that, I just thought of something...."

"What?"

"Marilyn doesn't know yet; I'll have to fill her in, she's at the hospital with Joe Murphy."

"Is Joe okay?"

"I hope so. He collapsed on the job today while chasing a stickup guy."

"Do you want me to come along, Pete?"

Shaking his head, Pete answered. "No, Dean, I think I can handle it, but thanks. I'll keep your number handy."

"Okay. I'll say a prayer for you both."

The two friends hugged. Dean went back into the Lieutenant's office, while Pete got ready to head to the hospital. Father, please put the words in my mouth that your daughter, Marilyn, will hear. Fill her with your spirit, that she will have the strength to endure the news of our brother's death.

Lt. King collapsed into his chair as Rev. Dean walked back into his office. "Reverend, I need your strength. Tell me…convince me…that I didn't cause that officer's death."

Dean had been a Lutheran minister and Police Chaplain for thirty two years. During that time he had seen more than his share of death and destruction. He rode the streets with some of the toughest cops on the job, guys and gals that were seemingly invincible. Yet when faced with a tragedy like that of a fellow cop's death, or that of an innocent child, they melted like butter on a hot skillet.

Two years ago, during an armed standoff with a kidnapper, Dean was on the scene of the incident, stationed inside the Command Post. Lt. King was the on-scene commander, and during the five hour drama Dean was able to take the full measure of the man. He found him to be a battled tested veteran who knew his job and his men very well. King was the quintessential leader—he led from the front. When it was time to make the entry, King went through the door with his team. He never expected any of those in his charge to do anything that he could not or would not do himself.

Dean shut the door to the office, grabbed a chair, pulled it directly across from King and sat down. They were like two generals seated on either side of a mock battlefield, about to discuss strategy. "Listen, Lew, we both know that you did the right thing in the case of two guys who failed to do their duty. They left their fellow officers out in the cold…harsh to say, but that's what it boils down to."

Rubbing his forehead, King replied. "I know, Reverend. What I'm second guessing myself about is whether or not I should have recommended having them busted back to uniform in addition to suspending them."

"You can second guess yourself all you want, but it's not going to change the outcome. Remember, your men are loyal to you for a reason—they trust you. If you asked any one of them who they would prefer to go through a door with, they would all answer: Lt. King. Just as the Father has blessed us all with free will, you give that same latitude to your squad. They can choose to do the right thing or not. But when they make the wrong decision, there must be consequences for their actions. Had you not disciplined those two men for not doing their job, your squad would be wondering: What's wrong with the boss? Why has he allowed that to stand?"

King mulled that over for a moment. "I guess you're right. I didn't do anything differently with them than I've done in the past with other officers who have screwed up. It's just so sad; I never expected that Geraci would take his own life over something that in time would be forgotten."

Reverend Dean leaned forward on King's desk. "That's the key, Lew, you never expected it...no one did. He never mentioned suicide to anyone. You can't fix something if you don't know that it's broken. Don't blame yourself for this; you don't own any of it. Grieve for the loss of a brother officer; pray that the Lord will give him rest. Be supportive of the men and women on your squad, and the family of Detective Geraci, but above all, continue to be a man of faith and the leader that you must be while you are the Commander of this unit. Your squad expects that from you."

Sitting straighter in his chair, as if a heavy burden had just been lifted from his shoulders, King responded. "Thanks, Chaplain; it's what I needed to hear. I'll get back on track...I need to for the sake of my squad."

"Good," said Dean, as he looked through King's office window and out into the squad area. "Your guys are looking to you for direction."

King stood up, which was his non-verbal clue to Reverend Dean that their business was finished. He walked to the door and grabbed the knob. "How do you do it?"

"How do I do what?" Dean asked.

"How do you stay sane after witnessing all of the carnage that surrounds police work?"

"I never get used to it," said Dean, "if that's what you're getting at. Each death or serious injury involves someone that is a child of God. Whether it's the good guys or the bad guys, they're all His children. It's tough to witness, even tougher when it's someone that you know. But I ask the Father to fill me each day with His Holy Spirit, that I might have the strength to endure, and the wisdom to help those that are in need of his grace."

"You've got a much tougher job than I do, Reverend. May God be with you."

Dean walked through the doorway. "Thanks. Say a prayer for me; Chaplains need them too."

King shut his office door, about to get busy with the month's schedule when the phone on his desk rang. "Violent Crime Unit; Lt. King speaking."

"Lieutenant, this is Leticia from the Chief's office. Please hold for the Chief...."

A minute later, King's boss, the Chief of Detectives, came on the line. "Have you seen the twelve o'clock news?"

His mind instantly jettisoned into a code red condition, King replied, "No, sir, I've been in meetings."

"Well I did; it's not good. Seems the media has found out about our rapist and they did a big piece on it a few minutes ago. Apparently the folks that clean the office buildings downtown have their own labor union—they're all over this thing demanding action right away. They're saying the city's 'gripped by fear.' Now the Mayor's office is pissed. C'mon up; we need to put something together to catch this dirt bag right away."

"Yes, sir," answered King. He hung up the phone, grabbed the case file and headed toward the stairway, completely forgetting about Detective Geraci's death. *Time to focus on the next crisis*

~ 33 ~

The Hospital

"You're looking better, honey, how do you feel?" Marilyn sat on the edge of the bed in the ER where they had spent the last several hours.

"I'm doing okay; I think that the IV really helped. My doctor warned me that taking in fluids was vital while undergoing chemo. I thought that I had it covered…guess not."

Marilyn had given a lot of thought to her idea of moving in with Joe to help him with his struggle. She was indecisive until today, when she saw him laying on the sidewalk. Now she was convinced that she needed to be with him. She just had to figure out how to somehow get *him* to understand that he needs her there. She took one of his hands in her own.

"Joe, I need to discuss something very important with you."

"Sure, Mar, what is it?"

Drawing his hand to her chest, she said, "Joe, I love you very much."

Smiling, Joe replied, "I know that honey. What's to discuss?"

"No, not that. I care about you and I'm worried about what's happening to you while you're undergoing treatment. Today could have been disastrous. What would have happened if that creep took your gun? He could have killed you."

"I know; I was surprised at how quickly I lost all my strength. It kind of scared me."

"Exactly," she said. "Can you talk with the Watch Commander about that inside assignment, at least until you are strong enough to work the street again? Sgt. Castro said that it's all but a done deal anyway—they want you inside. They appreciate your dedication, but it's dangerous for you to be on the street, Joe, for you and the other guys working with you."

He looked at the wall beyond Marilyn for a moment, as if the answer were written there. "I guess you're right. Maybe that was a sign from Him today, telling me to dial it down a notch. I'll give the boss a call tomorrow and ask him to set it up."

Marilyn leaned forward and kissed him. "Thanks honey."

The nurse walked in to get a temperature and blood pressure reading. "Hey you two wait till you get home for that stuff," she said jokingly. She got his readings and was gone several minutes later.

Sitting back down on the bed, Marilyn said, "I have one more request Joe."

Cocking his head to one side, Joe replied, "Now what, you want me working half days?"

"That's a great idea, but no. Hear me out on this…. Your

treatment is going to get worse before it gets better. You're going to be so weak some days that you may not even be able to get out of bed. I would never suggest what I'm about to say, were it not for your illness…Joe, I want to move in with you."

Joe lay back on the bed and stared up at the ceiling for a moment, then turned his head toward Marilyn. "Are you serious?"

"Yes. Joe, honey, you need someone to help you. You're all alone in that house, what happens if you have an emergency? How would you get help?"

"I'd call 9-1-1."

"C'mon, Joe, you know what I mean."

His smile disappearing, he said, "It's probably a good idea Mar, and I don't mean to be presumptuous, but I didn't want us to 'be with each other' until we were married."

A big smile on her face, Marilyn joked. "Oh, we're not going to 'be with each other' as you put it."

Joe stammered. "No, no, I didn't mean…."

She took his hands. "Listen, honey, I'm just kidding. You and I have discussed what we want in this relationship. You know that I've made a promise to Him to change my life. I won't give myself to anyone unless it's in marriage. But this is serious; the best way for both of us to endure this challenge is to face it together. Besides, I'll go crazy in my apartment by myself wondering if you're okay."

"Wow…."

With a quizzical look on her face, Marilyn asked, "What's wow?"

Joe shook his head. "I'm just so blessed…so overwhelmed by you. I never thought that I'd ever have these feelings for another woman after I lost Pat. I didn't think that I still had the capacity to love someone the way that I loved her. Then you came along, at a time in my life when it seemed like the sun had set on my chance at truly loving another woman. All I did was work until I was so tired that I'd go home and collapse on the sofa, then get up the next morning and do it all over again. My life had no meaning; I had nothing to live for. Now I have you."

She stroked his shaved head and said, "I think that God has blessed us both, honey. We came to the same crossroad together, each of us looking for someone—He made it happen."

He kissed her gently and asked, "So when are you moving in?"

"How about tomorrow?"

"That's fine," said Joe. "I'll make sure the linens in the guest bedroom are fresh."

"Don't worry about that. I can make myself comfortable. Your job is to rest and get well."

Suddenly, Pete pulled the curtain aside. "Hey, Joe, you look great; so do you, Bens. I expected to see you flat on your back, brother, but not with my partner."

Chuckling, Joe said, "She won't leave me alone."

Pete walked over to the side of the bed and gave him a hug. "So, how do you feel, my friend?"

"Much better, Pete. I guess that one of the reasons that I collapsed was not enough fluids, but the IV has taken care of that."

Marilyn stood up. "So, partner, did you get our paper finished or do I have to go in and work some overtime?"

Pete's demeanor changed, the smile was gone. "Bens, I have something to tell you: it's about Geraci."

~ 34 ~

The Parking Garage

His needs were becoming more frequent, the urges more compelling. His confidence had grown with each conquest. *The last one was too long ago.* The thrill of finding the next victim was almost as good as the eventual act itself. He craved the danger and excitement his new avocation afforded him.

He had totally dominated the woman by the dumpster—she had been powerless to stop him from doing whatever he wanted. As always, he had been successful in showing *her kind* how superior he was, and more important, why it had been wrong to humiliate him. But as he scoured the streets looking for more women, he noticed that there were hardly any to be found—at least any who were alone. *They must be finding a different way to get to work.* As he drove the bus routes searching for them, he found men only. And, of the few women that he had spotted, they had all been accompanied by males.

He abandoned the neighborhood and made his way

downtown. *They may be scared, but they still have to work.* As he drove, he scanned the skyline of the city, its steel and glass silhouettes reaching high into the ebony atmosphere. With their bright twinkling lights, the tall buildings made a postcard-like imprint against the onyx background of the night-time sky. He smiled. Darkness was indeed his ally.

One structure grabbed his attention as he drove North on Clark Street—the State of Illinois Building. The seventeen story edifice was rife with offices, all of which had to be cleaned. *This would be a fertile hunting ground.* He parked his car and began a search of the area. He would have to go to them now; he still had much work to do to purge the pain that they had inflicted upon him. Like a hungry animal searching for a meal, he set off on foot looking for the weakest member of the herd.

As he scoured the almost empty streets he was drawn to laughter coming from a bar just ahead. Two attractive young ladies exited the business hanging onto each other, their voices much too loud for the public way. It was obvious that the duo had had too much to drink. He ducked into a darkened alcove and watched as they joked and lingered lazily outside the doorway before saying their goodbyes to each other. Singing a tune that was unintelligible, they continued with their bizarre duet for several minutes. Then, after a quick hug, the women left in separate directions. Just a few doors away from the bar was a parking structure. One of the women opened the door to the stairwell and went inside.

Moving quickly, he silently traced her steps like a jaguar stalking its prey. The open staircase allowed the sounds of the city to permeate the structure's hulking concrete shell and served to mute his footsteps. She reached the second level still in party mode; the woman once again began to sing. The man fixated on her athletic figure. With drugstore-blonde shoulder length hair, a form-fitting top, and a too short skirt that accented her long, lean legs, she was by far the most attractive of his choices thus far. *This will be most enjoyable.*

With only a few cars remaining in the lot this late at night, it was a good bet that he would not have to worry about witnesses. As she approached several of them parked alongside each other, he pounced on her, knocking the woman to the ground between two vehicles. The amount of alcohol that she had consumed had dulled her senses and caused her reflexes to be slower than normal, giving her little chance of fending off her attacker. A fist to the side of her head was all that he needed to gain control. Like a bird in the mouth of a cat, the woman realized escape was near impossible. Not wishing to further incur her attacker's wrath, she lay limp on the ground.

With barely an effort he tore off her clothes, leaving her exposed from the waist down. She watched helplessly as he began to unbutton his pants. But as he was about to teach this one the same lesson that he had taught the others, he suddenly heard the sound of someone driving his way. The woman heard it as well, for she began to scream and reached up for him. Before he knew it, a golf cart-like security vehicle was all but on top of him. He crouched between the vehicles scanning for an escape route; he spotted an exit sign in the corner, not thirty feet from where he was at—it was his only chance. As he stood to make his escape, the woman grabbed one of his legs around the ankle. Yanking his leg violently from her grasp, he lost his shoe in the process.

With no time to retrieve it, he sprinted toward the stairwell. The security guard quickly drove his cart directly toward the man. Reaching the door an instant before his pursuer, the hunter, now turned hunted, flung it open; it swung wildly, catching him on the side of his head and causing a deep gash. The wound quickly yielded blood.

Attempting to heft his overweight body from the cart, the aged man knew that it was a futile gesture. With pained steps he made his way to the top stair and looked downward—this race would not find him the victor. The man, blood dripping from his wound and leaving an inculpatory trail, had made it to the first floor and out into the night. Realizing his limitations, the guard abandoned any attempt to chase the offender and went back to help the woman.

Returning to where he last saw her, he found her sitting half naked against her car. Before he could say anything to her, the woman suddenly raised her arm and proudly proclaimed, "I've got that bastard's shoe!"

Like a cockroach reacting to the flip of a light switch, the man quickly scurried back to his vehicle. Fortunately he encountered not a soul as he made his retreat. He climbed back into his car and turned the ignition. *Damn that bitch!* He pulled away from the curb scanning for any cops that may be on his tail—nothing. Within a few minutes he was back on the expressway, sans one shoe, heading further away from what was now his first failed outing. He looked at his head in the mirror—not enough for a stitch, but enough to create an instant stream of blood. *Damn her…someone will pay for her disrespect!*

~ 35 ~

Casey Esposito

Driving to the south suburb of Oak Lawn to interview the latest victim of the serial rapist, Marilyn slowly shook her head in disbelief and said, "I still can't get over Geraci's suicide, Pete. He was basically a good cop, who made a great detective. Sure, he screwed up that night at the ball park, but that's not something to end your life over, is it?"

Pete exited the Dan Ryan Expressway at 95th Street and headed west. "You're right, he was a good detective," he offered. "He and Carone had a great clear up record in the unit—King said they had a ninety-two percent clearance rate. And from what I hear, Geraci was religious about taking care of his elderly mom as well. He took her shopping and out to dinner on a regular basis."

"So what am I missing here," she said, throwing her hands up. "How do you toss all of that away?"

"I don't know, partner. Maybe there are some other things

that we aren't aware of that were going on in his life. All we can do is pray for him and the family members that are grieving their loss."

"Amen," said Marilyn, "I have been praying...not only for him, but for Joe as well. He looks worse, Pete."

"I know. Seeing him lying in that hospital bed yesterday really brought his illness home to me. Just between you and me, I don't think that he should even be working inside. I think that he should stay home until the chemo is finished and he's well on his way to recovery. I'm glad that you've decided to move in with him while he battles this thing."

Her voice quivering, Marilyn replied, "Pete, there's just so much going on now—Joe's disease, Geraci's suicide, and our case keeps getting worse and worse—I feel like I'm being smothered by it all."

Stopping for a traffic light, Pete reached across the seat and put his hand on her shoulder. "Listen to me, Bens. Joe needs you to be strong; he needs your help. Now is not the time for weakness. And I need you to be strong as well. We have to solve this case and stop this guy before he attacks any more women. To do that, we have to keep our heads in the game; we have to think logically and stay focused. We can't do that if we're worried about other things."

"I know, Pete, I know. It's just that two weeks ago, everything in my life seemed so perfect. I had a great job, a great partner...my love life was finally at a place where I hoped that it would always be. Then suddenly, it's like I'm teetering on the edge of a very steep cliff trying my best not to fall off."

Pete headed south on Laramie Avenue toward their latest victim's address. "All I can say, Bens, is that life is not without challenges. Everyone has hurdles to overcome, it's how we choose to get over them that determines our quality of life and our trust in the Creator."

"You're right. I hate to sound like a whiner, besides, Joe's challenge is far greater than mine. Thanks for putting things in perspective for me."

Pete parked their unmarked unit in front of the address and the partners walked to the front door and rang the bell. Seconds later, a young woman with peroxide hair pulled tight in a bun, and attired in a pair of too-small running shorts with a midriff tank top that showed off her tiny waist and pierced navel, answered the door. "Can I help you?" She asked, while chewing and cracking her gum.

The two detectives showed their IDs. Marilyn announced their office: "Chicago Police; we're here to speak with Casey Esposito."

"That's me," she said, with a smile that revealed perfectly sculpted teeth, whiter than the snow on the peak of Mt. Kilimanjaro. Stepping aside while gesturing for them to enter, the woman said, "Come on in...I just finished my workout. Gotta keep in shape, ya know?"

She led them into the living room, the walls covered with a bright yellow paint that caused the light to reflect off of them and onto the clear plastic covers that sealed the couch and chairs. Even the lamp shades wore plastic protection. It was obviously not a room that had welcomed many guests. As they sat down together, the crinkling noise of compacting plastic made for a cacophony of sound that seemed surprisingly appropriate for the moment.

Marilyn began. "Miss, we're here to talk about the man who

attacked you last night."

"Yeah…look at the side of my head," she replied, while pointing to a bruise by her temple. "The guy sucker-punched me; I never had a chance."

Marilyn continued. "Miss Esposito…."

"Call me Casey," she offered, "that's my nickname—well, at least to most people. My boyfriend calls me 'Legs'."

"Okay, Casey. Is it possible that the man who attacked you may have been in the bar with you, and that you may have even spoken with him?"

"Nah, not a chance," she said, cracking her chewing gum, "I woulda remembered the creep. Anyway, he wasn't my type. I woulda blown him off."

"So, you had never seen this man before; he was not a co-worker?"

"Uh-uh, he's just some dude who thought he could get some of this," she said as she spread her arms apart, pointing both index fingers at herself and glancing downward.

"If I may…what type of work do you do? I take it you're not part of a cleaning crew."

"A cleaning crew? Heck no, honey…I'm a professional. I graduated from business school downtown." She held out her hands and said, "Do these nails look like they clean offices?"

"No, they don't. So the man was a complete stranger. Tell us what happened…how did the attack occur?"

Looking in Pete's direction, the woman uncrossed and crossed her legs as she began. "Me and my friend, Nicole, stopped for a few drinks after work. She just broke up with her boyfriend, turns out the guy was cheatin' on her with his old girlfriend. So, ya know, we just thought a few drinks at the karaoke bar would cheer her up. Anyway, we got rollin' and wound up stayin' later than we wanted to." Licking her lips, she looked toward Pete again. "I started singing and some dudes in the bar started buyin' us drinks. Before we knew it, it was almost midnight."

Pete cleared his throat and asked, "Miss Esposito...."

The woman lowered her gaze and fluttered her long lashes at Pete while once again crossing her legs. She interrupted, "I'm Casey, remember?"

Shifting uncomfortably in his seat, causing the plastic to respond in a most unpleasant manner, Pete continued. "Yes, Casey...uh, you're positive that no one left from the bar with you and Nicole—it was just the two of you."

"Oh yeah, I'm positive," she said, fixing her gaze on him. "I mean, a couple of guys came on to me, ya know, but I just played 'em for drinks."

Marilyn steered the girl's attention back her way. "So both of you leave the bar; what happens next?"

"Well, we hang out in front of the joint for a couple minutes just to hug and say good-bye, then she goes back to where we work, she's got a permanent parking spot under the building—takes care of the Parking Boss, if ya know what I mean...and then I go down the block to the garage where mine is parked. I'm up on the second floor so I take the stairs...I like to walk up the stairs—keeps my legs toned," she said, as she straightened both of her legs and rubbed her hands over them, giving Pete a glance at the same time. "So I get up to the second floor and start walking toward my car. Next thing I know, bam, somebody jumps me and knocks me down. I'm on the ground and I look up at the guy—bam! He hits me upside the head."

"Did you lose consciousness?"

"Naw, I been hit harder than that. But I'm kinda high, ya know? So I think the best thing for me to do is play possum. I let him think that he knocked me out; I just laid there. The dude starts rippin' off my clothes—panty hose, thong, and my mini that I just bought last week—it was designer. That pissed me off more than him hittin' me."

"Okay," said Marilyn, "you're on the ground, he's got your clothes off; what does he do next? Did he rape you?"

"Oh, he wanted to, I mean look at me, most guys would give anything to have something like this, ya know?" Cracking her gum, she continued. "Anyway, the whole time I'm sneakin' looks at the dude. He seems like he's in good shape, but man, he's not my type at all."

"You mean, facially?" Marilyn asked.

The woman paused, "Facially…what's that?"

"The way that he looks…his face."

"Oh; yeah, no man, he's ugly. Anyway, I'm eyeballin' this guy the whole time, and I see he's got one weird looking eye—like he's lookin' in two directions at the same time. I'd never be caught dead with someone like him. Anyway, I see him openin' his pants, but before he can 'do me,' Jimmy comes drivin' up in his golf cart. The guy looks up and sees Jimmy, then decides to take off. I grabbed his leg trying to stop 'em, but he yanks free and runs to the stairs. I guess ol' Jimmy knew he couldn't catch 'em 'cause when got out of the cart and looked down the stairs, he just got back in and came over to help me."

Marilyn glanced down at her notes. "The police officer that filed the report indicated that you had one of the man's shoes."

"Yeah, he was in a big hurry to get outta there, he never even tried to get it from me."

"Good job, Casey. Between the shoe that you hung onto, and the blood that the man left at the scene, we're going to have some very good evidence to work with. All I need now is for you to give us the best description of this man as you can."

The woman gave them a description of her attacker, and as the officers got up to leave Marilyn said, "You've been very helpful, Casey, this information will go a long way in assisting us to discover this man's identity. We're thankful that you weren't hurt. Other than the bruise on your head, you don't seem to have sustained any injuries."

"I told ya, I been hit harder. But just between you and me," she said, while winking at Pete, "I told my boss that I'm kinda screwed up from it so he gave me the week off."

Marilyn handed her card to the woman as they made their way to the front door. "If you think of anything else, please call us. We'll be in touch with you to advise you of the progress in the case."

She glanced down at the card, and looking at Pete, she asked, "Is this your number too?"

"Uh…yeah," Pete stammered, "you can reach either one of us at that number."

As Pete walked past her to the door, the woman stretched her shoulders backward, causing her breasts to jut forward. "Gotta stretch after the workout, otherwise ya get stiff. Know what I mean?"

Marilyn cast a long glance at Pete and then back to the woman and said, "I know *exactly* what you mean, Casey. Thank you for your help; we'll be in touch."

The partners got into their vehicle and pulled away from the curb. "Man, I'm glad to be out of there," Pete sighed.

Smiling devilishly, Marilyn replied, "Oh, I bet that you are. You're fortunate that you weren't alone with that woman—you would have been the victim of an attack."

Pete pointed their car back toward the freeway. "Once again my partner saves the day for me."

"Yeah, I think 'Legs' was smitten by you. I better handle all contacts with her in the future."

"I agree."

~ 36 ~

Denny Wilson

Their interview completed, Pete and Marilyn were on their way to the Loop. They had arranged to meet with Jimmy, the night security guard, who had witnessed the attack on Casey Esposito. He was pulling a double shift today at the parking garage, and he welcomed the opportunity for a break from the monotony of riding his golf court up and down five floors. So rote was his task that he often found himself forgetting what floor he was even on; he drove in robotic fashion.

As Pete exited the Stevenson Expressway and drove through historic Chinatown with its massive gateway, Marilyn's cell phone rang.

"Hello, this is Detective Benson."

"Hi, Marilyn, this is Professor Wilson. How are you?"

"Oh, hi, Denny; I'm well, thank you. I'm out working on the case that I discussed with you a while back. We just completed an interview with the latest victim."

"Oh…another one? I was afraid that might happen. Are you available to stop by and visit for a bit? I have some conclusions that I would like to share with you about this individual."

"Hold on a sec, Professor. Marilyn looked over at Pete and said, "Pete, it's Denny. He's the profiler at the University of Illinois Chicago that I told you about; he wants me to stop by. Can you drop me at the university and then handle the interview with the security guard?"

"Sure; I'm interested in what he has to say about our guy."

"Thanks, partner." Marilyn put the phone back up to her ear. "Denny, I'm in the area; I can see you right now if you're available."

"That quick? Okay, as long as you don't mind that I'm still in my workout attire. We just concluded a basketball practice."

"No problem," she laughed, "what's a little sweat between friends. By the way, how are the Flames looking for the coming season?"

"Well, it's only summer league ball that we're engaged in right now, but we've got a couple of kids who've transferred in—we're looking for twenty points a game from each of them."

"That's great," she said, "see you at the gym in about fifteen minutes."

Marilyn ended the call. "Thanks, Pete, I hate to leave you alone to do that interview, but I think Denny can help fill in some of the blanks that we have about why this guy does what he does, and maybe give us a motive."

Pete turned onto Roosevelt Road toward UIC. "I hope so, the more we know about him, the better chance we have of arresting him and putting an end to his brutal ways."

He pulled over in front of the Flames Athletic Center, across from the UIC Pavilion. "Give me a call when you're finished with the professor."

Marilyn got out of the car. "Will do, partner; good luck with your interview."

***

Smiling warmly, the Professor/Basketball Coach greeted Marilyn with an outstretched hand. "Marilyn, it's great to see you again. You look fit, as usual."

"Thanks, Denny," she said, returning her own smile as she sat down. Looking around the room, it was difficult to discern if the walls were even painted, so numerous were the photos and plaques that covered them. Coach of the Year, Tournament Champions, Division Champs—the honors were seemingly endless. "Denny, you're going to need a larger office soon. You're out of wall space to hang any more awards."

"Thanks," he said, a crimson color rising up from his neck and painting his face a bright shade of cherry. "They all represent tremendous effort from talented kids who've added to the proud tradition of this school. I only channeled their energies in the proper direction."

Marilyn stood and moved closer to a news article that hung on the wall: *Prof Helps Cops Nail Predator*. "I remember that one, you were really spot on with your profile."

"Yes. I'm proud of that case. Your colleagues came to me with several investigative reports and follow-up interviews regarding that individual. I was consumed with that guy; one of the children that he had molested was the daughter of a faculty member. What a relief it was when he was finally arrested."

She sat back down in her chair and readied herself to record whatever information the Professor may have that might help her and Pete catch their offender. "Okay, Denny, tell me your thoughts on our rapist."

Wilson sat down in his black cushioned swivel chair, leaned back, and made a steeple with both hands, placing them in front of his mouth. "I've studied all the reports that you gave me, and I looked at your notes from the interviews with the victims and their descriptions and perceptions concerning the individual who attacked them. I found your notes extremely valuable; that information was not contained in the reports themselves."

"That's right," said Marilyn. "We only document the facts; we never include any conjecture or assumptions in an official report, nothing that we cannot prove to have happened or to be true."

"I understand…that would most likely be attacked by the defense at trial."

"Exactly."

Wilson brought his hands down from their former position and put them in front of him on his desk. He leaned forward and continued. "This man seems to fit a classic profile of what we consider to be a psychopath."

"You mean a sociopath?"

"Well, the two terms are sometimes used interchangeably," he answered. "It's estimated that about one percent of the population are psychopaths—scary isn't it?"

Marilyn nodded.

"They have an inability to learn from their past mistakes, and more often than not, they will get satisfaction through antisocial behavior, following through with their criminal, sexual, or aggressive impulses. Individuals with this disorder gain gratification through their antisocial behavior and they lack remorse for their actions.

"But all psychopaths are not alike," he continued. "Some may have a bit of control over their impulses and desires, others may not have any. We find that psychopaths who are highly narcissistic seem more prone toward violence. Dr. Robert Hare developed an actual checklist, called the PCL-R, which has been of great value in defining psychopathic individuals. He listed a number of traits that are common among those who are diagnosed. After reviewing your case, a number of things come to mind: lack of remorse, promiscuous sexual behavior, cunningness, and a need for stimulation, these all seem to describe the man you are looking for."

Busily writing, Marilyn looked up only long enough to answer, "Yes, it does."

Wilson continued. "Hare calls these types, 'intraspecies predators.' To satisfy their needs and to control others, they manipulate, intimidate…they may even seem charming before they resort to sex or violence to control others. What's most important is their lack of guilt. They have no conscience—the fact that they have harmed someone or ruined another's life, is of no consequence to them. They are dangerous because of their lack of humanity, the very thing that allows all of us to live civilly in our communities. In psychopathic people, compassion is completely missing."

Shaking her head, Marilyn responded. "Wow, Denny, you make this guy sound like a monster."

"You could say that," he nodded."

"Can these people ever be cured?"

"The short answer is, no. Unfortunately most of the studies have been done using the prison population; it's very difficult to diagnose this disorder in the general public. But suffice it to say, we've learned that punishment and behavior modification does not improve the condition. In fact, psychopaths will become even more cunning in their behavior, even more adept at manipulating people, including those that are treating them. The condition is considered both incurable and untreatable.

"These are extremely dangerous people, Marilyn. They care not about any consequences for what they do. In fact, you might consider them to be out of touch with reality, in that they have a sense of invulnerability—they don't believe they will ever be caught or injured as a result of their activities."

Marilyn turned to a fresh page in her notebook. "Denny, if you can, give me a thumbnail sketch of who we're looking for."

"I'll try," he said, glancing down at his own notes. "He's obviously male, probably white; age...35-40, average height, and dark hair. He is infatuated with his body—look for him to be a member of a gym, where he can show off his physique. He's probably obsessed with things like hair, complexion...might even use a tanning booth. The fact that he doesn't kill his victims; he stands over them at the completion of the act, tells me that he wants them to see who it was that dominated them. The sex act itself, while important, is secondary to being able to control the woman that he's chosen to violate. It's almost as if he's on a mission to punish these women. The only reason for that conclusion is that it seems that he's picked a certain segment of women, 'cleaning ladies', for lack of a better descriptor. For some reason, he dislikes them. He may have had an unpleasant interaction with one of them in the past which triggered contempt for all cleaning people."

"Will this guy ever stop his attacks at some point?" Marilyn asked, with a sigh.

"No. Once he gets going, once he feels the power and he basks in the gratification from hurting helpless women, his need to continue will only become stronger."

"You paint a bleak picture, Denny."

"It is bleak. I just hope that this information will assist you in capturing this sexual predator before he kills someone."

"Me too." Closing her notebook, Marilyn got up to leave. "Thanks so much, Denny, you've been a big help."

"You're quite welcome; stop by anytime. I enjoy this type of work."

"I will. You can grab that shower now; sorry to have made you wait."

"It's okay; I've got some student-athletes coming by shortly for some counseling."

"I don't know how you do it—teaching, coaching, *and* counseling?"

He smiled and led her to the door. "I wouldn't do it if I didn't love it. Most of these kids will turn out to be success stories after they graduate. It's our job to guide them and keep them on the right path to ensure that outcome."

"Sounds like a higher calling to me."

"It is; I think that all of us have a responsibility to the generation that will follow our footsteps."

"You're a good man, Denny. God bless you."

"Thanks. Bye, Marilyn."

***

A short while later, Marilyn was back in the car with Pete. They discussed the professor's analysis as they drove back to the office. "It sounds plausible to me, Bens," said Pete, as he melted into the amoeba-like rush hour traffic. "And it explains why he would single out women who clean offices—that had me stumped."

Marilyn closed her notebook and put it into her case. "Yeah, and the narcissism element…this guy is definitely in love with himself. If he tried to come on to one of these women at his office or somewhere else and was rebuffed, that could have triggered something in his sick mind to seek revenge on all of them."

"Crazy driver!" Pete slammed on the brakes to avoid smashing into the car in front of him. "How do people do this every day…?" Checking his outside mirror, he quickly moved into another lane. "I like Wilson's angle about the gym. I think that we should take that composite image that we have and hit the fitness centers on the Southwest Side."

"I agree; chances are that he's a member at one of them. We just have to find which one."

Marilyn grabbed her cell and dialed Joe's number. It went right to voice mail, indicating that it was probably turned off. She hung up and dialed the 8th District desk sergeant's number.

"Chicago Police, Sgt. Castro, how may I help you?"

"Sarge…Marilyn Benson here."

"Hi, Marilyn, how are you?"

"Fine, Sarge. I was trying to reach Joe, but he didn't answer his cell phone. Is he in the station somewhere?"

"No; he went home a couple of hours ago…said he didn't feel well. I told him to go ahead—he didn't look good, seemed very weak."

Marilyn rubbed her forehead and closed her eyes. "I was afraid that this would happen. His doctor started radiation along with the chemo; he said the cancer wasn't shrinking. It's really knocking him for a loop."

"That explains it. You know, Joe doesn't talk about his illness. He goes about his day just doing his job, not complaining or whining. I've got some guys that call in sick when they have a little cold, whereas Joe would come in every day even if someone had to carry him. He's my kind of cop."

"I know, Sarge, he's such a good man—so dedicated."

"Hey, how are you and Pete coming along on that rapist? Any good leads?"

"We're getting closer," she replied. "We've got a good composite and behavioral profile now. I think between our legwork and the Chief getting impatient about this creep being on the loose, things will be coming to a head very soon."

"Good."

Pete exited the freeway at 35th Street and headed toward the office.

"Gotta go, Sarge, thanks for your help."

"Bye, Marilyn."

Arriving at the building, he parked in the rear lot and they got out of their vehicle. Marilyn looked over the roof of the car at him. He read the concern etched on her face.

"Pete, would you mind if I called it a day? I should probably go home and check on Joe."

Nodding, he replied. "No, Bens, go ahead. I heard your conversation with Castro. I'll finish up the paper and see you in the morning."

"Thanks, partner, you're the best."

As she walked toward her own car, she turned to him and said, "Keep the prayers coming; for some reason I'm just not feeling good about what's happening with him."

"I will, Marilyn. Beth and I have had him on our prayer list ever since we first learned of his condition. Be patient and have faith."

"I'm trying…I'm trying…."

***

She pulled into the driveway and parked behind Joe's car. Her normal routine would find her at the gym about now, a practice that she had trained herself to follow since she first put on the uniform, but her concern for Joe moved her workout down a notch on the list of priorities. She unlocked the front door and found herself inside a house completely devoid of any noise. She set her bag down by the door and quietly walked over toward Joe's bedroom.

Pausing at the threshold, she saw him lying in bed, on top of the covers. He was still in his police uniform, only his gun belt was missing—it lay on the floor a few feet away. *He must be totally exhausted.* Tears began to pool in her eyes, as her heart felt the pain that only one who dearly loves another feels when their loved one is hurting. She felt a cornucopia of emotions—love, tenderness, anxiety, anger, and fear. *Father, please place your healing hands on Joe. Has he not suffered enough?*

She moved to the bed and quietly lay down beside him, her chest to his back. Placing her arm around him, as if she had the power to shield him from further pain and harm, the two spent the next hours clinging to one another. At one point Joe opened his eyes, but not a word was spoken between them. Communication was accomplished through feeling alone; the simple knowledge that they had each other transcended reality and consequence. In this moment there was no cancer, no hurt, only two people with hopes of a future together and faith in a loving Father who would see their dream realized.

The minutes and hours passed unnoticed. The harsh, hot light of the summer sun, morphed into a gentle luminous lunar glow that softly filled the room, each item in it taking on a silver sheen. For Joe and Marilyn, the world had suddenly become encapsulated into a twelve by fifteen space that held them cocoon-like—free from the horrors and challenges that had been their lot as warriors. Now, they floated safely on a cloud of innocent bliss, neither one anxious to break the reverie. For the moment it was a utopia envisioned only in dreams, but their dream, at least on this night, became reality.

~ 37 ~

The Run

Saturday morning dawned with the promise of a two day respite from twelve hour days for Pete and Marilyn. The past week had found them working long hours, but thankfully gaining traction on fleshing out the identity of the man responsible for the fear felt by those who labor cleaning offices. Pete's wife, Beth, welcomed the opportunity to spend time with him. Togetherness had been a commodity in short supply since the genesis of the serial rapist case. Now, she and the baby would enjoy family time with the man whom they both dearly loved.

As was his routine, Pete had awakened early and left the house for his workout. Like a junkie craving his next fix, Pete's body thrived on exercise. On those rare occasions when he was not able to squeeze in a workout, he felt lethargic and slow. Some people use caffeine for their morning jumpstart; Pete's rush of energy came from endorphins released while exercising.

This morning he had arranged to run with the pastor, Fr. Mike. The two friends had just turned the corner at 103rd and Kedzie and were now headed toward the gym at St. Xav's where they would finish. Despite having already logged three miles, the pair chatted like two buddies seated across from one another at a table, an indication of their fitness level.

Pete wiped a wave of sweat from his brow. "Father, I know that you try to keep up with all of your parishioners, have you heard any updates on Joe Murphy's condition?"

The priest focused on crossing the next street before answering. "I know that he has cancer, but I'm not certain of his present condition. Last thing that I heard was that he had begun chemo."

Pete picked up the pace somewhat as their effort brought them closer to the gym. "The latest is that Joe's doctor started radiation along with the chemo—he said that the tumor wasn't shrinking. Apparently, Joe's body isn't handling it all that well; I guess that yesterday he was forced to leave work early due to exhaustion."

Father Mike matched his friend stride for stride. Without a challenge having been articulated, the runners took turns accelerating, the pace was becoming race-like rather than that of a routine workout, neither one wanting to back down.

"If Joe is trying…to prove something…he needn't bother," said Mike, now gasping from the exertion. "All of us who know him…recognize…he's hard-working…dedicated. I spoke with him…early on…it was his intention to work…'til he was no longer able to do so."

A quarter mile from the finish, the friendly run became a duel, each athlete pushing the other to go faster until the oxygen debt became a bill that neither could pay. They ceased their banter and reached the doors to the gym simultaneously. Bent over, and struggling to re-inflate lungs depleted of air, the two friends basked in the glow of sweat and satisfaction.

"Oh, wow, Pete thanks for a great run. You really pushed me that last quarter."

"Me…? I was trying to keep pace with you. I was praying…that you didn't have another gear, I was maxed out."

"Yeah, right. Anyway, Pete, I think that Joe will probably get worse before he gets better. From what I know about his disease, it's not only a killer, but it is a punisher as well. He's in for a tough fight. But maybe with Marilyn by his side he has a better chance of coming out on top. In any case, I will be praying for him at daily mass."

"Thanks, Father, I know that he will be comforted in knowing that. Oh, by the way, have you heard that Susan O'Hara is seeing someone from church?"

Pulling his shirt up and wiping the perspiration from his drenched face, Father Mike responded. "Yes, in fact, I suggested that she attend the coffee gathering after mass on Sundays. I thought that it was probably a good idea for her to have more exposure to adults. She was spending far too much time alone at home with her children. She is suffering emotionally and needs healing. Being socially active will only serve to help her travel down the road to wellness."

"I agree." The two had recovered sufficiently and conversed normally once again. "Beth seems to think that if Susan can find someone who can love her and the boys as much as Joe did, her grieving will become somewhat ameliorated."

Nodding, the priest said, "Beth is probably right. Susan won't find anyone to replace Joe, but she may find a man that will love her and the kids just as much. The Lord has a plan."

"I know that for a fact," said Pete, with a big smile.

Father Mike offered his hand for a handshake. "Gotta go my friend, the altar servers will be at church for a meeting in an hour or so—I've got to clean up."

"Okay. Thanks again for a great workout. If you don't mind, may I have a blessing?"

"Of course," the Priest folded his hands in front of him and prayed. "Dear Lord, I ask that you extend your blessing to your child, Pete. Protect him from all harm as he toils in your name against those who would commit acts of evil on the innocent and defenseless. May you grant him strength in his battle with Satan; bless his sword and shield, that no wickedness may conquer him." He raised his right hand and made the Sign of the Cross over Pete's bowed head while saying, "May Almighty God bless you, the Father and the Son and the Holy Spirit, Amen."

Pete made the sign of the cross mirroring the priest's actions, and replied, "Amen."

The two men, each on a mission of saving souls in their own fashion, went their separate ways. Though it appeared that each man walked alone, their faith ensured that the Holy Spirit accompanied them. Their bodies and faith re-invigorated, God's Warriors were battle ready.

~ 38 ~

The Sunday Paper

Marilyn finished frying several strips of bacon and was about to prepare the scrambled eggs. She had been up early on this Sunday morning and had already completed her workout. Joe had experienced a rough day on Saturday, unable to do much of anything other than sleep and watch TV for a couple of hours. She had not seen him eat anything, preferring to drink only water. Recognizing that he was becoming weaker not only from his treatments, but also from his poor appetite, she was determined to start this day with a big, healthy breakfast.

As she broke the eggs and began to scramble them, Joe appeared in the kitchen. Waking up hungry, like a bear from a winter's hibernation, he walked up behind her and gave her a hug. "Good morning, Mar, is any of that for me?" He asked, while kissing her on the cheek.

"There's as much as you want, honey." She poured the mix into the pan and turned to him, returning his kiss on the lips.

"Good, I'm starved."

"You should be; you didn't eat anything yesterday."

Joe walked toward the front door, while saying over his shoulder, "I know, yesterday was a blur. I hardly remember anything about it." He opened the door to retrieve the morning paper from the porch. Coming back to the kitchen, he placed it on the table and read the headline: *Rapist On The Loose, Mad man targets cleaning ladies.* "Uh oh...this can't be good. Marilyn, you need to see this."

She set her spatula down on the counter and walked over to where Joe was standing. Picking the paper up, she took several minutes to read the story that occupied much of the top fold. "King's going to be hot when he sees this," she said, as she followed the story inside. "I'm sure the Chief will be all over him today or tomorrow, he'll want him to start a full-court press."

"Maybe you should call Pete and give him a heads up."

She set the paper back down. "Good idea." She went to her bedroom to retrieve her cell phone and punched the key to Pete's speed dial. He picked up on the third ring.

"Good morning, partner, did I wake you?"

"Of course not, I've been up and running already. Now, I'm just sitting here enjoying a cup of coffee and looking at the most beautiful sight in the world—my wife and son."

"You are a blessed man, Pete."

"I know; God's been good to me."

"Have you seen the paper this morning, partner?"

"No," he replied, "but I'm guessing from your call that you

have."

"Your guess is correct. Our case is all over the front page of the Tribune. I read the story; the heat is on, Pete. There's a Hispanic group, LAVA (Latinos Against Violence and Aggression), demanding that the Mayor do something to protect the female workers who travel downtown to clean offices after hours. Monday they're going to stage a rally at City Hall."

Pete set his coffee cup down and got up from his chair to pace. "Oh boy…that's all we need. I'm guessing that King will be called on the carpet to explain what's being done."

"Yeah, and then he'll be told that it's not enough."

"Right," he sighed.

"All I can say is, enjoy your day off, it may be the last one we see for some time."

"I hear ya. I guess we'd better get ready to head over to Mass while we still can. You and Joe have a great day."

"I'll be happy just to get some food into him today. Yesterday he didn't eat a thing."

"Just remember what he's going through, Bens. Chemo and radiation changes one's whole outlook on everything, including food."

"Thanks, I will. I'll see you in the morning…unless King calls us in sooner."

"Okay. Thanks for the heads up—good luck today with feeding Joe."

"Okay…bye."

Finishing up a glass of apple juice, Joe said, "I guess Pete hadn't seen the paper."

"No, it's a good thing that I called him."

Marilyn put four slices of wheat bread in the toaster oven, and then prepared two plates with scrambled eggs and bacon. A minute later the toast was done. She buttered Joe's two slices heavily, wanting to get as much fat and calories into his body as possible. Bringing the dishes over to the table where Joe sat reading the paper, she set a plate in front of him and said, "Here you are, sir, your breakfast is served."

Marilyn blessed the meal.

"Thank you, this looks great. I'm so happy that you're here. I know that this is not the arrangement that either of us wanted, but just know that I truly appreciate what you're doing for me."

She leaned down and kissed him on his bald head. "No thanks necessary, hon. We'll do whatever it takes to get through this thing—together."

"I know, but there may come a time when I become much worse. I want to thank you in advance."

She sat down across from him and took a sip of coffee. "Joe, baby, please…stop with the thanks. I'm here because I want to be here. I love you; there's nothing that I wouldn't do for you."

He swallowed a forkful of eggs, paused, and said, "Mar, I don't know what I'd do without you. If yesterday was any indication of times to come, I don't think that I can even make it into work, much less do anything beneficial while I'm there."

"That's okay, honey. No one expects you to; I'll call you in sick tomorrow. You have an appointment anyway, and I'll find out about extended sick leave. You shouldn't even be driving to and from the treatments."

Joe sat quietly for a minute, as if pondering Marilyn's last statement. Before he could respond, Marilyn continued. "I'm going to call a friend of mine—Leslie. I told you about her earlier. She's lives in my apartment complex. She's home during the day, and I know that if I asked her, she would be happy to take you to your appointment."

He put his fork down and momentarily stared blankly out the window. "I never thought that it would come to this…that I would be so dependent on others. I don't like this feeling, Mar. I'm so frustrated with being sick," he said, his voice breaking slightly.

"Joe, all we can do is ride this thing out and pray that His plan is for you is to get well and return to normal. In the meantime, accept help from others. You are blessed to have people that love you and want to be of assistance. Let it happen, let them minister to you. You've done it before, helped others in need. Now it's your turn. Get out of God's way; turn it over to Him, completely."

His eyes moist, voice quivering, he looked at the woman who meant so much to him. "You're right. I need to be more accepting of His plan for me. I need to be grateful for the fact that there are others who care and want to help. I need to pray that I might be more understanding of those who want to help."

"We'll both pray," she said. "In fact, do you feel up to going to Mass at Queen's this morning?"

"Sure, but first let me try to finish this breakfast that was prepared especially for me by someone whom I absolutely adore."

They sat quietly eating while reading the paper and enjoying spending time with each other. For now, things were seemingly normal; the cancer fear temporarily swept out to sea like a piece of driftwood on a beach, visible only if one strained to find it. But just as a storm turns serenity into calamity, the illness attacking Joe's vulnerable body would rise up and strike again—testing his resolve and his faith.

~ 39 ~

The House of Paine

They survived Sunday without hearing from Lt. King, but neither Pete nor Marilyn believed that this storm would pass without drenching someone in the waters of blame. Pete had phoned his lieutenant advising him that Marilyn would be in late, she would take Joe to his treatment and arrange for Leslie to take him home. In the meantime, he would make the rounds of the gyms in the area where the attacks occurred, showing the composite drawing to the owners in hopes that someone might recognize their wanted subject.

He struck out at Gold's Gym, Powerhouse, and Bally's, no one was able to make an identification from the likeness that he showed them. He thought that perhaps he should expand his search to include the near south suburbs. While driving east on 59th Street, he decided to go to the office and regroup. Suddenly, his eye caught sight of a store front sign: House of Paine. Underneath the wording was a heavily weighted barbell bent in a semi-circle. He had not seen this gym listed in the

Yellow Pages. He did a quick u-bender, parked his car out front, and went inside.

In marked contrast to the chrome and glitz of the nation-wide franchised gyms, this sweat emporium bore all the markings of a mom and pop establishment. Walking through the front door, his nose took in the stale, musty odor that hung in the air like a cloud of invisible noxious gas, not over powering, yet enough to insult the olfactory senses. Floor to ceiling mirrors hid walls badly in need of repair; the few spots without mirrors bore peeling paint behind radiators and pipes that no doubt worked futilely in the winter to warm the austere interior. Although still early in the day, the air conditioner-less business had already begun to exceed the temperature outside. A single pedestal fan in the corner labored in vain, standing like a lone soldier facing a battalion of advancing enemy troops, a battle lost before it even began. Dozens of old, somewhat rusted iron dumbbells, barbells, and weight plates littered the creaky wooden floor. Posters of an earlier generation of bodybuilders hung from the rafters, old and faded, like the men they portrayed.

Pete stopped just inside the entrance where a glass display case separated the business area from the exercise floor. Inside were fitness magazines, vitamin and protein supplements, tee shirts with the gym's logo, and energy bars. Seated on a stool next to a soda machine, was a barrel-chested man with a round face resting atop a short, squat neck. He sported a huge handle bar mustache that seemed strong enough to support someone hanging from either end. He wore a dirty tee shirt with the words, "POW/MIA Bring 'Em Home." The words were superimposed over a map of Vietnam. The shirt stretched tightly over his heavily muscled arms which served as a canvass for patriotic tattoos: the Marine Corps logo on his right arm, and the Unites States Flag with an eagle's head on the other.

"Morning, brother, are you the owner?"

The man folded his arms across his chest. "You a cop?"

"Yes, sir, Detective Pete Shannon," he replied, as he presented his ID to the man.

"Thought so, you're too clean cut to be anything else, 'cept maybe a insurance guy or somebody pedalin' Jesus. Yeah, I own this place."

Pete put his Detective ID back in his pocket. "Well, I'll tell you something sir. I wouldn't mind being any of those other things that you mentioned, especially someone pedaling Jesus."

The man got up from his stool and took a couple of steps forward. He placed both of his hands flat on the display case and leaned forward on them. His arms responded to bearing his weight by turning into two granite pillars, the veins popping out like runners from an ivy vine crisscrossing their surface. "You former military?"

"Yes, sir, Army."

His demeanor visibly relaxing, the man stood upright and let his hands rest by his side. "Good; I'm a Marine…served in Viet Nam. Had to leave the Corps on a disability—shrapnel from some gook who threw a frag grenade at us."

"Sorry to hear that."

"Yeah, at least I made it back alive—couple of my buddies didn't. It's no big deal. Army, huh? We used to have to pull you guys' butts outta rice paddies when Charlie had you pinned down. You Army dudes just don't know your limitations." The man picked up a cigar from an ashtray on top of the window ledge and placed it in his mouth. The malodorous smoke did little to mask the putrid air saturating everything inside this anachronistic facility. Extending his hand to Pete he said, "Butch Paine's my name, thanks for your service to our country."

Pete shook the man's hand, wincing from his grip that felt like the jaws of trash compacter. "Nice to meet you, Butch." Pulling the composite sketch from his notebook, Pete laid it on the counter facing Butch. "Have you ever seen this man?"

He picked up the drawing, took a quick look, and then set it back down. "Don't even need my glasses for this one. That's Serge."

Pete felt his heart speed up. "You know this guy?"

"Yeah…used to work out here all the time, early in the mornin' before most anybody else was here—even me."

Getting his pen out, Pete started to take some notes. "You said he used to work out here…what happened?"

Butch chomped on his cigar then sat back down on his stool. "I kicked his butt out 'bout six months ago. I got a lady comes in to clean the joint once a week; she cleans the toilets and sweeps up. I pay her under the table, cash, cuz, ya know…she's got no papers."

"She's illegal?"

The man folded his arms across his chest, wrinkled his brow and said, "I ain't here to dime nobody out that don't deserve it. This conversation ends right here if you're lookin' to lock that girl up. She's a hard working lady, tryin' to make ends meet; got herself four kids."

Realizing that he was in danger of alienating his best lead so far, Pete continued carefully. "No, sir, don't misunderstand me. I'm not here looking for illegal immigrants, that's not my job. In fact, I'm here to help them. The guy that I'm looking for has attacked a number of them. We haven't been able to identify who he is—that's why I need your help. He's injured a couple of them quite severely."

"Good, then we can do business. Tasha's been with me 'bout three years now—good worker—easy on the eyes too, if ya know what I mean. That's the problem. She got a good figure for somebody that's had four kids. Guess she works so hard she burns lots o' calories. Anyway, I come in one mornin' and find her sweepin' up over by the squat rack...guys use lots o' chalk over there...gets all over the floor. So I say good mornin' to her and she don't' answer. I walk over to see what's up, and I see she's been cryin'. I say, 'Tasha, what's wrong.' So she tells me. Says 'Walleye,' that's what we call Serge 'round here, he was comin' on to her, tryin' to hug and kiss her."

"He sexually assaulted her?" Pete asked.

"I guess he was lookin' to get in her pants, but she told him that she don't do that kind o' stuff—she's married. She got real mad and told him that he was ugly and that even if she wasn't married, she wouldn't be with somebody like him. He got angry, started yellin' and shovin' her around. She thought he was gonna rape her, till another customer come in to work out. Walleye took off right away."

"Did you report the incident to the police?"

"Hmph...." Butch gave Pete a sideways look. "What good would that do? Then I got the cops lookin' at her for bein' here illegal, then they're bustin my chops for hirin' her. Besides, he's probably illegal too. Nah, I just told him next time he came in that he was banned; told 'im I didn't want 'im here anymore, that if he came back I was gonna kick his ass, if you'll pardon my French."

"Why do you think that he may be here illegally?"

"I can spot 'em; there's lots of folks 'round here don't have papers. That's why I don't keep much records, most of 'em lie to me anyway. Walleye had that commie name; talked with that foreign accent—he ain't foolin' nobody—'specially me."

"Butch, do you have this guys address or phone, anything with his personal information?"

The man reached over to a shelf on the wall next to him and took down a ledger. Opening it, he found the page that he was looking for and said, "All's I got is his name: Serge Petrov. I keep track of when they join and when they pay their dues. I don't use no fancy computers or keep lots o' records. If somebody don't pay, I give 'em a few weeks to get the dough. After that, I kick 'em out till they come up with it. I gotta eat, too."

Sighing, Pete asked, "Would you say that the sketch looks pretty close to what Petrov looks like?"

Butch glanced down at the drawing. "Yeah, that's pretty much him, even that goofy eye."

Pete picked up the sketch. "Tell me, Butch, why do you call him Walleye?"

"Cuz the guy's got that one eye that always looks off to the side. He didn't like that nickname, got pissed whenever anybody called 'em that. But I tell you what...he thought he was a ladies' man. Oh yeah...we only got a few gals work out here, it ain't like them big gyms if ya know what I mean, but he'd try to come on to 'em. Thought he was all that. I guess when Tasha told 'im to get lost, he freaked out. She was really scared after that."

"Do you know what type of car Walleye drives?"

"Nah, but probably some foreign job. Said he don't like American-made cars; said they ain't built as good. That pissed me off. Japs'r makin' everything nowadays, pushin' the American workers right out. You won't find any foreign made stuff here."

Pete glanced down at Butch's wristwatch, noting that it was a Japanese-made Casio, but held his tongue.

"What about this woman, Tasha? Do you think that I might be able to speak with her?"

Butch shook his head. "Nope, don't work here anymore. She never came back after that; I guess she didn't want to face Serge again. She didn't know that I tossed 'im out."

"Do you know Tasha's last name?"

"Uh-uh, we was strictly business—she cleaned the joint and I paid her cash when she was done. Didn't keep no records, if ya know what I mean?"

"Okay, you've been a big help. Here's my card, if there's any way that you might possibly be able to come up with his address or phone—anything that will help me track him down—please call me."

Butch took Pete's business card, gave it a quick look, then put it in his pocket. "I'll see what I can do. I been here a long time, know lots o' folks 'round here. Maybe I can come up with somethin'."

Pete offered his hand reluctantly, remembering the man's last handshake. "Thanks for your help, brother."

The man clamped down on his cigar and Pete's hand at the same time. "No problem. Say...ya know I give coppers a break here if ya wanna join. I take fifty bucks off the dues."

He pulled his hand from the crushing machine, and replied. "I'll think about it, Butch. Thanks for the offer. Call me if you come up with anything."

"You got it." The man waved as Pete walked out into the fresh air. He breathed in deeply, trying to replace the fetid oxygen that had filled his lungs while inside the House of Paine. *Butch should be paying people to work out here, not the other way around.*

Twenty minutes later he was walking into the squad area. Looking over toward King's office, he saw Marilyn sitting in a chair across from King. When the lieutenant saw Pete come in, he instantly stood and signaled for him to join them. *Uh-oh, something's about to happen.*

~ 40 ~

The Lakefront

"I really appreciate this, Mom. The boys love when you and dad babysit—they love their nana and papa." Susan's mother sat on her daughter's bed and watched while she put her jewelry on. "And thanks for offering to cook dinner for them."

"You're welcome, dear. You know that dad and I treasure spending time with our grandkids. So…you and David…you're spending lots of time together?"

"I don't know, Mom, maybe not lots of time but we have gone out frequently. We enjoy each other's company; he's a beautiful person. I'm really becoming quite fond of him." Susan decided that the first pair of earrings did not compliment her outfit and tried on a different set.

Her mother shifted on the bed. "But don't you think that you should be dating many people, rather than just one?"

There, this pair is perfect. She gave a final look in the dresser mirror and then sat down on the bed next to her mother.

"Mom, I know what you trying to say. I know that you're worried about me, but you needn't be. I'm a grown woman; I'm not some impressionable teenager."

Susan's mother took hold of her daughter's hand. "I know, honey. It's just that ever since Joe died I've been worried about your future. I pray each day that God will direct your path, that you and the boys will have a normal life. I don't want to see you get hurt."

Having heard it all before, she patted her mother's hand in a role reversal of sorts, the child reassuring the mother. "Mom, I want the same thing. God didn't put us here to live by ourselves; he made a man and a woman so that they could share, so that they could raise families together, to be there when one partner needs help or consoling. I want that again Mom; I don't want to be alone. David might be that person, I don't know. But if it turns out that he isn't the partner that I'm looking for, then I'm sure God will send me down another road toward someone else. I have faith that He is with me on this journey, I can't be afraid."

"I'm such a worry wart," said her mother as she hugged her daughter. "You'll understand better when your boys are older and start to date, then you'll see your protective instincts take control of your otherwise rational self."

"That's a long way off. For now, I'm just trying to keep them safe in the backyard."

They laughed and got up from the bed then made their way to the living room. "Where are you off to tonight?" Susan's father asked.

"David's taking me downtown for dinner and then a stroll along the lakefront. The weather is clear and warm, it should be beautiful."

The doorbell rang and the boys ran toward it in en masse, each trying to be the first to open the door. Joe Jr., the oldest, was the first one there. He pulled it open to let David inside.

"Hey, guys," said David, as he scooped up the young ones. "How is everyone tonight?"

Susan walked over to rescue him from the attack of the munchkins. "Everyone is just fine, David. C'mon in, let me introduce you to my parents."

He walked from the hallway, a twin in each arm, into the living room where Susan's parents sat.

"Mom…Dad…this is David, the man who I've been telling you about."

He set the boys down and walked over to Susan's mother first. "Very nice to me you, ma'am." Then going over to her husband, he shook the man's hand firmly. "Nice to meet you, sir."

Surrounded by the four boys, David stood there not sure whether he should sit down or stay where he was. Susan's father broke the silence by asking, "My daughter tells me that you're an Army man, you seen combat?"

"Yes, sir; I've done several tours in the Middle East."

"That's a tough theatre," the father replied. "Guess you had it pretty rough."

"Not any rougher than any other soldier anywhere else. When you're away from home fighting for your country it's never easy."

"David, David, tell us about it, did you have to shoot

anybody? My Dad shot some bad guy…."

Susan quickly ran interference for her date. "Boys, boys, David will tell you a story some other time. We have to get going; we have reservations at a restaurant downtown."

He got down on his knees and hugged the twins, then did the same with little Joe and Pete. "Tell you what fellas…this weekend, if you Mom says that it's okay, we'll go to the park to play and I'll tell you a few stories about some children that I met in Afghanistan."

One of the twins, Mike, said, "Ackgannisdan, what is that David?"

The adults all chuckled. "Afghanistan is a country that's far away, Mike. The kids there don't have nice homes like we have here. Lots of times they go to bed hungry because there's not enough food to go around for the whole family."

"One time Mommy made me go to bed without a snack," little Mike offered.

Smiling, David said, "Then you know what it's like to be hungry."

"Okay, boys, we have to be going. Nana and Papa brought a video along for you to watch, and I made some chocolate chips for your snack tonight. Be good; I'll kiss you good-night when I get home."

"Okay, Mommy," the chorus sang. She gave them each their own hug and kiss, then ushered David toward the front door. "Bye, Mom and Dad, thanks again."

"Nice to meet you, folks," David added.

They walked down the front steps to David's car. He opened

the door for her, then went around and got in himself.

"That wasn't so bad, was it?"

"No; your parents obviously love you and their grandbabies. God's been good to you."

"I know He has, although I must admit that this past year I've struggled with my faith. When Joe was killed I was looking to blame someone, my first thought was that it must be God's fault—he let it happen. I'm ashamed to admit that, but my tears didn't allow me to see things very clearly. When I finally stopped crying and feeling sorry for myself, I realized that it was no one else's fault except the guy who shot Joe. After that, things got better. I recognized that He was right beside me, just like He's always been. He is such an awesome God."

Driving north on Pulaski toward I-55 which would take them downtown and onto Lake Shore Drive, David looked over at her. "I'm amazed at your faith, Susan. The man who you loved, the father of your beautiful children, was murdered, yet you accept it without question."

"Yes, David, I have to accept it as part of His plan. I don't know what He has in store for me or the boys, but I can't turn away from Him—if I do then I'm surely all alone. He told us in the Bible that He would never leave us; I believe Him."

"I see why your husband was so attracted to you."

"What do you mean?"

"You're beauty isn't just your appearance, it's your persona...your aura. There's radiance, almost a glow of love and truth that surrounds you. It's what attracted me to you when I first saw you at the coffee service at church that Sunday—it's purity."

Feeling her face flush, she hoped that David couldn't see her blushing in the dim light of the dashboard lighting inside the car. "David…stop, you're embarrassing me."

"I'm sorry…wait…no I'm not. I mean what I'm saying, Susan. You are such a beautiful human being. I feel blessed to be with you."

"Thank you, David."

They drove the final ten minutes in silence, enjoying the magnificent Chicago skyline on one side, and the beauty of hundreds of boats on the other, each one dancing in place upon the water in the harbor, their lights aglow, complimenting a brilliant full moon that bathed the night in a gentle hue.

~ 41 ~

Operation Cleanup

Pete dropped his things on his desk as he walked toward King's office. There was a message laying on it which he picked up and carried into the office. *Have to read it later.*

Good morning, Shannon, I just started filling your partner in on our plans to go with an undercover operation on your rapist.

"You mean a decoy?"

"Yes, it's what the Chief wants. That protest over at City Hall yesterday got the Mayor all lathered up. It wouldn't have been too bad, except for Reverend Jesse Blackman joining the fray. That got his attention. Anyway, he had the Superintendent on the phone and chewed him a new one from what I understand. Predictably, the boss then chewed out the Chief who then promptly took it out on me. The long and short of it is this: he wants us to set two undercovers out, one in the southwest neighborhood; one downtown in the area of the last attack."

"Okay…when does all this take place?"

"Yesterday; he wants this to happen ASAP. I've already told Benson that she will be one of the decoys and I'm waiting to hear back from Lt. Borelli on the other one, her name is Sanela Latarski."

Pete and Marilyn turned to each other, "Sanela?"

King looked at them. "Yes, Sanela Latarski. She's a sergeant, just recently been promoted, but the Chief likes her and told me that he wanted her as one of the undercovers. I spoke with Borelli this morning about her. He was not happy about having to give her up; he thinks the world of her. You two know her?"

Marilyn nodded. "She's a good friend, Lew. She worked on Pete's case when he was shot by Rosato."

"What about Marilyn, sir?" asked Pete. "Isn't it a bit unusual to have one of the detectives working the paper on the case to be one of the UCs?"

"Yes, except when the Chief tells you that that's what he wants. He knows about the job you both did at Wrigley Field with the guy that was ripping off the senior citizens. He liked that; he has faith in you." King gathered the papers together that he had been referring to and put them in a box on the corner of his desk marked, "Current Case Files." His desk was immaculate once again. "Besides, most of the female UCs the Department has are tied up on that prostitution sting they've got going at the McCormick Place Convention Center. That's about it for now. I'll get back with you two when I've firmed up a plan for Benson and Latarski. In the meantime make sure the file is up to date—you'll be spending a lot of time out of the office."

Pete and Marilyn got up and were about to leave when Pete suddenly remembered something. "Sir, all this may be unnecessary."

King looked at Pete, his eyebrows raised. "Huh, what are you talking about?"

"I was checking out some of the gyms on the southwest side this morning, showing our composite sketch around. I found this hole in the wall joint called, The House of Paine, a small privately owned gym. The owner ID'd our guy."

"Great, Pete!" Marilyn said, patting her partner on the back.

"You're kidding…." King said, with a huge smile.

"Before you get too giddy about the news, let me clarify. I haven't run the name through NCIC yet for one thing, so I don't even know if it's bogus or real. For another thing, it sounds like this guy might be an illegal immigrant from Russia; supposedly, his name is Serge Petrov. The owner of the gym had no address or phone for him. That's another thing, the gym owner looks like someone who still thinks it's 1970. He doesn't trust the government and therefore doesn't keep any comprehensive records."

King was on his feet now. "Well, it's a start. Good job, Shannon; get going on that name check and run him through the ICE database as well. Maybe they've got some background on this guy. I still need to turn the ship in the direction of the UC operation. So until we get some positive ID on this guy, we're moving forward with Operation Cleanup."

"What?" Marilyn asked, cocking her head and staring at her boss.

"Operation Cleanup, that's what the Chief wants this investigation to be named. He says it sounds good when he can refer to some type of operation with a catchy name. He says the

Mayor likes stuff like that."

Pete and Marilyn smiled at each other and headed toward the door.

"Shannon, let me know what happens on the name check."

"Will do, sir."

They went back to their desks to work on their case file. Pete finally looked at the phone message that he had picked up earlier.

Call Elizabeth Willman. 445-1901 Important. Witness saw your guy.

Frowning, Pete looked over at Marilyn. "Bens, do you know an Elizabeth Willman?"

Hesitating a moment to think, she replied. "No, I can't say that I've ever heard that name. Who is she?"

"I don't know, but I have a phone message that says that I should call her; she said that she has a witness who saw our rapist."

"Well, what are you waiting for partner—call the woman."

***

As soon as the two detectives had left his office, King's phone rang. "Violent Crimes, Lt. King speaking."

"Jerry, it's Sgt. Grey."

"Hi, Amy, what's up?"

"Turn your TV set on—now—channel two; the news is interviewing some wacky blonde chick who says that she was attacked by the same guy who raped the Latino women."

King grabbed the remote from his top desk drawer and pointed it in the direction of the flat screen hanging in the corner of his office. He pressed the proper channel and joined the interview in progress.

News anchor: You say this man tried to rape you? What happened?

Casey Esposito: I was going to my car in the downtown parkin' garage close to where I work. Me and my girlfriend, we were celebratin'. She just dumped her cheatin' boyfriend so we stopped for a couple o' drinks after work. We finished up and I go to get my car from the parkin' garage when this dude jumps out o' nowhere, hits me with a sucker punch, and then tries to rape me.

News anchor: But you were able to fight him off?

Casey Esposito: Oh yeah; the guy was strong but I work out all the time…I mean you can tell, right?

News anchor: Uh…yes, you look like you're in great shape. (The camera pans back to get a full body shot of the woman while she poses for the camera.

Casey Esposito: Thanks, I get a lotta compliments on my body. My boyfriend calls me Legs, says they go all the way up to my…well, you know what I'm gettin' at. I guess you can't say ass on TV, right?

News anchor: Right…I mean no…continue, Miss Esposito.

Casey Esposito: So the guy rips my skirt and thong off while I'm on the ground, I mean he ruined that skirt, it was a designer, ya know? Then he's getting ready to take out his you-know-what, but the guard comes along in his golf cart and scares him. He tried to run away, but I grabbed onto his leg and ripped his shoe off. The cops said I did good.

News anchor: It certainly sounds like it. Well that was a close call; we're glad that you're okay. Thank you, Miss Esposito. There you have it ladies and gentlemen, another innocent working woman assaulted at her job by a vicious thug who police have yet to capture. How long will this reign of terror continue; how long will the women in this town be gripped by fear? Join us tonight when we get reaction from the Mayor's Office on the latest developments in the investigation.

King hit the off button.

"You've got to grab this guy soon, Jerry. The media is having a field day with this one."

"I know, Amy. I'm trying my best. See what you can do to safeguard the UC angle on this. If the news gets out that I've got undercovers out, this guy will hole up some place and we'll never find him."

"Okay, I'll see what I can do. Good luck, Jerry."

"Thanks, I'll need it."

***

Pete and Marilyn were at their desks doing as King had ordered—Pete was completing the interview form documenting his meeting with Butch this morning, while Marilyn busied herself with getting the name check started. As she filled out the request, her personal cell phone rang. She looked at the caller ID and saw that it was her friend, Leslie.

"Hi, Les; did you get Joe home from the treatment okay?"

"That's why I'm calling, Marilyn. The doctor decided to admit him; he didn't accept the treatment well at all—he got very weak and became unconscious. They decided to keep him for a couple of days to run some tests and see why he is reacting so adversely to the chemo and radiation."

Marilyn hung her head and ran her hand through her hair. *Dear Father, be with my beloved, Joe.* "Are you still at the hospital?"

"No, the doctor told me that I may as well leave. He said there was no sense waiting around since Joe wasn't aware of anyone being there anyway."

"Okay, Leslie, I'll get there as quickly as I can. Thank you so much; you're an angel."

"No need for thanks, sister. Please call me when you get an update on his condition. In the meantime, I'll get a prayer chain started for Joe. We'll get him well one way or another."

"Thanks, Les, good-bye."

Pete swung his chair around and faced Marilyn. "I heard. Forget about the paperwork, I'll take care of it. Get over to the hospital and see what's going on with Joe. But just know that today is probably the last normal day that we'll see. My sense is that King wants this UC operation to start tomorrow night."

"Pete, I hate to do this. It seems like I'm dumping everything in your lap all the time, yet you haven't complained a bit."

He slid his chair over next to hers. "Bens, you were there for me when I needed you, when Beth and I were having our problems—you picked me up. When I was shot, you were there for us, again. Let me help you now. I see the pain that you're in; I know how much you love Joe."

A solitary tear slid down Marilyn's cheek, landing on her blouse near her heart, as though it might extinguish the burning that she felt. She reached out for Pete's hand and squeezed it tightly. "Yes, I want your help, I suddenly feel like it's all too much for me; I'm torn between Joe and my job. I'm praying about it, but He doesn't seem to be hearing me. I'm neglecting you and this case, and I think that Lt. King probably thinks that I'm ducking my assignment. Pete, what should I do?"

"He hears you, Bens; He's listening. He'll answer you when He knows the time is right. It's His will, not ours. Let's pray and then you get over to the hospital."

"Okay, Pete."

The two friends bowed their heads and he began:

Dear Father God, we bless and honor your name. We know that you are an awesome God, one who is kind and compassionate. We pray that you will shower favor upon our loved one, Joe. Heal him of his pain and affliction. And we pray also for your child, Marilyn. Give her the strength that she needs to care for Joe and still do your work. Send your personal warrior, St. Michael, to join us in battle as we search for the Evil One who has attacked so many innocents. Shine your light on us, Dear Father, help us to find Satan in whatever dark hole he is hiding and help us bring him to justice. Fill us with your Spirit and your Grace. In Jesus' name we pray…Amen."

"Amen," said Marilyn. She gathered up her equipment and made her way out the door. Pete would have to run the situation by King again, but he recognized that as much as his boss was sympathetic to matters such as these, there was a limit to how long he would allow it to go on. Pete sensed that the limit was just about being reached.

~ 42 ~

Elizabeth Willman

Pete was on his way downtown, having spoken with the woman whose name appeared on the message that had been left on his desk. She said that he should meet her at the intersection of Rush Street and Grand Avenue, near the Conrad Hotel, where she would share some information with him about the person who had been attacking the cleaning women. Twenty minutes later he spotted a young lady, wearing a Milwaukee Brewers tee shirt, standing in front of the hotel. He pulled his car alongside the curb, rolled his window down, and asked her, "Are you Elizabeth?"

"Yes…Detective Shannon?"

"That's me."

The woman quickly hopped in the front seat, causing Pete some apprehension. "Wait a second…." He never let anyone that he didn't know get in his police vehicle without searching them first. And even though this woman had contacted him with an offer of help, his experience told him to stay with practices that work. He looked her over—tight fitting shirt, shorts that were probably running apparel, gym shoes, and a fanny pack. The clothing, ostensibly, hid nothing. "Do you mind if I quickly look through your fanny pack, for my safety and yours?"

"No, not at all." She removed it and handed it to him. He quickly looked through the contents. Finding nothing that could be used as a weapon, he handed it back to her. "Sorry about that, ma'am. I do that with anyone who gets in my car."

"That's quite all right, no offense taken. I know that you're just doing your job. I wear this pack so that I can carry my pocket-size Bible wherever I go. I feel lost without it. Can you pull under Michigan Avenue? I'm looking for a homeless man named Mark Bradley; he told me that he knows you."

His interest piqued, Pete pulled out into traffic and drove east around the corner underneath Michigan Avenue. He quickly recalled his last contact with the man. He and Marilyn had interviewed him about his run in with the rapist, when Bradley had mistakenly been charged with that offense.

"Pull over by that dumpster, Detective," she said, pointing to an area that had fencing designed to hide the garbage station from the well-heeled Chicagoans that had to pass by this piece of prime real estate.

Pete slid the car close to the area that she had pointed out. "Let me see if he's here," she said, as she got out of the car. She walked over by the enclosure, looked inside, then quickly came back and got in the vehicle. "He's gone. I met him here a couple of days ago; it was raining. On days when it rains or snows, homeless people like to use the undergrounds—here and lower Wacker Drive—to stay warm and dry."

"Where do you think he's at right now?"

Shaking her head, the woman replied. "He could be anywhere; homeless people are like nomads sometimes. They wander around the city until they find a place where they feel safe. It may work for them for a few days or weeks, until someone either forces them to move or their gut tells them to find a new spot."

"You seem to know quite a bit about them, Elizabeth. Do you have time for a cup of coffee? I'd like to have you explain your contact with Bradley, and hear about your background, if I may."

"I'd love to."

Pete drove around the block, coming out on top of North Michigan Avenue. He found a coffee shop a couple of blocks away where they went inside and found a table near the window so that Pete could keep his eye on the street. He ordered two coffees and got his notebook out to record Elizabeth's comments.

"So…tell me about your conversation with Mark Bradley. How did you discover his involvement with my case?"

She put some cream in her coffee, took a sip, and began. "I was out with our bus. I'm a social worker; we send a bus around on the midnight shift several times per week with food, drinks, clothing, and blankets. We hand them out to the dozens of people who live on the streets. I don't know how some of them would make it without our help. Anyway, it was raining so we hit the undergrounds, knowing that most of our clients would be there trying to stay dry. We pulled up to that dumpster area that I had you drive to, and Mark was there along with a couple of other men. They were sharing a bottle of wine."

Pete interrupted. "Tell me how he looked, did he seem healthy?"

"No, not really; he was thin, unshaven, and raggedy looking. My guess is that he's probably an alcoholic."

Frowning, Pete replied. "Really...? Last time that I saw him he looked pretty healthy, even though he had been on the street for a couple of months."

"I think that he's fallen on hard times, Detective. He's had a couple of run-ins with some street thugs who stole the few personal belongings that he still had—his sleeping bag, a couple of articles of clothing, and his watch. I think that he's afraid of his own shadow now. I gave him a blanket and a rain jacket, and we brought him on the bus and fed him a meal. That's when he opened up about knowing you. Incidentally, you must have made quite an impression on him; he spoke highly of you and your partner.

"He told me that you gave him your card and said to call if he ever saw the rapist again, but he unfortunately lost the number, and quite frankly, he doesn't have the means to even make a phone call. That night, about an hour before we helped him, he told me that he saw that same guy again. He was walking in the area of the Conrad Hotel. There's an employee entrance to the hotel in the underground. He said he knew for a fact that it was the same guy because this fella apparently has one bad eye. Mark told me that he hid in the dumpster area so that he wouldn't be seen, but he said that he was scared to death. Apparently, this guy gave Mark a beating as he lay sleeping one night in a vacant building."

"Yeah," Pete sighed. "Mark was unwittingly taking a nap in the area that our rapist wanted to use for an attack. He gave him a couple of powerful kicks to ensure Mark would leave and not come back."

"He told me about that," she said, nodding. "He said the guy was pure evil. I spent some time with him after he finished telling me about that night, we prayed and talked about the Lord. Mark has lost a lot of worldly possessions, but he hasn't lost what's most important—his faith. All he needs is for someone to give him a chance. If he could get another job, I'm sure that he could turn his life around."

Pete finished his cup of coffee and signaled the waiter for a refill. "Elizabeth, you sound like a very compassionate person. Your work with the downtrodden is truly a blessing. What's your background?"

Their waiter poured them each a fresh cup. She picked hers up and blew on the now steaming brew and answered. "I'm a licensed Clinical Substance Abuse Counselor, and I'm studying for my doctorate in Police Psychology. I've been working with offenders in the correctional field for about eight years, but I've discovered that my real passion lies in helping law enforcement officers."

"Wow, you're a busy woman."

"You could say that," she smiled. "And a few nights a week some of my colleagues and I drive the bus around the downtown area, ministering to the needs of the homeless. I look at it as a way to give back some of the blessings that have come my way."

Pete pointed to the woman's tee shirt. "Milwaukee...?"

"That's my home; my mom still lives there. But for the time

being, Chicago is my new home while I'm working on my degree. Actually, Chicago's not that much different from Milwaukee, except that it's much larger. But I love running along the lakefront or down North Michigan Avenue; it's a beautiful city."

"Yes, it is." Pete took his business cards from the pocket of his suit coat and handed a couple of them to her. "Elizabeth, it would be a big help to me if while you are out on the streets at night you'd continue to look for Mark. If you do see him, give him my card again. Better yet, if you don't mind, let him use your phone to call me. I don't care what time of day it is; I would really like to speak with him about the person that he saw the other day. We need to arrest this guy as soon as possible."

She took the card from him. "I will certainly keep my eyes open for him."

"Thanks. Can I drop you anywhere?"

"No, I live around the corner on State Street. Besides, I'm not going home. By the way, are you a member of the Fellowship of Christian Police Officers?"

"Yes."

"Good, maybe we'll run into each other again. I'm an associate member."

"That's great," he said, as he laid several bills on the table and got up to leave. "You've made my day, Elizabeth. Thanks to the information that you've provided, I know that our bad guy is probably looking for a new victim in this vicinity. We can focus our efforts down here, rather than try to work two separate areas of the city."

They walked out the front door together into a blanket of hot humid air, more suitable for Miami than Chicago. Pete's coat made him feel like he was in the sauna at the gym. "This heat is burdensome," he remarked. "Wish I was dressed in running apparel like you are. This coat and tie just doesn't get it on days like these."

"I know what you mean…I'm wearing this for a reason—I'm off for my run." She took off jogging down the sidewalk toward the lake, waving goodbye as she disappeared into a blob of humanity rushing in directions known only to each individual, but nevertheless, creating a living mural on a canvass of big city concrete.

This might be the break that we need. Pete got back into his unmarked unit and headed back to HQ feeling just a bit more confident about Operation Cleanup.

~ 43 ~

Visiting Joe

Joe was asleep when Marilyn walked into his hospital room. *He doesn't look like my Joe, but I know that he's inside that person, somewhere.* Not wanting to disturb him, she lingered just inside the room, holding back the impulse that gnawed at her soul telling her to rush to his bedside and comfort him. She closed her eyes and reminisced about the days when they first met. They were at Pete and Beth's backyard barbeque, the one where her friends proudly announced Beth's pregnancy. Joe was there; shy, almost to the point of being timid. He was still numb back then, even though the loss of his wife had happened years before. He seemed almost surprised that Marilyn would approach him. When she spoke with him she saw the haunted look of a man who was without hope, without a goal.

They began seeing each other, first for conversation over coffee. But they quickly found common ground—their faith. All that Joe needed was for someone to rekindle the flame of belief that had burned so hot within him before the tragedy, but had become a mere ember due to his pain. Marilyn was that person. Her love for the Lord, her steadfast love of the Savior, sparked that fire again in Joe. Thereafter, they were constantly together. Now, just like the thief who comes in the night unexpectedly, Joe's health and the couple's serenity had been taken.

"Can I help you," asked a nurse, who came in to get Joe's vitals.

"No, I'm his girlfriend…I guess…I mean his fiancé…well not officially. I…uh…I'm sorry; I mean we haven't' really announced anything. Ugh, I'm running on making no sense at all."

"What's your name?"

"Marilyn."

"Well, Marilyn, I'm Peggy. I'm glad that you're here, Joe is a sick man."

"Hi, Peggy; can anyone explain to me what's wrong with him? He came in for his regular treatment this morning and now here he lies, worse than when he arrived."

"Just a moment." The nurse recorded the blood pressure, took his temperature, and read the monitors that Joe was attached to. "I'm not sure what happened with Joe this morning," she said. "Sometimes patients undergoing chemo and radiation have adverse reactions that will put them down for a couple of days. It's very stressful on the body. I'll try to get a doctor to come in and give you a better explanation. In the meantime, someone will be by shortly to draw some blood; we need to keep an eye on his white cell count."

"Thanks, Peggy." The nurse gathered her chart and left the

room. Marilyn moved to the chair in the corner and sat down. Although she hadn't worked out today, nor even put a full day in at work, she felt exhausted. The stress and anxiety from the pressure of being a new detective suddenly working the biggest case on the squad, coupled with caring for Joe, was all beginning to take its toll on her. She sank into the comfortable padded chair, laid her head back, and closed her eyes.

A short time later someone was tapping her on the shoulder. "Miss...Marilyn, wake up please." A man dressed in a white coat, most likely a doctor, was trying to awaken her.

Forcing her eyes open, blinking as she tried to focus and adjust to the light, Marilyn responded. "Yes, I'm awake."

"Peggy told me that you wanted to speak with a doctor about Mr. Murphy. I'm his doctor; I have a few moments now, or should I come back later?"

"No, please stay. I'm sorry...must have drifted off for a few minutes. Can you tell me about Joe's problem? Why is he having such a hard time with his treatment?"

"Well, Marilyn, the nurse told me that was your name. May I call you that?"

"Yes."

"Good. There are some things that I'm not clear about with Joe's cancer. He does have a cancerous tumor. We agreed to treat it with drugs, and then we also added radiation therapy to the treatment, hoping that it would be unnecessary to perform an operation. This duality, chemo and radiation, is extremely taxing on the human body. Chemo is toxic. Poison flows through one's body, attacking not only the cancer cells, but also the healthy cells. Although it's considered routine, it's anything but—some patients are very close to death from the chemo, even while it does the job that we want it to do. It's my hope that we can contain Joe's cancer before it metastasizes someplace else. That's why I'm attacking it aggressively. The down side is the havoc it that it wreaks on the patient. Believe it or not, Joe's otherwise good health was a factor in choosing this path.

"My original diagnosis was Stage I, but subsequent tests have indicated that it's likely Stage III; the cancer has spread to nearby lymph nodes, but not to other parts of the body. I'm still hopeful that our strategy will arrest any further spread, but Joe's going to get pretty beat up in the process."

"Oh, dear Jesus," Marilyn shook her head. "Doctor, I'm his primary care giver, but I'm a cop—actually a detective. My job has me working long, odd hours and shifts. I can't give him the attention that he needs. What do you recommend? Would it be better for him to be in the hospital during the treatment?"

He glanced over at Joe who began to stir. "Joe's condition will dictate that. Right now he's much too weak and ill to be sent home. I'd like him to stay for at least the next week. I have some more tests that I need to administer, and he needs to be strong for the next round of chemo."

"Okay, that sounds reasonable. I'll feel much better knowing that he's someplace where he will be watched 24/7." She took out her business card and handed it to him. "Please include my contact information on his records…here's my cell number," she said, pointing to the card. "I'll be here as much as I can, but please call me with any changes or problems."

The doctor took her card. "I'll make sure that it's included on his chart. For now, the best thing that you can do is to be upbeat, no doom and gloom. It may not look like it right now, but Joe is a tough guy—he's a fighter. He's doing the best that he can to get through all of this and get back on his feet. Your love and support will go a long way to help him come out a winner."

"I'll do that and more. We'll both be praying each day that God will guide you and give Joe the grace that he needs to endure and be victorious."

"Great; I'll keep you updated as much as I can. It was nice to meet you, Marilyn."

"Mar…? What are you doing here?" Joe mumbled, as he struggled to wake up.

She got up and went to his bedside. She gave him a kiss, hugged him, and then whispered in his ear. "I came to be with my best friend and lover. How are you, honey?"

She sat down on the bed. "I've been better," he said. "What happened? Last thing that I remember was the chemo line being hooked up."

Holding his hand, she answered. "You've had a rough day, Joe. The treatment apparently caused you to pass out, and the doctor decided that he wanted to admit you. He's going to run some more tests which will require you to stay in the hospital for a few more days."

"Mar, this thing is really kicking my butt. I knew that it would be a battle, but I thought that I would put up a better fight. I guess that God has me right where He wants me."

Bending down, she kissed him again. "You are putting up a good fight, but the doctor said that the treatment that you're undergoing darn near kills some patients. Don't worry about it, just relax and let these people take care of you. They can do a much better job of it than I can."

"I miss you," he said. "That's the worst part of being sick, I can't be with you."

"I miss you too, sweetheart. Don't worry; when you're healthy again we'll make up for lost time."

Joe struggled to sit up. "Hey, how's that big case going?"

"Too fast. Our guy has the Latino community up in arms. LAVA had a protest at City Hall that riled the Mayor, who jumped all over the Superintendent…well, you know the rest. Anyway, King is putting me and Sanela out as bait on Operation Undercover."

"What? You're working the paper, how are you supposed to work undercover as well?"

"I know what you're saying, but apparently the Chief specifically named the two of us to go under. King couldn't change the man's mind."

"Oh, Mar, now I'll be worried about you roaming the streets while this animal hunts you."

She shook her head. "No need for that. Joe, you know I can take care of myself. Besides, Pete will be out there along with other backup. We'll get this guy."

"Sometimes I wish that neither one of us were cops."

"C'mon, Joe, you know that police work is in our blood. We wouldn't know what to do if we weren't cops."

"Yeah, you're right. I guess that's just me being frustrated, talking. I can't wait until I can get back to my normal routine."

"You will, honey, don't you worry. You'll be back stronger than ever."

A woman wheeled a cart in with a supper tray. "The doctor said that you need to eat something, Mr. Murphy. I'll leave this here and come back for it later." She maneuvered it close to his bed and then left the room.

Marilyn took the cover off the plate. "Ummm, mashed potatoes, meat loaf, and green beans, are you sure we're not at some fine restaurant downtown?"

"Oh yeah, what a four star meal…."

She took the fork and put a serving of potatoes on it. "Here you go, down the hatch."

Joe reluctantly allowed her to feed him. After a few mouthfuls he had her stop. "That's enough; it's not sitting well."

"Okay, we'll leave it be for a while then try a bit more later." She pushed the cart aside and crawled beside him in bed. "This will have to be our together time, Joe. Let's be thankful for this opportunity that we have. I've missed you, honey; I need you."

"I need you too. It sounds corny, I know, but the day just doesn't seem complete unless I've spent some time with you…until I've seen your beautiful face."

She kissed his cheek, then took the bed control and hit the button that lay them flat. They closed their eyes and held each other's hand, content to be with the person that meant everything to them. For the moment at least, the sounds and noises from the hospital were but white noise to them-- meaningless. All that mattered was that two people very much in love shared a vision of a wonderful future together.

~ 44 ~

Anger

He was like a caged animal, nervous, pacing, and reluctant to search for another woman since the news broke about him. The interview with the blonde woman downtown angered him. *Stupid bitch!* She was at his mercy until the security guard had interrupted him. She should have felt his power; he was so close. Now he was feeling the need again, stronger, driven, almost like a junkie in search of a vein. He must find another woman and teach her a lesson. This next time he would be smarter—and ruthless. No more playing around; no toying with his prey. He would no longer use the sock with the ball bearings. It was a good weapon early on, but now he needed something more reliable. Besides, it was too difficult to take out of his pocket and then put back inside once he struck his victim with it. No, he would simply use his strength, his own overpowering brute force. But he would also bring his knife. There weren't going to be any more witnesses. That's what almost caused his downfall. He would take no more chances.

Once he dominated them, took what he wanted, he would gut them just like he did when he went hunting in his own country.

Downtown...that's where they were now. That's where he would hunt. The underground...away from all the eyes that might catch him busily at work, he would use the darkness to his advantage. Soon...soon....

~ 45 ~

To Catch a Rapist

"Alright, everyone, pay attention," King said, in his most authoritative Marine Corps voice. Coffee in one hand, and a notebook in the other, he gathered his troops to issue instructions. "Tonight we kick off Operation Cleanup—the brainchild of the Chief of Detectives. He's handpicked the two undercovers: our own Detective Benson, and Detective Sergeant Sanela Latarski, from Lt. Borelli's shop. If anyone has any heartache over this, save it, I've already been shot down by the Chief when I asked the same questions that you more than likely have running through your mind."

Pete and Marilyn looked at each other, and then at Sanela who was seated across from them.

King continued. "The fact is that the UCs are excellent cops and investigators, and frankly, no one's doing them any favors putting them out on the street as bait for this sick individual that we're after. And, that's why the backup on this assignment is going to be crucial. Here's how I've broken it down:

Shannon and Martinez, you'll be Benson's backup; Anderson and Johnson, you'll tail Latarski. Briggs and Moran, you'll be in the van with our Tech guy, Tony Zilis, who's down in the shop double checking the monitoring equipment."

Bobby Briggs stood up. "Hey Lew, this Zilis guy's not a cop. Why does he have to be on the street with us?"

King put his notebook down by his side and looked directly at him. "Because I've got two cops' lives on the line out there; if the equipment goes belly up, I need someone that can fix it—fast. Zilis could wire the Sears Tower to glow neon green if I wanted him to—he's an electronic genius. Does that answer your question?"

"Yes, sir." Briggs sat down.

"Yeah, Bobby, and make sure that you're not listening to the Pirates game instead of the police radio," joked Moran.

"Yeah, they'll kick the Cubs' butt all over Wrigley," Briggs fired back.

"Alright, knock it off. I want the van to be tucked away somewhere in between the two locations that I've decided to target. Shannon came up with some fresh intel yesterday from a woman downtown. Based on what she told him, our guy appears to be scoping out the area near the Conrad Hotel on Rush Street, right around the underground entrance beneath North Michigan Avenue. Benson, you'll be working that area. Latarski, the last place our bad guy hit was in the vicinity of the State of Illinois Building, you and your backup will concentrate on that area."

"Yes, sir."

"Both of the UCs will be wearing wires. I hope that I don't need to stress the importance of monitoring the devices at all times."

The squad looked around at each other, remembering the night that Carone and Geraci had fallen asleep when they were supposed to be Pete and Marilyn's backup.

King turned the page on his notes. "Benson, your backup will drop you at a bus stop on Michigan Avenue, just south of the Loop. I want you to sit by the window during the ride so that you're visible in case our guy is looking for victims on busses; and then get off at Wacker Drive. Walk north on Michigan to Grand Avenue, where you'll take the stairs to the underground. Take your time once you're down there and slowly walk to the employee entrance. One of the victims was listening to an iPod when she was attacked, so I want both you and Latarski to wear the same type of earplugs. I'll give you an access badge to open the electronic door when you reach the building. Once you're inside you can go to room 413 and just chill out until 6:00 am, at that point I want you to retrace your steps to the bus stop. I'll have the route written down for you, but you'll end up on the southwest side at an apartment building. You'll go inside to Apartment IE; just hang there until I release you."

"Yes, sir."

"Latarski…."

"Sir."

"Your team will drop you off at Hubbard and Clark Streets. Get on the bus going downtown and get off at Lake Street. Same thing as Benson; sit by a window. Take your time; walk around the State Building and then use the access badge that I'll give you to go in the entrance on Clark Street. There's a security office on the first floor; they'll be expecting you. Then it's the same drill. Leave at six and retrace your steps. Take the bus to North Avenue where a UC vehicle will pick you up.

Any questions?"

Briggs' hand shot up. "Sir, how long will we be working this operation?"

"Until we either catch this idiot, or the next crisis overshadows this one."

"Thank you, sir."

Lt. King closed his notes. "We've got a couple of hours before we kick this thing off. Double check all of your gear, make sure that everything is working properly. You two UCs—with the exception of the last victim, the others were dressed in slacks and blouses or tee shirts. In other words, they looked like cleaning people. Make sure that you dress accordingly. Get ready and be safe."

***

Her mouth dry from the tension, Marilyn grabbed a bottle of water from her shoulder bag and took a drink. She looked at her reflection in the bus window, feeling very much alone as she moved steadily toward a possible appointment with a madman. She silently said a prayer to St. Michael that he would be with her tonight.

While the huge behemoth lumbered northward, Marilyn thought about Joe, lying ill in the hospital. She couldn't get him to eat any more from his dinner tray before she finally had to leave him yesterday. But she could hardly blame him for not eating. His treatment had made eating mechanical, something done only to survive rather than to enjoy, everything tasting the same—metallic. With his bald head and shrinking body, he was morphing into a child-like version of his former self.

Get your head in the game, Marilyn.

The bus approached the designated stop and she got up and stepped down toward the door. The air brakes hissed, like a serpent coiled and ready to strike, as the bus came to a stop. She got off and walked toward the stairs leading to the underground. Wanting to appear nonchalant, as if this was here daily routine, she tried hard not to look around, but her eyes darted here and there trying to find anybody who might be the suspect. She slowed her normally quick pace to what seemed like a crawl, giving her more exposure time should anyone be watching her.

Walking down the stairs she entered the subterranean world of underground Chicago. Dimly lit, the day's traffic exhaust still hanging like a cloud wrapped around the countless numbers of support pillars, she spotted the employee entrance to the hotel. She walked across the street illuminated by an eerily blinking yellow traffic signal that seemed to be sending a message of caution to her, rather than the traffic. Looking around the area, she spotted the dumpster where Pete had said that Mark had been seen. She stopped about a hundred feet short of the door and rummaged through her bag, trying to stay in harm's way for as long as she could without being too obvious about it. She pulled out the access badge and proceeded to the entrance and then went inside. *Safe....*

Moving immediately to the bank of elevators just inside the entrance, she took one to the fourth floor where she proceeded to room 413, opened the door, and went inside. Closing it quickly behind her, she let out a sigh of relief and then went over to the bed and sat down. She was conflicted; the weight of the unknown had been lifted from her, albeit temporarily, she had not been attacked. Yet she needed the assault to occur so that they could end this reign of terror. She dialed Pete on her cell phone.

"Pete, it's me; I'm up in the room."

"Good...I guess. Did you see anyone?"

"No, I tried to look around without appearing to do so, but I didn't see anybody. There wasn't any traffic either."

"Yeah," he replied. "We did a quick drive-by just before your bus arrived. There were a couple of cars that drove through the area, but none seemed suspicious. We spotted several vehicles parked down there, but didn't see any heads sticking up. It would have been too obvious to get out and look inside any of them."

"Okay," she said, collapsing backward on the bed. "Do me a favor, Pete. Call my cell around 5:45; I need a nap—I'm exhausted."

"Will do. Hey, partner, you never told me about your visit with Joe yesterday. How's he doing?"

"I don't know, Pete," she said, staring at the ceiling. "I spoke with the doctor who told me that Joe's cancer is actually Stage III. He's treating it aggressively, hoping that he'll kill all of the cancer cells. But he acknowledged that the treatment is probably testing Joe—pushing his tolerance to the limit. He woke up while I was there and we talked. I was able to feed him a few forkfuls of food, but he is losing so much weight...."

"That's too bad. I guess there's nothing that we can do except continue to pray that this treatment will ultimately make him well."

"I know, Pete, believe me, I've been praying non-stop. It seems like that's all I've been doing lately. I hope that the Father doesn't think that I'm whining."

"I doubt that. He loves to listen to His children. Things will work out, Bens. Get some rest; I'll call you."

"You're the best, Pete, thanks."

Within a few minutes, she had fallen asleep, surrendering to the urge to completely escape from the reality of her life at the moment. For a while it was peaceful and nourishing, her body completely given over to the trance-like state of sleep's rejuvenation. But then she saw him, attacking her…knocking her to the ground. She was overpowered and held fast by the weight of his body. Her arms pinned close to her side, she was unable to fight back…helpless. No…No…! She screamed, waking herself up from the terror—sweating—afraid.

She sat up, shaking. *Thank God; I was only dreaming.* She grabbed the remote from the nightstand and switched on the TV, not wanting to risk another frightful vision. The Evil One was in her head.

***

He was satisfied that this was the one; another stupid woman listening to her music. *They make it too easy.* She was attractive and nicely built, well worth the wait. Tomorrow night he would satisfy the hunger building within him. Time to teach someone a lesson…

~ 46 ~

Someone Unexpected

Lt. King had his troops assembled once again in the unit bullpen. "Listen up. Last night we had some activity with the UC Operation, although not quite what we were hoping for. Latarski was accosted by a couple of drunks who came out of the bar just down the street from the State Building. In fact, it's the same bar that our last victim, the blonde woman who keeps reminding us that she has legs, was visiting on the night that she was attacked. These two idiots started hassling Latarski and the backup units had to intervene. We wound up locking them both up for Disorderly Conduct, just to get them away from the area. I don't know if our bad guy witnessed any of the action or not. If he did, our cover's blown on the UC end of the investigation at that location, and possibly for the whole operation. Anyway, good work by the tail guys."

Sanela nodded in their direction, as Detectives Anderson and Johnson smiled at one another.

King continued. "Over at the hotel, Benson made it into the building without incident and then left this morning by the same route. Backup reports a couple of cars driving in the area just before she arrived, and a few parked underneath, but they didn't see any bodies walking around."

"Hey, boss," Briggs said. "I noticed that when Benson hit the underground the signal got kind of weak. I mean, we still heard her walking and all, but there was some static."

King looked toward Zilis. "Tony, what do you think?"

"It's not perfect down there, Lieutenant. Some spots are better than others, but I can't tweak it any higher. It's as good as it's going to get."

"Okay. You guys on backup are just going to have to concentrate—no good times radio. Understood?" Everyone nodded.

"Alright, if there are no other comments or questions, same drill tonight. I hope that we didn't spook our guy last night. Stay safe."

The meeting broke up and Sanela went over to Marilyn. "Are you doing okay?" Sanela asked, as she took one of Marilyn's hands.

Marilyn replied, "I'll be much better after we nab this character. I don't know about you, but waiting for this guy to attack me is driving me up the wall."

"I know, but that's not what I meant. Being bait is bothering me too, but I'm talking about Joe. How are you handling that?"

Marilyn took her friend by the hand and led her to a room off of the squad area that is normally used for interviews with witnesses and arrestees. She sat down in a chair along the wall;

Sanela did the same.

"It's the worst. I'm so worried that I'm going to lose him. He's getting weaker each day from something that's supposed to be curing him. I spend time at the hospital with him, and then go to work and try to focus on my job. It's not good...not good at all."

Sanela put her arm around her friend and cradled her head on her shoulder. "Mar, I know that you're going through a tough stretch right now. All the odds seemed stacked against you. It's especially difficult to focus on your job when a loved one is suffering. Just know that you have friends who love you and are praying for you."

"Thanks, Sanela. I know that I have many people lifting prayers up for both Joe and me, but it just seems like there's no relief." She said, as she sat up to wipe a tear away.

"It's always darkest before the dawn, my friend. And remember, Paul tells us in the Bible that God won't test us beyond our strength. He's throwing a lot your way right now, but you can handle it, Marilyn. You will be victorious."

A smile appearing on her face for the first time in a long time, Marilyn answered. "Where would I be without my faith and my friends? God is good, and I guess that without these tests, our faith would be meaningless."

"Absolutely; be strong and be confident that He is with you—always."

"Thanks, Sanela that was just what I needed to hear tonight. Good luck at your location; may God bless you."

"And may St. Michael be with you, my friend."

***

Headlights. He ducked down behind the steel box that housed the electrical connections for the underground power. He was too close to his goal to blow it now. The vehicle passed without stopping. If last night was any indication of the woman's schedule, she should be coming down the stairs in a matter of minutes. His excitement was building; he couldn't wait to show her his power.

***

Although not as edgy as last night, her stomach was still roiling nevertheless. Her visit with Joe today was uneventful. The doctor was keeping him hospitalized for observation and running blood counts several times per day, his white cell count continued to be much too low. The only change was that they had begun feeding him through a tube inserted directly into his stomach. Since Joe had trouble eating, they decided that he wasn't getting enough nutrients, ergo the food port. When she left his room he had been sleeping.

She looked out the bus window. They were passing over the Chicago River; her stop was just ahead. She put the faux earphones in place and then went to the front door. As she waited for the door to open, the bus driver said, "Ma'am, is everything okay?"

She turned to him. "Why do you ask?"

"Well, I've never seen you on my route before, but last night and tonight I had this sense that you were in some kind of danger. I can see it in your face. I have two daughters; I'm pretty good at reading facial expressions."

Not wanting to blow her cover, yet touched by this stranger's concern, she answered. "You're very kind, sir. I'll be okay. I have a loved one who is very ill, I'm worried about him."

Nodding, he answered. "I knew something was bothering you. I'll pray for your friend's recovery."

"Thank you."

The door opened and as she stepped from the bus, the driver added, "Joe will be fine, and I'll pray for you too, Miss—for your safety. I'll be with you." He waved and closed the doors, propelling the monstrous vehicle forward. "What...what did you say?"

Too late, she watched as the bus taillights became but mere specks as they blended into a kaleidoscope of city colors. *I'll be with you?* At that moment she knew that the Lord had just reassured her of His presence.

She walked once again to the stairway that would carry her below into the danger zone. But she now felt at peace. *If it is to happen at all, let it happen tonight. I can do all things through Christ who strengthens me.*

Reaching the bottom, she walked slowly along the street, casually checking the parked vehicles that she passed by. Screeeech....! A car burned rubber at the flashing red light, causing Marilyn to turn and look in that direction. Suddenly, there was a blow to her head. She tottered for a moment, trying to maintain her balance. She dropped her bag and caught a glimpse of her attacker—*it's him!* She tried to focus, tried to say something to alert her backup. But at that moment the man struck her once again, knocking her to the ground. He grabbed her hair, the force of it bringing tears to her eyes. The man jerked her into a sitting position, went behind her, and placed his arms underneath hers. He dragged her away from the street behind the power box and pushed her down on her back.

"Pe..." Before she could scream Pete's name, the man covered her mouth with his hand, forcing her head to turn sideways and into the ground. He sat on top of her, pinning her arms close to her side. *The dream....*

Struggling, squirming, she tried to move into a better position to free herself, her face scraping along the ground as she did so, as the man's weight ground her skin into the concrete. The attacker took his other hand and ripped open her blouse, exposing the wire. She looked sideways at him as his eyes grew wider. It was then that she saw the eye. He yanked it off her body, the tape that had held it in place taking bits of flesh with it. He threw the wire against the steel box. "You try to trap Serge? You will see no one gives me disrespect."

The rapist struck her again; Marilyn bit the hand that covered her mouth. "Ow! Stupid bitch!" The man reached behind his back and produced a knife. He held the blade against her throat. "You think you are better than Serge? You will find out." He put the blade between her chest and bra, and then brought the blade up, cutting through the fabric as easily as a diamond cuts glass. He yanked off the remnants of her blouse and bra.

"Pete...Pete." He struck her again, harder, the blow causing her to almost pass out. She felt him move down her body, his hands beginning to work on her slacks. *Pete, where are you?*

As he began opening her pants, she saw a figure appear behind the man. The stranger jumped on her attacker's back, knocking him from on top of her. They fought for a few seconds, the man on his knees striking the stranger in the face. He paused and then Marilyn saw the flash of a blade…silence. In an instant, Marilyn sat up and reached down between her legs to her ankle holster. She drew her five shot revolver, pointed it toward the man, and fired two rounds at him just as he was turning his attention back to her. The man held his ground, continuing to stare manically at her. She focused on his bad eye and fired again. The man fell over, his knife falling harmlessly to the ground.

The gunshots, amplified inside the concrete cave, the sound ricocheting from pillar to pillar, drew security from the hotel. They quickly called 9-1-1 for the police and an ambulance. Several seconds later, Pete was at her side. He took off his police windbreaker and put it on Marilyn to cover her nakedness. "Are you okay?"

"Yes," she said, trying to regain her strength and equilibrium. "He tore the wire off; I couldn't signal you." The side of her face was raw with abrasions. "I guess that I must look a sight," she said,

He took out his handkerchief and pressed it against her face. "I knew something was wrong, your timeline was off. We started to move when you didn't call, telling me that you had made it inside the hotel. In fact, Tony the tech guy had a hunch that the wire wasn't working. We were a block away when we heard the shots. Looks like our case is solved — good job, partner."

Pete, that man lying next to the bad guy…he saved my life. I was pinned to the ground, helpless, that guy jumped on top of him and knocked him off of me."

Pete looked at the body lying on the ground next to the rapist. "Bens…it's Mark Bradley."

Pete went to him and turned him over. He checked his pulse and saw that he was still alive. By now the ambulance had arrived. Pete signaled for them to come his way. "Work on this guy first—he saved a cop's life."

The paramedics stopped the bleeding and hooked up an IV. They secured Mark on a stretcher and then placed him in the back of the ambulance. One of them did a cursory examination of the other body lying on the ground. "No hurry on this one; he's going to the Coroner's Office."

"Can you stand, Bens?"

"I think so, but I'm shaking all over. It's just now sinking in—everything." Pete helped her to his unmarked unit to allow her to regain her composure, while they waited for another ambulance to arrive, along with the Crime Lab and a Shooting Team. "Pete, I think St. Michael was with me tonight."

"What do you mean?"

"Before I got off the bus, the driver said that he knew that I was in danger. He told me that he would be with me. Before I could ask him what he meant, he drove off."

"Amazing," said Pete.

"Something else…. He told me that Joe would be okay. Pete, I told him that I had a loved one who was ill, but I never told him Joe's name."

Pete simply stared at his battered partner. "Are you sure that's what you heard?"

"Positive. Pete, I've been praying like you wouldn't believe, begging Him to hear me. Tonight I felt Him; I knew that tonight was the night. I wasn't sure how it would turn out, but I felt confident that I would be okay, that I would survive because He would be with me."

"God is good." The two partners sat in the car, silent for a few moments until Marilyn said, "Pete, let's pray."

"Great idea." They joined hands and he began:

"Dear Father God, we thank you the gift of faith, without which we would never know you. You are an awesome God, a Father who never leaves his children's side. Thank you for protecting Marilyn, for St. Michael's intercession, and for your child, Mark, who risked his life so that Marilyn would live. We pray that you will grant him a swift recovery from his wound, knowing that his sacrifice will put him in your favor once again. We pray also for our dear friend, Joe, that you will heal him and have our hearts grow lighter. We praise your name; we love you and bless you. Thank you for honoring us by allowing us to toil as your warriors. Amen."

There was much to do before they closed the case of the serial rapist. A mountain of paperwork awaited them, but right now it was to time to reflect and give thanks. The Evil One had been defeated, and a city "Gripped by Fear" had been freed from another demon.

Epilogue

Marilyn's shooting was ruled justifiable by the Shooting Team and the Coroner's Jury. Lt. King recommended her for the Award of Valor for her actions that night. Several weeks after the shooting, she attempted to learn the identity of the bus driver who spoke with her. Although she gave a full description of the man to them, the Chicago Transit Authority insisted that no one matching that description was driving that route on the night of the incident.

Pete continues to work as Marilyn's partner in Lt. King's unit. He and his wife, Beth, enjoy spending time with their son, Pete, Jr. They are excited that Beth is pregnant with their second child.

Joe finally responded to treatment, but not before his weight had dropped so low that he was transferred to the Mayo Clinic. His treatment was intensified, but he was eventually found to be "cancer-free." Upon returning to Chicago, he and Marilyn became officially engaged. He has returned to the police department, full-time.

Susan and *David* are still dating. She is happy and confident enough to be including her children in some of the activities involving David. Her mother no longer asks her if dating David is the right thing to do.

Elizabeth Willman was granted her PhD and is now employed by the Chicago Police Department as a Police Psychologist. She was honored by the Chicago City Council for the information she provided to Pete.

Mark Bradford survived his knife wound and works for a local ministry, helping the homeless at a shelter downtown. He also was honored by the Chicago City Council for saving Detective Benson's life.

Serge Petrov, the now deceased rapist, was found to actually be *Serge Popov.* He had escaped his native Russia, after having been convicted of rape and attempted murder. Before his death, he had shared an apartment on the southwest side of Chicago with two other illegal Russian immigrants. The trio made a living by selling cigarettes on the black market. Fingerprint and DNA analysis positively identified Popov as the perpetrator in all five of the attacks.

Maria Gonzalez, the rapist's first victim, never recovered. She was eventually moved to a nursing home where she remains in a coma.

LaVergne, TN USA
27 December 2009
168159LV00002BA/53/P